HAWK WITCH

THE BONEGATES SERIES

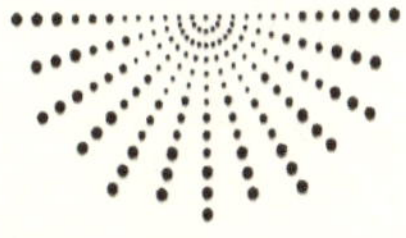

ASHLEY MCLEO

MERAKI PRESS

To those friendships that just don't quit.
My SA ladies. Love you gals so much!

CONTENTS

"Serves the old bugger right!" Branna Penny, the "it girl" of Dublin, shrieked with delight as she took her turn to cover the ex-provost's eyelids with a lurid shade of red lipstick.

I watched as other graduates climbed the stone statue of George Salmon, itching for their turn to deface the slimy bugger. Though it pained me to agree with Branna, this time we were of the same opinion.

"Aren't you going to join in on the fun, Lan? If I were a Trinners girl, I wouldn't want to miss a chance to get back at the spiteful fart."

My best friend—my only friend—Finnegan Fairchild appeared at my side, bringing with him whiffs of leather and moss that mingled in the crisp November air. He grinned as he took in the graduation ritual he'd explained to thousands of tourists as a Trinity College tour guide.

Young women in line for their turn to deface the statue turned to stare. Finn, well versed in ladies' stares, winked.

A couple swooned on the spot. Gag.

"Right," I scoffed. "You know I'm nothing like them. They only ever want to talk to me to get closer to you. You're why I have no girlfriends."

"So why do you have no guy friends? Besides me, of course. That's obvious. Who wouldn't want to be my friend?" Finn raised a playful eyebrow before pressing on. "Have you brewed up one of your witchy potions to keep the lads away?"

I swatted his well-muscled shoulder. "Oh, shut it! You know I don't brew up potions. I'm no healer. I suppose I'm too awkward for them. Or I give off serious daddy issue vibes."

Finn shuffled his weight and frowned at the mention of my father. Silence descended, and he turned to stare at the riotous scene before us. Not wanting to make him more uncomfortable, I turned, too.

Lipstick graffiti caked the provost's face now, and shades of red bled down his neck. By the time the queue finished, George's socks would be crimson. It was the provost's penance for shouting against women entering the college, even while he unwillingly signed the admittance papers. A humiliation his likeness suffered in accordance with Trinity's staggered commencement ceremonies year after year.

"You know, Lan, those girls shouldn't have used you to get my attention. It was a foul thing to do."

Finn never knew what to say when I spoke of my father, even peripherally, so he often changed the subject. Not that he hadn't listened to me in the past when I'd brought my father up, wondering where he was, what he'd be like, and what of myself I'd find in him. Finn *had* listened. Probably for longer than most people could bear, but the guy could only take so much.

The idea of a man abandoning his child made Finn profoundly uncomfortable. Despite the death of his biological father before Finn's birth, my best friend had grown up with a stable family.

For me, abandonment was a confusing and painful fact of life that most people thought I should be over by now. Then again, most people didn't have issues with magic *and* social anxiety.

"That's not fair now, is it? I've used you nearly all my life to pass as normal." I attempted to swing my arm over Finn's shoulders. Even at my above-average height, it was a stretch.

Finn bent his knees obligingly and an uncharacteristic splash of pink stained his high cheekbones. "That's different. We're best friends. You can lean on me whenever you need." He slithered his arm atop my shoulder, and I laid my head there.

From the top of the statue, Branna and two other girls paused in their selfie marathon to stare me down. I sighed, recalling how they had asked me to coffee our first year at Trinity, and for a few weeks, I'd thought I'd made real girlfriends. Soon enough, it became clear they only talked to me to be around my best friend. When I mentioned their behavior to Finn, he dropped them straight away. They still hadn't gotten over the burn.

At least I wouldn't be seeing them again after today. They were all staying in Dublin and working the fancy jobs they'd acquired between term ending in the spring and graduation in the fall. Though attending university in the city had been fun, I missed the countryside. I couldn't wait to get the hell out and doubted I'd return soon.

A LOUD SCREECH FILLED MY EARS AS I OPENED MY CAR door.

"I'm coming, Naela," I yelled, my mouth spreading into a wide smile.

The screeching paused for a heartbeat before sounding again, more insistent this time. My bloody bird was a diva sometimes.

Grabbing the bags I'd packed so I could stay at Finn's flat the night before graduation, I ran to the front door and pushed it open. I threw everything on the floor.

"Mam! I'm home!"

"Hi, darling!" My mother, Aileen Shea, appeared from her room. Her dark brown hair was up in a ponytail and only half her face was made-up for her shift at the hospital. Mam's gray eyes, eyes I'd inherited from her, popped against the red, puffy skin beneath them. She'd been crying.

"You all right?"

Mam made her way down the hall to take me in her arms. "I'm fine, darling. Just got a wee bit emotional on the drive home from your ceremony. Graduating from uni is a big accomplishment. I'm so proud of you. Gran would have been, too."

My eyes traveled past Mam to the other presence I felt whenever I entered our house. A photo of my gran was the first thing anyone saw when they walked through our door. Her familiar smile, the long gray hair, and her eyes that sparkled with mischief always tugged at my heartstrings. It was true she would have been proud. Gran had always been proud of everything I did, no matter how average.

"Thanks. I thought of her, too." It had been impossible not to think of Gran. I felt her absence daily.

Mam pulled away, but kept a hand on my shoulder, which she squeezed. "And I'm so sorry I couldn't stay longer to celebrate after you received your degree. I'm working with Dr. Cannon today. You know how he is."

"It's all right, Mam. Your patients need you."

There was no use in making her feel bad for having to work when I returned home sooner than she expected. I'd just wanted to leave the ceremony as soon as I was given my degree. Home had been calling.

"I'm surprised you didn't go out with Finn. Did his father have other plans for him?"

Finn's upright, English stepfather was a man of many plans. These included plans for Finn, for Finn's younger sister, and even plans for me. It was only because of Mr. Fairchild's connections, and Finn's determination that we attend university together, that I'd been accepted into Trinity.

My short brown hair swished from side to side as I shook my head. "Finn snagged a meeting with the head of the history department after graduation. Did it all on his own, so he's quite excited about it. He'll come by this weekend to celebrate but until then, he's busy schmoozing."

Mam laughed. "Who would have thought Finn Fairchild would straighten up so prettily? That one suffered from a double dose of original sin for far too long. It's good to hear he's taking after his stepfather a bit more."

I couldn't deny that my mate was a bit of trouble. Finn enjoyed shaking things up sometimes. Everyone knew it too.

She jerked a thumb down the hall. "I'll prep the spare room tomorrow. Will he bring Kane?"

"I didn't ask, but I hope so. Naela would love the flying partner. Speaking of Naela, I better see to her, so she shuts up."

I nodded out back where my Northern Goshawk had been screeching insistently for the duration of our conversation. Honestly, it was a wonder we'd been able to ignore her, but I supposed after living with a needy hawk for years we'd gotten used to it.

"Brilliant, darling. I'll finish getting ready for work." My mother kissed me on the forehead and disappeared down the hall.

I rushed out the back door. Two gold eyes latched onto me as Naela released her loudest screech yet. The bird was pissed I'd taken so long. She really was a pushy little thing.

"Sorry, Boss! I was saying hi to Mam."

The goshawk puffed up her feathers, annoyed at being second fiddle. My lips twitched up at the reaction, but I suppressed the smile. I didn't want to annoy her more. She might drop a mouse on my head. It wouldn't be the first time.

I pulled on my protective leather glove and went to open the mew—the specialized hawk enclosure that kept Naela from flying off to who-knew-where while I was gone. The mew worked most of the time, though, once I woke to find Naela sitting outside my dorm window. When I called to tell Mam, she'd burst into tears saying she'd been searching everywhere for Naela. I'd been a bit annoyed, but more amazed that Naela had broken free and sought me out, instead of taking her freedom as many hawks would.

"You're right. What was I thinking choosing Mam first? *You're* the boss." I unlatched the cage, and Naela flew out the door.

She zoomed above the treetops, did a few flips in the air, and plunged back down.

My lips flattened as her gray and white feathers disappeared into the woods behind our house. I placed my fingers in my mouth and pushed out a piercing whistle. Naela came barreling back toward me with incredible speed, and I flung my sheathed arm out to the side, thumb up. Seconds later I took Naela's weight as she perched, one talon on my thumb, the other digging into the thick leather covering my forearm.

"Nice to see you, too, Boss."

Naela turned to look at me, a chattering sound escaping her beak.

"Ah, right. How forgetful of me." I strolled over to the cooler where we kept her meat. My nose wrinkled from the stink as I fished out a cut.

Naela took the morsel and gobbled it down. A pleased noise worked its way up her throat.

"That good, huh?"

The bird inched a little closer to me. In hawk terms, it was basically a hug.

"So, you all right? Anything new?"

Naela tilted her gray head and in the gesture, I read what I wanted to. *Fine, thanks. Better now that you're back for good. Your mam's nice but she doesn't quite get me, you know?*

"I understand. You and Finn are the only ones who really get me."

Naela stiffened and her gaze sharpened upon me.

"*Obviously*, you know me better," I said reassuringly, and her stance softened.

The back door opened with a squeak, and Mam peeked out. "She never looks like that when it's me and her."

I grinned. "You off to perform miraculous healing now?"

My mam wasn't just a charge nurse but also a well-regarded healer in the witching community. If Western medicine failed her patients, Mam always offered an alternative route. It was easier to pull off as a night nurse because of less supervision. And as Mam says, in the dead of night when they're all alone, people will try about anything to heal—even witchy remedies.

"I hope so. You off for a walk with Naela? Better take it in while you still can. The leaves will be gone soon."

I nodded, already eyeing the woods behind the

house. It called to me so strongly that one would almost think I was a rumbler witch.

"All right, darling. How about we breakfast together?"

"Sounds perfect. Night, Mam." I was already envisioning the nice, quiet night I'd have after my walk.

Home had always been my sanctuary. Here no one could bug me or interrupt my peace. Of that much, I could be sure.

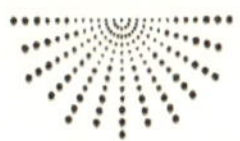

Water slipped off my skin as I rose from the bath, smelling of Mam's luxurious rose-scented bath oils. Using her oils, which Mam kept hidden deep in the cabinet, was my only rebellion as a teen and it persisted to this day. I huffed out a laugh at myself as I tossed the towel, evidence of my misdeeds, straight in the wash.

It was silly, really, feeling like I was getting away with something. I should have acted out a bit more at university. Finnegan would have been delighted to oblige me in that endeavor, but I just wasn't that kind of person.

Despite being close, Finn and I had very different routines while at Trinity. He went out, often with many girls chasing him. Or he ventured to The Long Stone pub with his guy mates for a pint. I preferred to watch a movie, read the newest science fiction novel, and—when I had to—study. On the weekends we hung out, we'd usually catch a picture together. Sometimes he'd even convince me to walk the streets of Temple Bar and watch the Guinness-soaked tourists for a laugh. My favorite pastime was when we'd drive a couple of hours west to be with Mam and fly our hawks.

Today, Naela and I spent hours in the woods before the damp cold became unbearable. She flew, and I watched and listened to the smooth beats of her wings on the air. I loved watching her fly, wished I could join her. Occasionally I'd experiment with my magic for light, but unfortunately, I was often left in the dark. To my chagrin, my power was rustier than I'd thought it would be.

I wasn't the best witch—likely not even in the top fifty percent. A part of me wondered if my light magic would be stronger had my family been part of a coven with another illuminator as a member. Instead, Gran taught me.

She had been a psychic, but not in the way humans thought of them. Humans rarely got that stuff right. A more apt description would be a mind witch. Since Gran couldn't work with light magic, she was technically unqualified to train me, though she was more qualified than any elemental witch in our area.

It had been difficult to decide whether to train to become a healer, a psychic, or an illuminator—the three of the seven holy sects of magic witches trained in if they weren't a born elemental witch. In the end, only light magic felt right.

And of course, I'd had no say in the matter pertaining to the single unholy sect of witching magic —the demon borns.

Demon borns were commonly thought of as cursed. They were so rare I'd never even seen one. Neither had Mam nor Gran. This was because there were no demon borns in Ireland. At least not on the official record. Most of their kind had been run out of Europe long ago. They fled to America for a new start.

As much as I liked to think I'd be open-minded if I met one, I really didn't know how I'd act. Mam and Gran had drilled into me they were as dangerous and untrustworthy as the demons their ancestors had fornicated with for power.

I'd never want to be a demon born witch. Trustworthy or not, they were freaky, and supposedly their eyes flashed red when they worked magic. I already had a hard enough time getting along with others. There was no need to add more strain to my social life, and I was pretty certain that crimson eyes would kill whatever good vibe I possessed.

Mostly, I wished I could have been born an elemental. I'd have labeled myself an earth rumbler, wind weaver, fire scorcher, or water diviner with equal glee.

Well, maybe I did have a *slight* preference for a weaver. To manipulate the winds, Naela flew on would be fantastic. I smiled at the thought of how fun that would be.

As if she could hear me thinking about her, Naela screeched outside. I waved, knowing that with her superior vision she could see me through the pitch-black night. It surprised me she was still awake after all our exercise. I'd fed her a full dinner, which usually lulled her right to sleep. I, for one, was completely knackered. It was time for sleep.

I was in my bed five minutes later. The spine of my newest sci-fi novel cracked satisfyingly as I opened it. Sighing, I snuggled deeper beneath the covers. I was still reading, fighting the pull of sleep with each word, when a screech from Naela ripped me out of my lulled state. The book flew from my hands as I shot up and clenched the duvet.

Shite. Was a foolish fox confusing Naela with a defenseless pigeon and trying to break into her cage? Bloody hell. Not again.

My covers flew off in a haze of frantic limbs and goose-down. I slipped into my robe and rushed through the house. Slowly, I peeked out the back door.

Only the blackness of our garden and the forest beyond stared back at me. I exhaled a bit of tension as I pulled on my wellies. Things looked okay, but I needed to check on Naela. If I didn't, she'd work herself into a frenzy and be up all blasted night. Grabbing the baseball bat Mam kept by the door in case of a prowler, I stepped outside.

A frigid gust of early November wind blasted a shiver down my spine. I jerked backward as Naela appeared from the darkness, the white of her feathers catching the moonlight. She swooped toward me and landed a second later. Her talons squeezed into the robe covering my shoulder when I didn't offer my arm.

"How did you get out again?" I whispered, wincing as her sharp talons dug into my skin.

An unnatural stiffness plagued Naela's stance and her feathers were ruffled. I followed her gaze into the forest and waited, my breath high and tight in my chest, my heart pounding violently. Nothing charged out of the dark at us, so I chanced another glance at Naela.

I gasped. Blood covered her right wing feathers. "You're hurt!"

Naela's attention lingered on the woods and she jutted her beak out as if preparing to launch at whatever was out there.

Taking the hint, I inched forward. She wanted me to get on with catching whatever did this to her—contribute my part in our hunt, as I did when her talons ripped through a rabbit on our walks, and she expected me to finish the job.

My steps were soft thanks to an earlier rain

shower. Each time they landed on the damp earth, I prayed there wasn't a man in the woods. Or that if it was a creature, I hoped it did not have large teeth or sharp claws. We made it halfway to the woods when something, a light, winked in the darkness.

Predatory eyes—my blood went cold.

Suddenly, tree branches rustled and shook. Whatever it was, it was on the move. Then, faster than I thought possible, an enormous bird soared from the depths of the forest. It came straight at us, its unwavering eyes glinting in the moonlight.

Naela squawked, an unusual, undignified sound.

Shite. Must be an eagle. I'd never known Naela to be intimidated by another bird. At well over five pounds and unapologetically alpha, she was—as my falconry mentor liked to say—"a beast of a beast."

I hoped my beast had not met her match.

My teeth ground together as Naela's talons sunk deeper into my skin, but I kept my eyes wide as the bird soared toward us, gaining speed. Instinctively, I lifted my bat. Hitting an eagle was the last thing I wanted to do, but I'd be damned if I let this bird attack Naela again.

The bird had emerged from the trees and was now close enough for me to see its plumage. My mouth dropped open. It wasn't an eagle at all, but an overgrown sparrowhawk. I braced myself. Sparrowhawks, while normally small, were bold. They were willing and able to bring down prey that hawks three times their size had trouble with. However, no sooner had I sunk into my stance than the sparrowhawk veered right and back toward the forest to swirl around Naela's mew.

Naela screeched in indignation, and I rolled my eyes.

"Quiet now. Don't draw attention to yourself. We want it to go away."

"Which I will do as soon as we've had a chat," a voice, feminine and commanding, cut through me.

Naela screeched again and flapped her uninjured wing.

A woman clad in a black robe emerged from behind Naela's mew. Her nose was long and sharp, almost beak-like. In contrast, her lips were full and soft. Her blonde hair flowed down her back in shiny waves and her blue eyes shone in the moonlight.

I blinked. Where had this woman come from? And where did the hawk go?

"You have quite the hawk there, Lana Shea. Clever. She took one look at me and knew I was not what I seemed. Opened the cage herself—I believe to defend you. I apologize for the injury to her wing. It was in self-defense." The woman glided forward, her movements graceful and her black cloak flapping.

"Stay back." I clenched the bat so tight that the grain of the wood was palpable. Her words registered belatedly, and my dark brows furrowed. Naela's injuries were from another bird, nothing a human could reproduce. "Are you telling me you were that hawk? Are you a shifter? And how do you know my name? Goddess be, this must be a dream." Witchy words my Gran used when she was stressed, flew out of my mouth.

"I come as a messenger. And yes, I am the hawk, and the hawk is me." The woman nodded, and I caught something odd. Her ears were pointed.

An elf, I realized. My brows scrunched together. Elves were rare—so rare I'd only ever seen one. That had been from a distance, and I hadn't been able to glimpse his ears beneath his hair. The sight of his magic, how he'd created a ward to protect a woman from getting mowed down by a bus, had been what gave him away.

Most species of fae lived on a different plane of Earth—Faerie. The ones who lived among humans were generally weak demi-fae. According to a book Gran had given me on the fae, the blood of demi-fae had been mixed with humans and other species of creatures over time, making them less magically potent and more human in appearance. However, this woman, whoever she was, appeared anything but weak.

"But, elves aren't shifters." My words died in my mouth as the woman transformed into the giant sparrowhawk and back into a woman. Showed how much I knew.

Naela's feathers puffed to unbelievable dimensions

and a low keening rolled out of her. I tucked the bat under my armpit and placed my hand on Naela's back. She needed its weight to soothe her frazzled nerves.

The woman lifted an eyebrow. "Ah, she's a familiar. Now I understand."

"No—we're just close."

A tinkling laugh flew from the woman's rosebud lips. "Lie to yourself all you want, witch, but I fought with that hawk not minutes ago. There's something more to her. As a falconer, you realize no hawk in their right mind would let a human pet them."

I knew that. I'd always thought it a quirk of Naela's, not a by-product of some magical bond we shared. I shook my head and the rest of my body followed with a shiver. Now that the adrenaline had worn off, the cold was seeping in.

"Whatever," I said, ready to move on. "Why are you here? What do you want?"

"What do you say we go inside, out of this dreadful cold, and I'll tell you exactly why I've come?" Her keen gaze sharpened as if she was about to go in for the kill. "Or rather, why your father sent me."

I jerked. The bat fell from its tightly tucked position between my arm and side. It thunked to the ground, but I didn't move to snatch it up. I couldn't take my eyes off this woman.

"What did you just say?"

"Your father sent me. If you'd like to know why, invite me in."

"Tell me here."

"Absolutely not." Her gaze leveled me. "The flight was long, and I'm sick of this weather. If you don't want to hear what I have to say, I'll leave."

My heart threatened to bust out of my ribcage. She couldn't leave, and I didn't think she was bluffing. Nor did I believe I could sway her. This woman gave off a strong-willed vibe.

"You won't hurt us or steal anything?"

"That's not my mission."

Odd phrasing, but then again, everything about this woman was odd. I waved for her to follow me into the house.

Naela refused to let me be alone with the elf, so I placed a leather gauntlet over my shoulder to minimize the talon markings I was sure I already had and let her come inside with us too. Mam would kill me if she discovered I allowed Naela in the house, but as long as Naela didn't fly about wrecking things, Mam would never have to know.

"Er . . . would you . . . like some tea?" The custom Gran had drilled into me when we had guests slipped from my lips as we entered the dining room. I didn't even have a chance to stop it.

I closed my eyes briefly, annoyed at myself. This woman was no guest, even if she was acting the part. Why was I treating her like one? She was an intruder. One with information about my father. Information I needed. I should be interrogating her, not getting her bloody tea. I pressed my lips together, reassessing my gut reaction and halting any words I might regret. I only needed a second to reconsider and conclude that would be the wrong move.

I absolutely should be getting her tea. I should be doing everything possible to get her to stay so she would tell me why my father sent her. Act the proper host, Lana, I told myself.

Still on edge, I tried to smile kindly at the elf. From the widening of her eyes, I suspected my smile didn't come off as intended. If my strained facial muscles were any indication, I probably looked a bit looney.

Instead of dashing off, though, the elf lowered herself into a chair by the table. She leaned back as if she were a queen, not some random elf shifter sneaking about my house at night. "Tea sounds lovely. What a rare treat."

Rare treat? Our tea was from a supermarket. This elf better not be expecting something fancy. If she did, she was at the wrong place.

It was a miracle I got the kettle on, my hands shook so hard. By the time I plopped two tea bags into mugs of steaming water, brought out the cream and sugar, in case she liked her tea that way, I thought I may pass out from anticipation. I made my way to the table, my chest tight, suffocating me. When I handed her the mug, the elf gripped it with glee.

I sat down across the table, brows furrowed. She was a strange one, that was for sure. My hands warmed as they wrapped around my mug. The heat and familiar scent of the tea grounded me, eased my shakes, and gave me the strength to proceed.

"Who are you and why are you here?"

"My name is Ellette. As I said, your father sent me." The woman reached into her ebony robes, and Naela keened a warning. "He requested I give you this."

"Shh. It's all right, Naela," I said when my hawk didn't stop making noise.

Naela tucked her head over her injured wing and stared at me with accusing golden eyes. Guilt washed through me. I'd been so intrigued by the elf, I hadn't even examined Naela's wing. I was a bad handler.

"I promise I'll look at it once she leaves," I whispered. Naela closed her eyes, mollified for the moment.

Ellette pushed a scroll of paper across the table. "Your hawk's name means 'little champion'?"

"That's right."

She raised her eyebrows. "Like I said, a familiar."

I ignored Ellette's comments, took the scroll, and unfurled it. My eyes scanned the document and narrowed. "What is this? A riddle? Some sort of scavenger hunt?"

She leaned forward and her voice was low when she answered. "It's a challenge and an invitation to meet your father."

The modicum of relaxation the tea had brought disappeared as my spine straightened. On my shoulder, Naela puffed up once again.

My eyes flew back to the scroll, running over the words. To my great dismay, I understood them no better than I had the first time around.

> Shamrocks encircle The Cross.
> Your clue lies within a stone,
> where the wicked are reborn pure.

"I DON'T UNDERSTAND. WHY WOULD MY FATHER SEND me something like this?"

"As I said, it's an invitation. Your father is inviting you to find him and get to know him. The clues are designed to lead you to him, should you choose to undertake the hunt—the challenge."

"But . . . why can't he ring me? Or show up crying at the door with a wilting bunch of flowers like a normal absentee father? And why did it take him so long to acknowledge I exist?" I said, unable to keep the exasperation from my tone.

Ellette's eyes crinkled at the corners, almost as if

she were smiling, but her mouth didn't move. "Your father is anything but normal. And he did not believe the time was right before. As for the challenge, your father wants to meet you only if you have the courage, intelligence, power, and most of all, the desire to do so. It's his way of making it your *intentional* choice, not a mere reflex. If you lack a true desire to meet him, you won't put in the work."

What the bloody hell? Who says that? I leaned back with a huff.

Ellette rose. "Now that I've performed my duty, I must be going. Thank you for the tea. What a delightful treat, one I shall remember for a long time."

My mind worked fast. "Are you going to see him? My father?"

Her blue eyes narrowed. "I am, but you'll have no luck following me. Follow the hunt. If you have what it takes, the clues will lead you to your father." Ellette opened the sliding door off the dining room and let herself out. The next second she'd transformed back into a sparrowhawk and soared into the night.

I stood there, rooted to the ground, wishing I could grow wings and follow.

CHAPTER THREE

Sleep eluded me, so when Mam's car pulled into the driveway around seven in the morning, I was wide awake.

I met her at the door. In my hands, an oversized mug of her favorite lemon tea, spiked with a wee bit of whiskey, trembled ever so slightly. The other hand clenched a mimosa—a prop to ward off any suspicion. My grip on my drink was so tight, it wouldn't surprise me if the dainty flute shattered.

Mam's eyebrows shot up. "You're up early! Or is it late? Still celebrating graduation, I see?" Her mouth broke into a grin, probably proud that I was finally showing signs of a typical twenty-something rebellion.

"Just couldn't wait for our celebratory breakfast!" My tone sounded too chirpy, and I cleared my throat.

"I added a wee bit of whiskey to your tea so you could celebrate, too."

And to loosen her tongue when I started asking questions about my father. No need to say that out loud, though. I'd be causing trouble soon enough. I winced, already not looking forward to it.

Mam had always been uncomfortable when I'd asked questions about my father, which, when I was younger, was often. I used to have vivid dreams about him. I'd wake up elated, sure he had finally returned, positive he wanted to have a chat and take me out for ice cream. Mam would become tight, irritated when I asked after him, and she had to explain it was all a dream—yet again.

I was around fourteen when Gran took me aside and explained why. She told me Mam felt ashamed of her actions. That she held shame for becoming pregnant after a whirlwind courtship that didn't pan out. Her shame deepened when she never heard from my father after calling and sending many letters, telling him he was to be a parent. It multiplied when she couldn't provide the first few years of my life and had to rely on Gran. It ballooned when she had to work so hard to make ends meet. Finally, Mam's shame imprinted on her heart when she missed most of my childhood firsts. It hurt to think Mam thought that way, when she'd given me everything.

Everything except for information about my father. The most I'd ever gotten out of her was that he looked like a porcelain doll with luminous white skin, shockingly blond hair, and intense gold eyes. The only remnants of him in me were the thin rings of gold around my pupils.

"What are we making?" Mam asked, taking the steaming mug and sipping my concoction.

"The works. Bacon, beans, hash, sausage, eggs, and soda bread. Just like old times."

Mam's face softened. I could tell she was thinking of our lazy weekend mornings at home with Gran. I wondered what Moira Shae would have made of our odd intruder last night. No doubt she would have read the shifter-elf's mind. My gran probably would have ended up with some fecking answers, not a million more questions, like me.

"Let me change and I'll start shredding the potatoes." Mam disappeared down the hall, her spiked tea in hand.

The bacon already sizzled in the pan when Mam slid into the kitchen on socked feet, a gleeful smile on her face. The mug hung loosely at her side, empty. Shite, I hated to ruin her good mood by bringing up my father. But I had to do this. I needed answers.

"Someone's happy," I quipped.

"There's a lot to be thankful for." She smiled and picked a few potatoes out of the cupboard and danced all the way to the sink. "I've been thinking we should take a little trip to celebrate your graduation! Do you fancy a trip to Spain? It'd be a chance to get some sun and out of this terrible cold. You reckon Finn or the falconry school would watch Naela for a long weekend?"

I whirled about, unable to keep up the pretense that this was a carefree breakfast any longer. "Mam—I've got a question."

Mam stopped dancing, placed a wet potato on a towel, and turned to face me. "What is it, darling? You all right?"

I dropped my eyes to the ground. "It's about my father."

For a moment, Mam stiffened like a deer caught in headlights. Then her shoulders fell, and she loosed a gusty sigh. "I'm sorry it's such a disappointment, but I haven't lied to you—"

"I get you don't know much, but there isn't anything—something *small* and seemingly insignificant—that you left out?"

Mam bit her lip. "You must understand, darling. Obie kept his past in the past. He often wanted to learn all about me. I was so young and flattered—and I'll admit a bit selfish—that I never inquired much about him. It was as if he popped into my life one day, luminous and charming as could be. He made me happy, and I was pleased to be in the moment."

She flitted her hand through the air, indicating instantaneous disappearing. "And then, one day, he was gone."

"How?" I didn't understand how someone could

just disappear off the face of the Earth. Was he some sort of super-spy or something?!

"I don't know. I googled him once when we finally got the internet, but nothing came up." She gulped loudly.

"That was it?" I couldn't believe that she'd just give up so easily. Mam wasn't like that. She was as tenacious as they came. Not one to give up on those she cared for either. And clearly, at one point, she'd cared about my father.

"No. I looked a few times, but my heart couldn't take much more." She gave me a sad smile. "Please remember, I learned I was going to be a young single mother soon after your father left. I didn't have time to run about chasing a man who abandoned me. A man who didn't respond to my phone calls or the dozens of letters I sent telling him he was to be a father. I had a little girl to raise. Once I got over my hurt, I had no time for someone who seemed to have disappeared off the face of the Earth."

Mam looked down at her hands. Shame washed over her like the sunlight pouring in through the kitchen window.

My heart broke. I'd pushed too hard and upset her. I hated that. "Please don't feel badly, Mam. I wouldn't normally bring it up, but . . ."

Her eyes met mine, curious. "Did something happen?"

I nodded. "Someone stopped by last night. A

woman, well . . . a shifter-elf. She told me my father wanted to meet me and gave me this."

I pulled the scroll out of my pocket, no longer rolled, but folded. I extended it to Mam.

"Your father *contacted* you? Through a *shifter-elf?* How in the bloody hell—?" Mam wiped her hands dry and took the paper, opening it up. Her eyes and mouth flattened as she took in the clue.

My stomach clenched at the reaction. She despised the sight of his handwriting; what would she say when I told her I wanted to find him?

"The woman who dropped it off claimed to work for my father. She arrived as a hawk and got into a fight with Naela—"

"Naela got in a fight?" Mam's gaze shot up from the paper.

Her shock was understandable. Naela regularly asserted her dominance, but she never got into fights.

"She's fine, just got a cut on her wing. I'm going to take her to the school when they open. More a bad shock than anything. Anyhow, the woman gave me this. Told me if I was brave, intelligent, and powerful enough, my father would want to meet me." My cheeks burned as I said the words. What sort of father made his children prove they were anything?

"Does this sound like something my father would have done? Or is this some arse or psycho trying to play a twisted game with me?"

I didn't know why someone would do such a

thing, but my lack of relationships and a general distrust of people made it seem plausible.

Another sigh flew from Mam, then she tipped her chin up and gazed at the ceiling.

"Mam?"

"I'm so sorry, Lana. You were always enamored with the thought of him. I knew this day would come —the day when you'd set off to find him. Now that it's here, I'm so emotional."

She sorted herself out and looked straight at me. "This sounds like something your father would do. He loved games and history. He even set up something similar for me about a week after we met. It was such good fun. I remember thinking no other man could be as creative and intelligent." Her voice cracked, and she shook her head.

"I don't know where he is, but if you want to go find him, I'll support you. It's your right to know your father. I'm just sorry I'm not much help."

A lump formed in my throat. It hadn't been my intention to make Mam feel awful. "No worries."

I took the clue back, its thick paper creamy between my fingers, and tucked it in my pocket. "I'm going to find him—figure out these clues. I can't help but think he may have some answers for me. Help me figure out what to do with my life. Maybe . . . uncover bits of myself I can't explain. Maybe help with my skittish magic."

Mam nodded, and then her eyes widened, "Lana —" Her tone was heightened.

"Hmm?" My tone rose to match hers. Had she remembered something important about the man she'd fallen in love with twenty years ago?

"The bacon. It's smoking."

Shite.

———

WOOD SCRAPED ON WOOD AS MAM PUSHED BACK HER chair and walked her dirty plate to the sink. "What time are you planning on taking Naela to get her wing mended?" She gave me a small smile. Though we'd spent most of our breakfast munching silently and thinking, Mam never could handle discord for long.

"When they open." The sooner I took care of Naela, the sooner I could devote all my attention to figuring out the bloody clue.

"How about an early dinner together tonight? Before I go in to work?"

There it was, the peacekeeper dinner, where Mam would act like this morning never happened.

"Brilliant, Mam. I'll be back by two at the latest. Naela's wing isn't too bad, even so, I want a second opinion."

I'd checked Naela thoroughly after Ellette left. What the shifter-elf said was true. It appeared she'd done enough damage to get Naela off of her and then retreated into the woods. I was still perplexed over *how* Naela had gotten out of her mew. After I'd found her on my windowsill at Trinity, we'd invested in a hawk-proof latch—but her escape was a matter for another day. A day when I didn't have so much on my mind.

Mam cleaned her plate and kissed me on the forehead before retiring to bed.

As soon as she'd gone, I pulled the scavenger hunt clue from my pocket. The words shot up at me, as much gibberish as the night before.

Was I smart enough to figure this out? I'd barely made the cut for Trinity and still suspected that Mr. Fairchild had a lot to do with my enrollment. I bit my lip as doubt crept in, only to be shattered a moment later by the vibration of my phone across the room. Wondering who would ring me at such an early hour, I abandoned the clue to get my phone. Everything clicked into place as I read the text flashing up at me.

I may not be clever enough to figure out these clues on my own, but luckily I was best friends with a brainy guy. I dialed Finn.

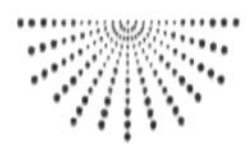

CHAPTER FOUR

"Please tell me you brought something else to wear," Finn groaned as I ran up the stairs to his Dublin flat.

"You think I'm carrying this garment bag because it's full of precious gems? Of course, I brought a dress, Finn!" I rolled my eyes. "I couldn't wear it in the car. The bloody thing took forever to steam. There was no way I was letting it get wrinkled on the drive here."

Finn welcomed me inside, a sandy blond eyebrow raised. "Someone's stressed."

"After last night, you bet I am." I shut the door to his bathroom, which unlike the few other men's bathrooms I'd seen was always spotless and smelled freshly cleaned.

"Good to see you too, Lan!" Finn called through the door, his voice cheery.

I shook my head. As if I hadn't just seen him yesterday. I'd already told Finn the events that had unfolded since graduation, and naturally, he offered to help.

For a price.

None of his go-to girls were available for a last-minute posh dinner party with the senior faculty of Trinity's history department. Finn, knowing I had no other plans, offered a trade: his help with the clue for my presence as his date at the dinner party so he didn't appear pathetic. He was a great guy, but a touch vain.

Seeing as I needed his assistance, I did what I had to do to make it happen. I'd spent the morning rushing Naela to the School of Falconry to check on her wing, then dashing back home to pack and prepare. The steaming of my black dress—the only dress I owned—had been a top priority.

Finn would *kill me* if I showed up for his fancy dinner slovenly dressed. As I needed his help with the clue, I didn't want him annoyed at me. Blessedly, the silk had not wrinkled on the drive to Dublin. Smoothing the water-smooth fabric over my stomach, I looked in the mirror.

Not bad for a rush job, I thought, taking in the way my soft gold eyeshadow and coat of mascara illuminated the ring of gold in my gray eyes. Even my hair was cooperating for once, its brown waves falling neatly to hover just above my shoulders. I stepped out of the bathroom, ready.

Finn whistled. "Excuse me, Miss. Who are you and where did my best friend run off to?"

I stuck my tongue out. In return, Finn flashed his charming, easy grin. He looked good, too. His tailored black suit accentuated his slim physique and made his blue eyes pop. No one would ever guess that the pair of us would rather tramp around the woods with birds of prey on our arms.

"You ready then?" he asked as he walked to where his shiny shoes were kept by the door.

"Just another mo'. Have to repack my bag." I pulled a tiny purse out of the duffel and stuffed it with my phone, lip balm, wallet, and the clue. Finally, I pulled on my black leather jacket, the only covering I owned that remotely went with my dress.

"Was that the paper you were talking about?" Finn nodded at my handbag. "The one that shifter-elf gave you?"

Though Finn was human, he knew all about the supernatural world. This was because as a child I'd had no other friends and needed to talk to *someone* about my world. Plus, it'd been an easy way to impress him, which when faced with the mountain of Finn's accomplishments, I'd tried to do as often as possible.

Thankfully, he loved keeping my secret. I suspected he incorporated it into his theories of why history played out the way it had. I had to admit that some of those theories seemed pretty bang on.

I held out the note. "Want to look at it?"

Finn's eyes lit up as he took the paper, feeling it between his fingers first and then opening it. "This is thick—like the paper of older manuscripts—not something you'd get in any old store."

His gaze scanned the page, widening with each word. "Your father really put in some thought."

Unlike most other times I'd brought up my father, Finn wasn't shying away from the prospect of talking about him. I suspected that was because *this* time there might actually be a solution. And if there was anything Finn loved, it was figuring out a puzzle. Plus, it would make me happy to meet my father. Or at least, I thought it would.

I rubbed the back of my neck. It had been a long ride across the country, long enough for many doubts to arise. "Don't you think it's a little weird, though?"

Finn's eyes lifted to meet mine. "Explain."

My arms crossed over my torso, pulling my leather jacket tighter around me. "It's just—one minute I'm sure I want to meet my father. I want to ask him all about himself and see what I can find of myself in him. Just meeting him may help heal so many wounds . . . change my life. Maybe it would even help with my magic. If he's an illuminator, he could teach me . . ."

I paused and shook my head, emotions warring inside me. It was ridiculous that I was conflicted now, when a possible solution had been presented, but I couldn't help how I felt.

"The next minute I'm wondering why I'd want to meet a man like him anyhow? He left Mam in the worst way. And why didn't he contact me earlier? Mam is sure this letter is from him, says it's his style. That tells me he had to know about me all this time. Or at least for a while."

Finn's face softened. He understood where I was coming from, how deep my wounds and dreams regarding my father were. "Lan, you've been wanting this your whole life. Don't doubt yourself now. Obviously, our situations are different, but if this was happening to me, I'd do it. I'd give anything to meet my biological father."

"There's no comparison," I said, my eyes locked on Finn. "Your dad would have stayed—if he could. Mine didn't."

"That's his loss, now, isn't it? Now it's our job to find him and show him what he missed out on." He held his arm out. "Let's get through the dinner and then we'll get started on this clue."

I nodded and took his arm, relieved by the pep talk and the knowledge that my friend had my back.

SURPRISINGLY, THE DINNER WASN'T HALF BAD. THEN again, being with Finn always made social gatherings easier. He had a way about him that made people want to be near him, talk to him, and indulge him. An infectious confidence that I lacked. Still, I was glad when it was over, and we could get started on working out the scroll's clue.

We were walking around the campus afterward—Finn trying his best to shake off one particularly enthusiastic professor who had taken a shine to him—when it hit me that this may be the last time I walked the grounds of Trinners. I don't know why I hadn't thought about it at graduation, probably because of the masses of people around. Or perhaps it was that being here now, in the evening quiet, was a more reflective time. Whatever the reason, I found myself tuning out the professor and staring at the two enormous Oregon maple trees growing in the middle of Library Square.

The trees were an anomaly, far larger than any others on campus, and rumors surrounded them. Some said their massive size was because the buildings all around buffered the maples from the wind and rain. Students with a darker edge liked to think the trees grew to such fantastic heights because they'd been planted atop old monastic burial grounds and were well fertilized by the dead.

Neither theory had ever fully satisfied me. Why, I couldn't say. But one thing was clear. The trees were different, mysterious, and I was fine keeping them that way.

"Bloody hell, I thought he'd never leave. Let me see that paper again." Finn's arm wrapped around my shoulder, and I jumped. He smirked and gave a little chuckle. "Wish I could have zoned out on Professor Windbag's talking as well as you did."

"If you could, you wouldn't be networking with the best historians in the country right now." The words flew out of my mouth unexpectedly. It was usually my job to diminish Finn's healthy ego, not inflate it. Still, there was no denying what I'd said was true. Finn had many familial connections, but he was also one of the hardest workers I'd ever met.

Finn raised his brow at the unsolicited compliment. "You may have had a touch too much wine at dinner, giving me compliments like that. Now, let's see that paper one more time."

I extracted the clue from my purse. In less than a day it had gone from a crisp rolled-up sheet to a crumpled, bent mess. I handed it to Finn, and he examined it. Minutes ticked by with only the sounds of Dublin to fill my ears. I watched Finn closely, trying to discern if he had any idea what the clue meant, but not wanting to break his flow. Finally, I couldn't take it anymore.

"Can you help me figure it out?"

"Course I can. I knew where we needed to go straight away. Just wanted to be sure I didn't miss anything." He looked up at me and winked. "Which I didn't. Getting there, though—especially tonight— will prove an issue."

I gaped at him. "You knew where I needed to go this whole time? And you still made me go through with dinner?"

"Aww, hush now, Lan," Finn said. "You had fun, I could tell you did. Plus, I needed time to figure out how we'd even get in, and you wouldn't want to wait any longer than possible. Unfortunately, I didn't come up with a solution."

I crossed my arms across my chest, unwilling to confirm I'd had *a bit* of fun. "Where are we going?"

"Shamrocks encircle The Cross. Your clue lies within a stone, where the wicked are reborn." Finn, always the showman, repeated the clue. "Don't you see, Lan? A cross, shamrocks, a stone not just any stone, and rebirthing the wicked can only mean one thing—a cathedral—more specifically St. Paddy's. Rumor has it, he's the one that came up with the shamrock insignia to ease us Irish barbarians into worshipping the Holy Trinity."

"St. Patrick's," I breathed, annoyed at myself for not thinking of it. Then again, at least I had an excuse. I was a witch and therefore not inclined to worship anything or anyone who tried to convert my people. Still, it had been rather obvious.

The shining moment of reveal over, my shoulders slumped. It was late. The cathedral wouldn't be open until morning, but I didn't want to wait until the morning. It was times like this I wished more than ever that Gran was still alive. She'd have been able to convince someone to open the doors.

Wait a minute . . . Gran.

I sucked in a sharp breath and grasped Finn's arm. "I know what we need to do. We need to call an earth rumbler."

CHAPTER FIVE

We'd been waiting thirty minutes when Gran's lifelong friend, Sean O'Connor, turned the corner of Patrick Street.

Time had not been as good to Mr. O'Connor as it had been to my gran, who was healthy and spry until the night she died mysteriously in her sleep. I'd avoided calling Mr. O'Connor or joining him for Monday dinners my last two years at Trinity for that very reason. That he was alive with his history of ailments while Gran was no longer with us seemed so unfair.

Despite my reasoning, a pang of guilt shot through me when Mr. Connor beamed my way. No doubt he had missed our weekly meals, especially after his best friend's death. I should have been there for him. How selfish I'd been, avoiding him to hide from my pain.

"Lana Shea! How I've missed that bright smile! I see you've chopped off all your hair. It's quite flattering." Mr. O'Connor held out a single arm for a hug, keeping the other firmly grasping his cane. My guilt multiplied as his trembling body melted into mine.

Was he strong enough to do what I was about to ask of him?

"Hello, Mr. O'Connor. I'm sorry if I woke you."

Mr. O'Connor pulled back, a look of incredulity on his face. "Dear, you could call me on death's door, and I'd answer! Plus, I never sleep anymore. Who's this young lad? He looks familiar." Mr. O'Connor squinted at Finn.

"Finnegan Fairchild, sir." Finn stepped forward and took the old man's hand. "I joined Lana for dinner at your house once. Best Guinness stew I've ever had—I still dream about it."

Mr. O'Connor's watery brown eyes widened. "Oh, I like him. You should bring him around when you stop by next, Lana."

A smug look crossed Finn's face, and I refrained from rolling my eyes. Like Finn needed another member of his fan club.

"I'll do that, Mr. O'Connor. Thank you for meeting us. I know I was vague on the phone, but I have a rather odd request I figured was best asked in person."

Mr. O'Connor raised his bushy eyebrows. "I'll do whatever I can to help Moira's granddaughter."

I steeled up the courage to push the words out of my mouth. Finn leaned closer, his certainty washing over me as his hand landed on my shoulder.

"Can you help us break into St. Paddy's cathedral? It's to help me find my father." I blurted the words out in one go.

Mr. O'Connor's hunched spine straightened. He turned from me to the imposing cathedral and back again.

"I must have misheard you, Lana. How could I—"

"You're a rumbler—able to manipulate earthly components—and the locks are metal. Gran told me a story once, about how when you two were younger you opened a lock." It was my turn to raise my brows. I was using the term "open" kindly. Mr. O'Connor may look like an innocent old man, but he and my gran had gotten into their own spots of trouble together.

"Hmm. Moira never knew when to keep her mouth shut," Mr. O'Connor grumbled, though there was an undeniable twinkle in his eyes. "You aren't planning on stealing or vandalizing any holy relics? I may not be Catholic, but that's where I put my foot down."

I shook my head so emphatically my hair whipped about my face. "No theft or defacing."

At least, I hoped not. I realized then that I really

had no idea where this was heading. I only knew it would lead me to my father.

Mr. O'Connor sighed and, finally, grinned. "Well, why not, then? I haven't anything else to do tonight, and a wee bit of mischief never hurt anyone. Moira always said you'd be called to meet your father one day. As usual, she was right. Which door do you want to enter by? A side entrance would be best—fewer witnesses."

"Brilliant, Mr. O'Connor. If I may ask, though, how are we going to get over the fence?" Finn gestured to the iron gates. "It's rather tall."

We all knew Finn was asking for Mr. O'Connor's sake. Finn and I could climb the fence. It was a polite question. One that reminded me that while Finn was a genius, he was not a witch.

Without answering, Mr. O'Connor led the way to a tree alongside the less traversed side entrance to the cathedral.

"Lana, do you think you can provide an illusion while I work? From the fence to this tree?"

It was night, which would make it harder because there was less light to work with. Of course, there was no way I would admit that around Finn. My illusions were one of the few magical talents I was proud of. I nodded, and Mr. O'Connor's eyes twinkled brighter. He was looking more like a schoolboy by the second.

"May take a minute," I said. "I'm out of practice.

Stand closer to the fence so we're out of the way of foot traffic. I'll let you know when it's done."

I closed my eyes, and the sounds of the men's easy chatter filled my ears, a welcome white noise. I was glad for their distraction. Audiences didn't suit me.

Most people thought a witch's power came as easy as breathing. And while that was the case for a majority of witches—the elementals and the misbegotten demon borns—it was never the case for me.

Like healers and psychics, illuminators like myself were born without elemental powers. Magical scholars had always considered us an enigma. We have access to magic at birth—can sense it humming in our veins—but must choose a specialty around age twelve if elemental powers still haven't cropped up.

Most non-elementals went on to become healers, which explained the plethora of cunning women throughout history. A fair few pursued psychic training and throughout history that was always the case. Psychics were the rarest of the holy sect of witching; only the unholy demon borns were rarer, and they didn't get to choose their power.

Illuminator magic, my magic, was the third option that witches could train in. Most chose it only after they failed at psychic training and healing. It was notoriously nuanced, and usually beyond frustrating. Over a lifetime, most lightworkers only learned how to manipulate a few slivers of the electromagnetic spectrum. Three spectrum domains out of eight were considered quite good.

Nearly all illuminators began their training in the visible light or white light range. It was so common illuminators dubbed white light the "base spectrum." From white light, one would learn to identify the energies of other spectrums. Once they harnessed them, they could weave them in with the base spectrum, like a braid, so their power would become visible to the naked eye.

Each spectrum woven into visible light gave off a distinguishing color. Infrared light woven with white light produced a red hue, while ultraviolet and white light made green. No one really understood how it worked—it simply was how it was. After all, magic wasn't science, even if it felt like it sometimes.

Even with a decade of training, I could still only produce the two most basic forms of illuminator magic: static mirages and flashes. Both skills were in the base spectrum. As for manipulating the rest of the energy in the electromagnetic spectrum? It may as well be elemental magic, because that's how close I was to working with it.

In my current situation, a moving illusion like a giant car crash would have been brilliant to divert attention. Unfortunately, my power wasn't up to snuff. A static illusion that moved with us, erasing us from view but not altering the landscape, would have to do.

I stilled, pooling my power deep within me, concentrating as I called white light.

The familiar sensation of stepping out of a black cave came over me, as it always did when I accessed the visible spectrum. The hardest part about illusions was getting the light to reflect the landscape I wanted. That it was dark out would only make it more difficult. Working light magic at night was murder because the illuminator had to control the brightness and saturation of the mirage. Give me an illusion on a bright, sandy beach over soft twilight any day.

A breeze blew my hair across my cheek, tickling the skin there as a group speaking German passed by. What they must think of me? A girl with her eyes closed while two men chatted around her?

Suddenly, I felt full, like I'd eaten too big a meal, but in my whole being, not just my belly. I'd reached my magical saturation point, the point where I couldn't harness any more light. I had to release it soon, else a glow would form around me.

I opened my eyes to make sure no one was coming. The nearest person was at least thirty meters away, their back to us. I raised my hands and let the light trickle out. Particles and waves wove and altered reality before me, creating a soft blur that solidified as the light settled to replicate the fence and background.

Suddenly, Mr. O'Connor and Finn were nowhere in sight. Only I, who could sense my power and knew where to find the seams where reality and magic met, knew where they were. I sucked in a breath of air and wiped a thread of sweat from my forehead as I joined them behind the illusion.

"We're invisible to anyone walking down the pavement."

"Good lass," Mr. O'Connor said, pride in his voice.

"Brilliant," Finn added, his eyes wide with awe as they met mine.

"My turn." Mr. O'Connor flicked his wrist and the tree beside us sprang into motion—its long branches stretching and reaching for us. The branches grasped Finn first. His smile was so wide he looked like he'd won a lifetime subscription to his favorite history magazine. The woody limb hoisted him over the fence and deposited him gently on the other side.

"You next, Lana. I may need help on my dismount. I want both you young ones there for me."

The tree's tiniest branches slipped around my waist. Mr. O'Connor was an experienced earth rumbler, and it showed in his finesse when he allowed the knobby branch to touch only the leather of my jacket and not my silk dress. When the tree scooped me up it felt strong, like it could toss me across the lawn of the cathedral, and yet gentle all at once.

I refrained from sighing at the ease with which Mr. O'Connor manipulated earthly elements. He'd probably been able to do magic like this all his life.

I was over the fence in no time, landing lightly on the grass with Finn's hands there to assist me. Mr. O'Connor made easy work of hauling himself over and landed without the aid of his cane, as if he were a man thirty years younger. The bit of magic seemed to have invigorated him and quelled his shakes. His eyes were alight with mischief.

"Will your illusion block us from sight as we move?" Finn asked.

I nodded. I may not be able to make objects or people move *within* my illusions, but making the illusions move *with me* was much easier. All I needed was to will it. I snapped my fingers, and the illusion moved as I stepped back, creating a mild blur at the seams.

"This is brilliant. You should do magic more, Lan."

I rolled my eyes, Finn didn't understand what it took for me to do the simplest tasks.

"Practice would make it easier." Mr. O'Connor added his opinion.

"Since I'm out of school, maybe I'll have more time. For now, let's get into the cathedral."

I turned before the men could say another word and walked across St. Patrick's lawn, pulling my illusion behind me and praying that this would work.

CHAPTER SIX

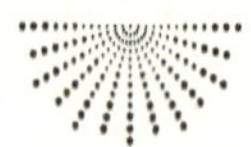

On light feet, we approached a side door.

"I'll take it from here, Lana," Mr. O'Connor said as he came up alongside me.

Magic poured out of his hands and into the lock. Faint clicking met my ears as Gran's friend worked the mechanism inside. The sounds stopped, and the rumbler grabbed the handle and pushed the door inward. I shook my head. When you could manipulate anything from the earth, it was as easy as that. Unbelievable.

"Wicked," Finn breathed.

The old man chuckled. "*Magic*. After you, Miss Shea."

I walked through the door and the men followed. As soon as no one outside could see us, the light that I had collected for the illusion pooled in my hands. Once again, we were visible and now that I was using the magic differently, my palms acted as a lantern. My fingers trembled from the effort and a sensation of heaviness washed over me. That wasn't a good sign. I was already knackered from what little magic I'd done.

What if this hunt took us to a dozen more sites that required magic? Would I be able to keep up? And if I couldn't keep it up and we ran into someone, what then? Mr. O'Connor wouldn't get anywhere fast with his cane. Could he tug at the metal in a person's blood so that they would pass out from the pain and we might escape? I had no idea. Nerves overtook me like a tsunami.

"We broke into a cathedral." My voice came out in a squeak. "What if we need to search in the catacombs? Or a priest's private room for the next clue? This could mean serious trouble. My father doesn't seem to be the playful sort, does he?"

"No, he doesn't," Finn agreed, "but I have an idea where we need to look. It's not the catacombs."

Thank goodness, because I hadn't a clue what to do after we got into the cathedral. The clue had pointed to a stone where the wicked were reborn pure. But practically this whole place *was* stone, which made the search seem impossible. I looked at Finn, urging him to go on.

"It's said that Saint Patrick baptized his followers in a well-spring which has long since been pillaged," Finn said. "A stone from the sacred well is on display here. A stone present at the rebirth of thousands of Irish pagans."

"Well, now that we know what we're looking for, shall we search?" Mr. O'Connor asked, his eyes still twinkling.

Here I was nervous about getting caught, and this old man was having a grand time. I needed to grow a spine. They were doing this for me. I straightened my shoulders, trying to radiate strength. I'd have to fake it till I made it.

"The sooner we find it, the sooner we can get out of here. I'll lead so we can see." I made my way down a dark hallway and toward a door at the end.

"Holy shite," I whispered as I pushed open the door. Reflexively, I clapped my hand to my mouth even as the grandeur of the cathedral's nave continued to assault my senses.

Finn loosed a low chuckle. "I'm sure St. Patrick would expect no less from a heathen."

I spun and glared at my best friend. "I've never been here."

"Sorry!" Finn held up two hands. "Teasing, Lan! Seriously though, *how* have you never been here? You lived in Dublin for four years."

My glare hardened. "I'm *a witch*, Finn. What use do I have for coming in here? Do you know what happened to my people during St. Pat's time?"

It was a weak excuse, and I knew it. At the very

least I should have stopped by for the cultural aspect, but that was beside the point.

"Right," Finn said, looking somewhat chastened. "Let's begin looking. Search for an old stone with a cross on it. I've seen it, but it's been years since I was here last. Whoever finds it, alert the others."

At his instruction, we split up. Finn took the front half of the nave where the priest and choir would stand during services. Mr. O'Connor and I split the sides and worked our way back.

I moved slower than the other two, still taking in the surrounding beauty. The cathedral was, simply put, amazing.

Its peaked ceilings resembled gorgeous, colored reproductions of a cave. There was mosaic flooring that featured Celtic crosses, leaves, and other designs in a pattern so intricate it took my breath away. But the showstopper was the stained glass all around us. Stunning images in a riot of colors were illuminated from the outside by the lights on the street. Although I couldn't name the stories or the people in the glass, their images told tales that were wondrous all the same.

Sure, the chairs looked uninviting and uncomfortable, and the cathedral had an old, unpleasant odor, but there was an undeniable calming presence to the place—even for a witch. I could see why people would travel near and far to worship here.

The abrupt sound of metal falling on stone ripped

me from my reverie. Turning, I found Mr. O'Connor standing on the other side of the cathedral, blushing scarlet and picking up a chair his cane had knocked over.

If anyone was in the cathedral, we could expect a visit soon.

Sure enough, a door somewhere deep in the cavernous cathedral creaked open and the sound of soft footsteps on stone followed. I ran at Mr. O'Connor and motioned for Finn to do the same. If I was to pull off another illusion, we needed to be together. I didn't have the power for three separate ones.

"Hurry, Lana," Mr. O'Connor whispered.

My jaw tightened as I called the light. The footsteps were growing louder, closer. Finn's familiar scent, suggestive of leather and moss, enveloped me as he joined us.

Magic radiated from me in an illusion far more complex than the ones I was used to, just as an old clergyman turned the corner three meters away. My teeth gnashed together as I held a mirage made up of chairs, the mosaic floor, the arched stone behind us, and a statue of a man who at that moment I was wishing never existed. Blood pounded in my ears as the clergyman shuffled about. At my side, Finn's breath was so shallow his chest barely moved, and Mr. O'Connor worried at his lip.

The clergyman took his time, peeking around

corners and checking locked cages with maddening thoroughness. Clearly, he was intent on ensuring all the church's relics were accounted for and not a stone was out of place. Once, he even sniffed the air and looked around, which gave me heart palpitations.

What if this clergyman was part shifter? It seemed unlikely, but I was sure stranger things had happened. Ten agonizing minutes later, the cleric shuffled away, muttering something about rat exterminators. The instant the door shut behind him, I released my hold on the light and gasped.

"Lana, my dear, are you all right?" Mr. O'Connor whispered.

I nodded. "I expect I'll sleep well tonight. That's more magic than I've done in months."

Mr. O'Connor lifted his brows. I didn't have to be a psychic to know he was thinking I should practice more.

"That was a close one. Especially when I think I spotted what we're looking for," Finn said, leading the way to the far back of the cathedral. As we drew closer, it became clear Finn was bang on. A large stone lay on the ground, inscribed with a Celtic cross and plaque which described it plainly as being a part of 'St. Patrick's Well.'

Finn and I knelt to examine the stone from every angle for an etching or a scrap of paper hidden in a crevice. All the while, Mr. O'Connor shined the light from our phones downward so we could see better.

"I can't find a thing." I fell back from my squatted position onto my rear, after my sixth go around the stone. "This must not be it." I paused as an exhausting idea rushed over me. "You don't think my father meant us to go to the actual well of St. Patrick, do you?"

"If that's the case, I don't think we'll make it there tonight," Finn said, running his hands through his blond curls. "My dad won't let me borrow his car this late. You're not in any condition to drive right now, and I know how you feel about me driving your car."

He was right. My hands were still trembling from my last use of magic. I felt weaker than ever. I'd probably fall asleep at the wheel. And yet, although Finn was dreadful at driving manuals, thanks to his stepfather who *only* bought automatic vehicles, I was almost willing to risk my clutch for this.

"Hmm." Mr. O'Connor, who had been paying little attention to our exchange, broke my train of thought with a hum. "All rocks have secrets and I suspect we have yet to plumb this stone's."

My brows furrowed at the rumbler turn of phrase. "We looked all around the stone a dozen times. It's not like it's so intricate we'd miss something unless it was ridiculously small."

"True," Mr. O'Connor said with a nod. "However, you neglected to look under it. What did you say your father hoped you'd be? Strong, clever, and powerful? Lifting this stone with no one noticing would qualify as all three."

I sized the stone up. It was massive and definitely heavier than Finn and I could lift. If we couldn't, I doubted my father could. "I don't think—"

"And there's the fact that I sense a thin disturbance in density between the two stones." Mr. O'Connor's eyes narrowed in concentration.

"What?"

"As a practiced rumbler, I'm attuned to the density of the earth and its components. There's something trapped between the stones."

Finn looked skeptical, but he still stepped forward to heft the stone. "I suppose I can give it a go."

Mr. O'Connor held up his hand. "No need. I have it under control."

A smirk slid over my face at Finn's taken-aback expression, only to slip right off a second later as the St. Patrick's well stone began to shake.

"Mr. O'Connor! Are you—?"

The stone levitated a couple of centimeters and scooted to the right, answering my question.

"Finn! Make sure it doesn't fall off that side." I instructed. Finn rushed to place a tentative hand on the side of the stone floating above the ground, ready to catch it at any moment. We didn't need the heavy stone falling on the tiled floor, bringing the cleric back —or worse, damaging the tile, which would be impossible to hide.

Between lifting us over the fence, breaking into the cathedral, and lifting this enormous rock, tonight was probably the most action Mr. O'Connor had seen in months.

Quiet as a church mouse, I nabbed one of the worship chairs from the back row and set it behind Mr. O'Connor. Like any proud Irish man, he shook his head and waved it away. Still, I kept the chair there, watching as millimeter by agonizing millimeter the stone shook and shifted. I was wiping Mr. O'Connor's damp brow with a hankie Finn had pulled out of his pocket when something glinted from beneath the stone.

"There!" I whispered. "It's a metal plate. Just a bit more."

I shot a glance at the old man. His chest heaved with the effort and even with the help of his cane he was wobbling. "Finn, could you take the weight of the stone? Just enough so it doesn't crash? That way Mr. O'Connor doesn't have to support it with only magic?"

Finn nodded, squatted, and placed his hands beneath the stone. One heaving gasp later, Mr. O'Connor's legs braced as he released most of the stone's weight.

"Thank you, Lana. I needed a wee reprieve. Now, if I can just get through this last push."

With Finn keeping the weight of the stone off the floor, the rest was easier. Not a minute later, a metal plate the size of a post-it note was exposed. I snatched it up, set it on the ground, and made to help the men. We'd barely gotten the stone back where it belonged when Mr. O'Connor's knees buckled. I jumped up from my crouched position, gripped him beneath the armpits, and lowered him onto the chair.

"Just like your grandmother, always knowing what's best for me before I do." Mr. O'Connor wheezed and gestured to the metal plate. "What does it say?"

I snatched the plate off the floor. Looping writing and two masculine silhouettes were etched in the metal.

> Seek your quarry between our heads,
> Men long dead, ideas widely read.
> Identity questioned to unlocke one's mind
> Boyle, transform, create, until your stars align.
> Aside Brian's harp shall you look,
> For your clue, found in a blue book.

Between our heads? Men long dead? Brian's harp? Oh, please don't tell me we're grave robbing next. I wasn't sure meeting my father was worth all that. But what was with the odd spelling? Boyle? Was my father thick and didn't know how to spell boil properly? Or unlock?

I glanced at Finn and, miraculously, his eyes were

alight with understanding. "Don't even tell me you know what this is talking about?"

Finn cracked a smile. "You would, too, if you showed tourists about campus every week. Or spent *any* time at all in the library."

I rolled my eyes. "No need to rub it in, Finnegan. Everyone knows you're a genius student. Just tell me! Where are we going, oh studious one?"

"Trinity's Old Library. Where else would we find the heads of a bunch of dead men and a book?"

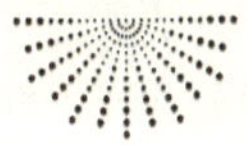

Lifting the three of us back over the cathedral's fence zapped what little energy Mr. O'Connor had left. He drooped as he touched down on the sidewalk. Finn took the old man's cane while the pair of us shimmied his weight on our shoulders.

"We'll help you home," Finn said. "Luckily, we won't need to break into the library." Together, we escorted the old man home.

"But, how will you get into the library without detection?" Mr. O'Connor protested a couple of streets from the cathedral. "You may need me to unlock a door again."

"Finn's a nerd. A huge one, actually. He has a plan." My friend hadn't told me about any plan, but I could tell by the look on his face that he had something up his sleeve. "Probably a brilliant one. I promise that if it doesn't pan out, we'll ring you."

Mr. O'Connor sighed, resigned to the fact that his night of abetting criminals for fun was over.

"And people worry over teenagers breaking the law," Finn muttered after we'd seen Gran's friend home and left his flat. "Seems that it's the old ones you have to look out for."

"He and Gran were two peas in a pod," I agreed, readjusting my dress and jacket, which had gone askew from bearing Mr. O'Connor's weight. "So, how are we planning on getting into the library when it doesn't open for hours?"

"My connections," Finn murmured, sending a text and placing his phone back in his pocket. I'd wondered why he'd been one-handed texting the entire walk to Mr. O'Connor's flat.

"Don't tell me the provost is going to let us in?" My eyes widened. Finn's family had friends in high places, but I doubted even he had the guts to ask the head of Trinity for that big a favor.

"You'll find out soon enough." Finn poked me in the side. "Let's catch a ride. My contact is already there."

Funny how when I attended university I rarely stepped foot in the library and now I was breaking in. I shook my head at the direction my life had taken as we walked the grounds of Trinity to the Old Library.

"There he is," Finn said when the visitors' entrance came into view.

I squinted. Before me stood a young man wearing baggy clothes and looking a touch disheveled. Definitely not the provost.

"Who is that?"

"The janitor. I met him at the pub and had a chat with him. Since then we've gone for coffee or pints at Long Stone."

"Must have been an interesting chat. What'd you talk about?" I'd known Finn long enough, and his tone suggested he was glossing over a juicy detail.

Finn adjusted his collar and a faint blush swept over his cheeks. "Colin wanted a few tips on how to ask a lady out. He said I looked like I knew a thing or two about wooing the fairer sex."

I groaned. Of course.

"Cheers, Colin!" Finn said, recovering from his embarrassment as we got closer.

"Thanks for meeting us so late. This is my friend Lana, the one I told you about with shite for grades. She's grateful you're letting her into the library. The primary source she needs to finish her paper and graduate is in there. She needs to get the paper in by noon and was going to finish it after the party we just left. She swears she saw the paper on the internet, but now the website's down, and she's running out of time. Bad luck, eh?" Finn shook his head at my supposed bad luck.

It took a lot to keep my mouth from dropping open at the outrageous tale. Still, for the sake of Colin, an innocent bystander to Finn's antics, I refrained. Instead of swatting Finn, I tried my best to look pathetic with a dash of anxiety. May as well pile it on.

"Thank you so much," I said. "My advisor will *kill* me if I don't get this paper done in time. He's already extended the deadline twice!"

"Twice? Finn's text said four times, but he likes a bit of drama, doesn't he?" Colin's mouth quirked up.

He didn't know the half of it. I should never have told Finn my fear that the second riddle referred to grave robbing. He'd been yammering away about cadaver heads deep in the basement of the library on the taxi ride over. I was *pretty sure* he was having a laugh watching me turn green, but I couldn't be *positive* until we found the blue book.

"It's no problem. Anything for a friend of Finn's. I'll be waiting by the front door so I can lock up when you're done. You said you only needed about twenty minutes, right? I have to be at me next job in a few hours and wanted a wee kip beforehand. Please touch nothing in the Book of Kells exhibit. You can go up that way . . . I'll wait down here." Colin pointed to the stairs off the gift shop, which bypassed the opulent Book of Kells exhibit. He looked nervous, which was understandable; his job was on the line if someone caught us.

"We won't go anywhere near the exhibit, I promise," I said. Finn must have given Colin some seriously valuable dating advice for him to call in this sort of favor.

We were halfway up the stairs when Finn spoke, his tone a touch exasperated. "What does Colin think we're going to do? Rush out of here with the Book of Kells under our arm? Like anyone could get it out of that queen-proof case!"

Whatever annoyance I was feeling at Finn for making me out to be a pathetic idiot vanished and I grinned. The outrageous story of Queen Victoria literally signing the priceless gospel was always good for a laugh. Since that audacious moment in history, the gospel had been placed in what the librarians and students now called a "queen-proof case." The case prevented further vandalism, whether from a royal or commoner.

"Heads . . ." I stopped a few steps from the top of the staircase as the Old Library opened before me.

Relief coursed through me as I stared at the white busts of scholars lining the shelves. "Finn, you are such a bugger." I pinched his arm, and he yelped. Served him right, having me think I'd be searching for the next clue in a room full of skulls.

We stood there a moment, breathing in the smell of old books and taking in the richness of the library together. It was a place unlike any other, with its domed, gleaming wood and the ethereal sense of knowledge that seemed to float in the air. Off the staircase stood a case housing the famed Brian Boru Harp, a medieval harp that was now an Irish national symbol—and on every pint of Guinness.

"Breathtaking, isn't it? Did you know this library is the largest single-chamber library in the world?" Finn asked, unable to keep his tour guide persona at bay.

I sighed. The moment was over. "Come on, let's find this book so Colin can get some rest." I pulled out the second clue and read the lines again. "Whose heads are we looking for then?" I asked, unable to come up with two people on my own with so little information.

"Robert Boyle and John Locke. Their busts are over here."

The misspellings clicked, clearing up my lingering confusion. I was about to release a sigh of relief that my father wasn't a complete idiot when I saw it. A tiny, blinking red light at the end of the library closest to us.

We were being recorded.

Grasping Finn's shoulders, I pushed him down into a crouch and he nearly toppled down the staircase.

"There are cameras in here!" I hissed.

"Shite! I'm sorry, Lan. Colin probably doesn't even realize, he has no reason to worry about cameras. And I was so busy mulling over the clue I didn't even think . . ." Finn trailed off, looking gobs-macked that his knowledge had failed him.

It wasn't his fault, though. Even if I'd only been here once, I should have known. This library was an icon of Ireland, a site that housed precious books one couldn't find elsewhere. Of course, there were cameras here. What had we been thinking?

"It's all right. We didn't crest the steps and expose ourselves. If it caught sight of us, the view wasn't clear."

Covering my face with my hands, I stood and took in the ceiling, looking for another telltale red light. As far as I could see there was only one other camera, on the very far end of the library. "There's another. Both pointed in the middle of the room. Once we get to the bookshelves, we'll be fine."

I crouched to Finn's level again and released a sigh laden with a mix of relief and weariness. "I don't have enough energy left for a full illusion, but I can blind them both. Lead us to the alcove as quick as you can," I said, already harnessing the light. It came slower than ever before, but soon enough it flickered in my hands.

Finn's eyes latched onto the glow of my palms and he nodded, looking relieved. Realization dawned that while I had almost nothing on the line and something dear to my heart to gain, Finn was different.

His being here, breaking and entering into two landmarks of Dublin, was putting his future as a professor of history at risk. A swell of compassion overtook me and I swore that even if working this magic brought me to the brink of passing out, I wouldn't put his future in jeopardy.

"I hope this book is still where your father thinks it is," Finn whispered. "If it's been moved, we'll have to search every alcove."

"Well, we best get started then," I replied, hoping the anxiety of maintaining my light for a long period didn't show. Raising my hands, I flashed a beam of light at each camera. It took a few seconds for my aim to stabilize, but as soon as I hit the lens we were on the move, cresting the stairs, and running down the long hall of the library. I trusted Finn to lead the way and focused on correcting my aim with each step.

We'd gone more than halfway down the long hall when Finn halted between two gleaming white busts. Still focused on maintaining my aim, I spared them a glance and only managed to read the names Robert Boyle and John Locke before Finn pulled me into the alcove. We were out of camera range. I let the light die in my hands, not willing to waste an iota of power that we may need to get out undetected.

"It sticks out like a sore thumb." Finn pointed up.

On the top shelf amidst a sea of brown and black spines was a tiny blue book. Pulling the ladder over, I climbed the rungs faster than I ever thought possible, grabbed the book, and descended.

The book was old and felt flimsy and grimy—as if

centuries of dirt had seeped into the startling light blue cover. I thumbed through its thin, browning pages, searching for my next clue.

A scrap of loose parchment broke free and fluttered to the ground at my feet.

Finn snatched the paper up, his blue eyes widening as they darted across the words.

"What? What does it say?"

"Lan, I think we're close. *Really* close." Finn shoved the clue beneath my nose.

Wrapped in bronze, you'll find the key.
Your gateway to new beginnings.
Deep within the fruit, you'll see,
a final token, bone-white—your winnings.

My eyes locked on Finn's.

"The Pomodoro sphere," I breathed, not needing his help this time. Most Dubliners, many tourists, and *all* Trinners students knew about the sphere. They would have seen the strange bronze sculpture in the courtyard outside Berkeley Library, the library most of the student population used for research.

There were many beliefs as to what the art installation represented, but I'd always liked Finn's explanation that the artist had been depicting worlds "torn apart and knitted together."

Even the mention of the word "fruit" hinted at

the Pomodoro sphere—which, besides being the artist's last name, translated to tomato in Italian.

"I think you're right. This must be the clue that tells you where *he* is. What else could 'your winnings' mean?" Finn paused. "You know, Lan, your father has quite a lot of flair."

My heart thrummed in my chest. I was so close. I was going to meet my father. I set the blue book on a random shelf. It was an act that would frustrate a future docent, but I couldn't bring myself to care. Bolstered by my excitement and nerves, light flashed in my hands. This time, it took only a second for me to aim, and we rushed out of the library to seek the final clue.

"As strange as the first day I saw it." I stopped and stared at the massive bronze sphere that looked like a cross between a sliced tomato, its seeds exposed to the world, and the Death Star.

Standing before the Pomodoro sphere at night was eerie. The lights from the library behind us reflected on the bronze and distorted our reflections to some-thing a tad monstrous.

I shivered and pulled my leather jacket tighter around me. Only when its warmth enveloped me did I realize how cold I'd been. The temperature outside had dropped from chilly to frigid as we crept into the wee hours.

"Show me the paper again?" Finn's six-foot-frame

leaned over my shoulder and I pulled the parchment out of my pocket.

"This must be it." Finn tilted his head. "I'm not seeing any superficial clues, but that's not a surprise. The paper says—"

"Deep within the fruit," I recited. "How else would you hide a clue in broad daylight with the assurance no one would touch it but the person it was intended for? For all my father knew this hunt could have taken me days."

I stared at the edges of bronze, meeting together and coming apart like mouths of jagged teeth at various places in the statue. There were plenty of crevices in which to hide a small bit of parchment. I turned to Finn. "In fact, it *would* have taken me days without you. Thanks so much for your help."

Finn swung his arm around my shoulder. The gesture was familiar—comfortable—which was what I needed in this life-changing moment. "I'm happy for you, Lan. And, I'll admit, curious to meet your dad, too. I hope I'll finally understand where you get your oddball side from."

Nothing could stop my eye roll. "Now that you've ruined the precious moment, what do you say you help me search?"

"After you, my lady," Finn swept his arm toward the sphere.

I took exactly three steps before whirling about to

face Finn once more. "But what if he doesn't like me? Or I don't like him? You know I don't have the best track record with people . . . I mean, you're basically my only friend." My eyes dropped to the ground at the admission. Although we both knew it to be true, I rarely said it out loud. That I'd done so twice in two days . . . well, it was safe to say I was having doubts about myself.

A finger hooked my chin, lifting it until I was gazing into Finn's eyes. Usually playful, at that moment they were full of compassion.

"Lana, there's *no way* your father won't like you. Especially after all the shite he put you through to get here. As for you not liking him, at least you've got a reason for it. If he's a right arse, give me a wink. I'll punch him in the nose and we'll be on with it. We can go back to our lives like he never existed. Either way, I'm with you."

A tear fell down my cheeks and Finn pulled me close, wrapping his arms around me. What had I done to deserve a friend like him? I listened to the beat of his heart, its steady rhythm centering me until, finally, I pulled away.

"Thank you for believing in me." I inhaled softly. "I'm ready. Let's do this."

Finn grinned at me. "That's my girl!"

I strode over to the art installation and plunged my hand into the first crevice I encountered.

Squinting into the depths of the Pomodoro sphere, I tried to spot anything my tactile senses might miss. Something about probing the inside of the statue felt wrong, and yet, my fingers persisted; traveling over blunt bronze and black teeth, wiggling into each crack no matter how small.

"Hit anything yet?" Finn asked, from the other side of the huge statue

"Not a thing."

"Me either, but some crevices are pretty small. It's a squeeze for my hand and I can't see past it. I'll shine a light on your side, then maybe we should move this way?"

How sad that I need technology for something I can do with magic. I shook the negative thought from my head. There was no reason to make myself feel worse about sucking at magic.

"Finn!" I squealed as he appeared around the corner, the bright light of his mobile shining right in my eyes.

"Sorry." The light plummeted to the ground and Finn grinned sheepishly. "Pull your hand out so we can get a proper view."

I did as he said, and he stuck his phone against the crevice.

"Looks all clear. Move it that way." I pointed in the direction I'd already been going.

Finn moved excruciatingly slow, but I refrained from urging him to go faster. At least he was being thorough. We'd made it about halfway around the sphere when I spotted it.

"There! Finn! Do you see that bit of white?" I pulled my arm out and pointed. My eyes narrowed as I tried to figure out what it was. It didn't look like paper. Perhaps a case holding a map or address? I supposed that was smart, this final clue being out in the elements and all. Had it been only a scrap of paper, it might have blown away.

The light swung in the direction I'd indicated, and Finn's face lit up. "What are you waiting for? Grab it!"

My arm plunged back into the statue, my fingers flailing around for the gleaming white object hidden there.

"You're almost there—a centimeter or two more."

Apparently, this section of the sphere was significantly deeper than the others I'd explored. I pressed my body against the statue, hoping it would lengthen my reach enough.

It didn't.

"Help me, won't you?"

Finn extended his phone-free hand inside the statue alongside mine. Within seconds he'd grasped the prize and was pulling it out.

But I couldn't wait any longer. My fingers flailed around inside the statue, desperate to know what it was, to take it from Finn and be the first to lay eyes on what my father had left me. My skin brushed Finn's, then something smooth, hard, and cool. A rock? My hand overlaid his, and I squeezed it tight, letting him know he could release.

Before he could comply, a peculiar fog rolled over us. I furrowed my brows and gasped as the world tilted. An intoxicating sensation overwhelmed me, like I was on a roller coaster going downhill at an unbelievable speed. Colors melted together, the air around us tightened until it constricted within my lungs, and the object in Finn's hand grew so hot that even with his skin as a barrier I felt it.

And everything spun to black.

CHAPTER EIGHT

My breath returned as the blackness lifted and my tailbone slammed into hard stone. The dizzying sensation that gripped me slowed.

Finn sat in a heap at my side, our hands intertwined with the prize we'd found in the Pomodoro sphere. Though it had been hot mere seconds before, it was a normal temperature once again. His pulse thundered as fast and insistent as mine against my skin.

I shook my head, trying to regain my bearings just as a sharp, hot pain radiated up my arm. I glanced down in time to see something being inscribed on my wrist in what resembled white ink. The symbol pulsed there for a second before nearly disappearing against the paleness of my wrist.

Is that a rune? But why?

"For Sinker's sake. There are two? Were the clues not specific to each person?" A deep voice asked.

I lifted my gaze and locked eyes with a striking hulk of a man. He was tall, dark as midnight, with long, curly hair that threatened to escape from its tie. His muscles bulged beneath the metal and leather armor, making him look every bit the warrior.

Behind the man stood a petite blonde of around twenty-five with pointed ears—another elf. The blonde wore the same mix of metal and leather as the man. It was attire one would think out of sorts with the delicate-looking woman. At least until you gazed into her eyes, which were green and dagger-sharp.

The woman moved forward, smooth and light as air. "No questions, Ryker," she said, though her brows furrowed, indicating she had many. "Remember the last time someone questioned His Majesty? One must have gotten through on accident. We'll figure this mess out later. The window of time is closing, and we're expected in the throne room. Wait here until the time is officially up in case another arrives. I'll show these two the way."

His Majesty? Throne room? Where the hell were we?

Ryker nodded, although he didn't look convinced. "Whatever you say, Ebba."

"Follow me," the blonde, Ebba, commanded before striding from the room.

Finn opened his mouth to say something, but shut

it again when Ryker extended his hands to us. I grabbed one, Finn the other, and Ryker pulled us up as if we weighed no more than children.

"You'd better move. Ebba's a fast walker." Ryker's deep voice rumbled through me, as imposing as the man himself.

"But . . . where are we? And what is this?" I asked, holding out my wrist before realizing the room we were in was even more intriguing than the rune etched on my skin.

It was stark white and sterile, even with the many torches burning on the wall and the lit fireplace. Chilly, too, as evidenced by the gooseflesh popping up on my skin despite the crackling fire. Two chairs and a table laden with a jug and half-finished meals of what smelled like roasted meat were the only furnishings in the room. There was nothing to do here but sit, talk, eat, and *wait.*

"You're in Lyonesse. The marks," he nodded to my forearm, "are language runes. They will allow you to understand and converse with others. Most of the fae in the castle can speak English, specifically the younger generations. However, a couple of the stodgy master healers refused when the king bid everyone learn English years ago—I assume in anticipation of your arrival."

I opened my mouth to ask why, but Ryker didn't let me interrupt and plowed on.

"Many fae subjects outside the castle don't under-

stand it either. His Majesty thought you might appreciate the automatic translation and the ability to
speak with others as you wish. The bonekey—the
thing that brought you here—was enchanted to
inscribe a rune on its bearer when they arrived at
Phoenix Castle. Someone can remove it later, should
you find it offensive. I apologize, but that's all I can
tell you for now." Ryker gestured down the hall. "I've
annoyed Ebba enough as it is by distracting your
attention."

I turned to find Ebba waiting down the hallway,
her hands on her hips.

"Wow." Finn gaped before he caught himself and
his trademark charming grin spread across his face

I shook my head. The woman was frustrated, and
Finn thought he'd try his hand at flirting? You'd think
Finn would latch onto the fact that we'd teleported
somewhere, rather than ogle a hot blonde.

"Come on." I grabbed his hand and pulled him
toward Ebba.

We were still a considerable distance from the
gorgeous blonde when Finn apparently came to his
senses.

"What are we doing, Lan?" He whispered. "Do
you know these people? What happened? One minute
we were at Trinity, then in a swirling hole of . . .
something, now we're here? Lyonesse? And they
tattooed us with a . . . language rune? Should we be
following these people's orders?" He paused and his

sandy blond eyebrows pulled closer together. "What happened to your eyes?"

"My eyes?"

"The ring of gold in your eyes. It's expanded. There's hardly any gray left."

Having no mirror, I couldn't confirm what he said, but nothing felt off, so I focused on the few facts I'd learned.

I didn't know what had happened, except that it was something magical and planned by my father. I was as confused as Finn, but there was no way I was admitting that. In our long history, magic was the only thing I could do that he couldn't.

Plus, he was here . . . wherever here was, because of me. I should put up a strong front—for now, at least. A white lie to calm Finn's nerves was at the tip of my tongue when I caught sight of the unbelievable.

Sucking in a sharp breath, I veered toward the window. The creature—with its spiraling gray horn atop a regal, glimmering, equestrian body—was mythology come to life. My breath stilled, taking in the beast I'd never believed I'd see—never thought it possible, because unicorns weren't real. At least not anymore. Centuries ago, humans hunted them to extinction. Yet, here one was—before me.

"Bloody hell," Finn breathed, joining me at the window. "It looks like it's got a bad dose of something. Don't you think?"

He was right that the unicorn looked sick—its ribs visible and gait lethargic. And weren't unicorns supposed to be glittering and white? Or gold, silver, or black? Certainly not a dull gray . . . I tried to recall the details from the stories Gran had told.

"You may gawk at unicorns later. We're on a tight schedule. Come now, the king is waiting." Ebba appeared at my other side, redolent of places where the ocean meets a forest: briny, fresh, and woodsy all at once.

Three more unicorns flashed through windows as we followed Ebba down a long, white hallway, but this time, I barely saw them. My brain whirred with wonder and questions. Was I about to meet my father? Or some king, as Ebba had mentioned? Was this just another step in the odd scavenger hunt he'd sent me on? If this was the moment I'd been waiting for my entire life, that led to more questions. Like where was Lyonesse on the map? France?

Ebba rounded a corner and suddenly we were standing before a massive door. Not just a door—a piece of art, crafted in white wood and veined with black marble and gold. My mouth dropped open as I took in the decoration more closely. The gold and marble were not running through the wood at random but had been artistically shaped, the black marble forming a phoenix with gold flames around it.

"Wow," I whispered.

Two men dressed in armor and holding swords

stood in front of the doors. After a nod from Ebba, they pushed them open, and we followed her into the grandest room I'd ever seen.

The walls were crafted of white marble and veined with gold, just like the door. Crystal chandeliers heavy with candles spanned the ceiling, providing light and the first flicker of warmth I'd felt since entering the castle. Large windows allowed dim light to seep in as the sun set. It seemed wherever we were; it was twilight. For the first time since entering the room, I inhaled. A scent I could not place lingered in the air, reminding me of elderberry and apple all at once.

Someone coughed and my attention was diverted to where it probably should have been in the first place. A crowd of people in regular clothes stood before us, and in front of them a throne sat raised above all.

Ornate gold sconces, empty of flame, led up steep stairs to an ivory throne. A king sat atop the throne, his tapered ears marking him as elven, one of the species of fae that looked most like humans. His skin and long hair were as pale as moonlight, indistinguishable from the pure white cloak hanging from his shoulders.

A strange sound, birdlike, hit my ear. The king reached behind him, waving a long-fingered hand, and the sound stopped. I peered around the king and gasped.

Perching behind the throne, partially in a shadow, was a large black bird with crimson tail feathers. Its glaring contrast to the king's coloring was startling. At the king's side was a younger man—his son, if his complexion and ethereal air were any indication. A third figure stood behind the throne too, dressed in a black cloak and hooded so that not a sliver of skin showed. As I watched, the hooded figure stepped forward.

"Well? Speak guard," a voice barked. It was higher than I would have imagined. A woman? "Is that the last of them?"

"It is," Ebba said, her lips twisting in a way that told me she did not appreciate the hooded figure's tone.

"And the allotted time has passed?" the king asked, intense gold eyes boring down upon our group.

Ebba's annoyance vanished, and she bowed. "Yes, Your Majesty. Ryker is closing the portal now." She ushered us toward the silent group of about a dozen people.

A quick once over told me we were quite a diverse group. We appeared to be from many backgrounds, though as a supernatural I could sense a common thread tying us together. Every person here, except for Finn, radiated supernatural power clear as day.

My gaze swept over the group, pausing longest on an albino young man of African heritage and the woman next to him who reminded me of a Pacific Islander. Or at least the ones I'd seen in movies—I'd never been near the Pacific in real life.

From where I stood on the opposite side of the group, I could feel the shifter energy vibrating from the pair. I even thought I could hear a low growl emanating from the woman. No doubt the environment had them on edge and they were suppressing the urge to shift. It didn't help that they were standing right next to each other, their animal aspects responding to one another. I wondered what type of animals they became.

"Splendid work," the king said. "Fall back, Captain Ebba."

Ebba fell in line with two other guards, positioned just inside the throne room door.

On her right was a woman who looked to be about my age, with ebony skin, white hair, and pure amethyst eyes that were as unwavering as the massive sword hanging off her hip. She was imposing as all get out. I'd hate to be the person who impeded that deadly, beautiful girl.

A man stood to Ebba's left. He appeared only a few years older than me, with dark hair and sea-gray eyes that popped in contrast to his tanned complexion. Wherever Lyonesse was, apparently everyone here was gorgeous.

I was about to turn back around when the throne room door opened, and Ryker slipped inside.

"Is it closed?" the king asked as Ryker bowed.

"Yes, Your Majesty," Ryker replied and went to stand next to the man who reminded me of a handsome matador.

"Splendid. We shall begin. Let me start by saying welcome to Lyonesse, the royal seat of the Fullfeathers. I am King Oberon Fullfeather. This is the Crown Prince, Casimir Fullfeather."

Someone shifted in my peripheral vision. A short, muscular redhead looked ready to burst out of the crowd, questions at the tip of her tongue. Next to her, a woman of Asian descent with tattoos running the lengths of her arms bit her lip, mirroring the nerves I felt.

The king took no notice of anyone's unease or confusion. In fact, he seemed overjoyed as he swept his arms wide in a welcoming gesture. "I've waited for this day for many years. To meet those strong, clever, and desirous enough to find their way here. To see who you've grown to be. I cannot tell you how pleased I am that my children have made the journey home."

CHAPTER NINE

The king's words rang in my ears like a riddle. Individually, they made sense, but not all together. A group of people who could not look more different if they tried were . . . siblings? Royal gold eyes locked with mine, and Finn's words came rushing back.

"The ring of gold in your eyes. It's expanded. There's hardly any gray left."

Gold—like King Oberon's eyes. I was *half-elf* —part fae.

"Oh, hellllll no." The shifter woman I could picture hula dancing on the Hawaiian islands crossed her arms, looking thoroughly unconvinced.

Then the redhead stepped forward from the crowd, her stride bold as brass and hands on her hips. She pointed a finger at the king.

Behind us, a commotion sprang to life. I twisted and my breath hitched. The young woman with white hair and violet eyes rushed forward, sword drawn. Other soldiers looked poised to do the same. My heart lunged into my throat. Oh no, what had the redhead done?!

"Halt," the king said, raising his hand.

The umber-skinned woman stopped just as quickly as she'd burst into motion. And yet, she remained hard-faced and poised to charge the redhead should she further threaten the king.

"She will not threaten me," the king spoke as though he was as sure of this as he was his own name. "She simply does not know our customs. Fall back, soldier."

The woman returned to the grouping of guards on the edge of the room. Other guards sheathed their swords. Slowly, my heart rate returned to normal.

"You're telling me we're all related?" The redhead swept her hand around.

There wasn't a hint of apology in her tone for the ruckus that had just happened. Although I was scared for her, I sort of admired that. If the violet-eyed soldier charged me like that, I'd have been blubbering an apology.

"If that's the case," the bold woman continued, "which I doubt, you have some explaining to do. And I, for one, would like you to start by telling us where the heck Lyonesse is? I've never heard of it." The young woman stuck her chin up in defiance.

Behind me, a guard sucked in a sharp breath.

The king, however, smiled. "Demanding your due. Yes, you are my daughter. As you are new here—unknowing of your place—I will give you the answers you seek, but let's make one thing clear."

Oberon stroked the throne with moon-white fingers. "As long as I sit upon this throne, *I* am the one making demands. You may ask for answers and I may deign to give them—or not. Now, tell me, daughter, what is your name and what power can you claim?"

Eyes darted to the imperious redhead. To her credit, the girl stood her ground as if she hadn't been put in her place by an elven king. Finally, she spoke. "Crystal Clawsin, part dwarf."

Oberon's smile grew, and he leaned back in his chair. "Superb. Prince Casimir—you could learn something from your brazen sister."

The prince, who until now had remained stone still, jerked his head in a sort of nod.

"Repeat your question," the king said.

"The girl asked where Lyonesse is, Your Majesty," the figure in the dark, hooded cloak behind the king supplied.

This time it was obvious that the person hiding beneath the hood was a woman. I wondered why she wasn't showing her face. Was she not human?

"A reasonable and intelligent question as her

family chose not to join their kind during the Sinking." Oberon tented his hands beneath his chin. Rings, heavy with gold and rubies, glinted on three fingers.

"Hundreds of years ago, when humans grew fearful of magic, fae of all species retreated." He shook his head as if regretting the choice. "They did so by sinking the islands of Earth to a dimension humans knew naught about. The fae pushed those islands together to make a continent—what we call Faerie."

"So you're saying *this* is Faerie?" Crystal looked unimpressed, though I couldn't understand why. I was stunned.

"Yes, a purely magical land," the king replied, his eyes twinkling. "And as you may imagine, creating this realm took an extraordinary amount of magic. So much, in fact, that it cost those who sunk Earth's lands their lives. Their sacrifice provided all fae species a haven. Faerie is still on Earth, but a different plane of existence. We call the dimension you hail from the 'Old Land' and Faerie is composed of five different realms. Lyonesse is one of the largest kingdoms in Sinkers Realm."

Finn and I shot looks of disbelief at each other. Sure I'd heard of Faerie, but had I ever imagined I'd go to Faerie? Absolutely not. This was bloody wild.

"If Lyonesse is on a different plane of existence and we are all related, it stands to reason that you went between planes and impregnated our mothers." Crystal pursed her lips, her disdain clear. "Why did you feel the need to go propagate the Old Land? Are you out of fae women here . . . sir?" She added the last bit as if it were an afterthought.

"Titles and transitions to something more intimate in the future can be awkward. You may all address me as sire for now." King Oberon rose from his throne and raised his arms.

The sconces lining the stairs caught fire. Flames leapt a meter high, creating the impression that King Oberon walked through hell as he descended the stairs. Lit by light, his features were a landscape of sharp angles and ghastly white skin. My heart rate picked up, and I inched closer to Finn, who grabbed for my hand and squeezed it tight.

"Your conception is a convoluted tale. There is a queen—Queen Pari of Buyan—determined to see the end of the Fullfeather dynasty. Queen Pari has taken all she can from my land and my people." Oberon stopped before a young man with a beaky nose, and bright red hair. He was dressed in plaid, reminding me of a lumberjack.

"Tell me, my son. What is your name and animal aspect?"

The man's light green eyes widened. "A—Arlo—and a golden eagle," he stuttered.

"As a shifter close to the land, perhaps you noticed

it, Arlo? The land outside leaves little desire for you to fly over, does it not?"

"No, sire. The land looks dead," Arlo replied, his face burning as bright as his hair.

A vision of the ill unicorn flashed in my mind. I'd been so transfixed by the creature and what was about to happen next, I hadn't noticed the land surrounding it.

"Dead, indeed. The desolation outside the walls of Phoenix Castle is a call to war against Lyonesse. A war waged by Queen Pari of Buyan. Long ago she stole the bonegate created for Lyonesse, wrought from the bones of the Fullfeather Sinker—your ancestor. Bonegates are magical portals between Faerie and the Old Land, but they are also *beacons* of power. They are the most important attribute a kingdom or free region in Faerie can possess." The king's lips turned down.

"Because of her thievery, Queen Pari has been siphoning off the life force and magic meant for Lyonesse for years. By the time I replaced my father on the throne, most of my subjects were weaker than those of previous fae generations. Many had difficulty conceiving children." He paused, as if in pain, and shook his head.

"I was not excluded from the plight of infertility. My son, Prince Casimir, is the only full fae child of mine to live, though many quickened in his mother's womb before him. He was a weak babe. It is a miracle he lived and even more a miracle he thrives now."

The king's eyes flashed to his heir, who was still sitting on the dais above. There was no affection in his gaze—only appraisal.

"It is preferable for a leader to have multiple heirs should anything happen to the firstborn. Faerie is a dangerous place. Death is far too common. I'd already lost more children than I could bear because of Queen Pari's malevolence. Thus, I hatched a plan. I secretly sired heirs with the women of the Old Land —women out of the reach of Queen Pari."

"So you just went around willy-nilly and knocked women up?" The Pacific Islander woman asked, her arms still crossed over her chest.

The king's gold eyes flashed, and for a second, I thought he was going to prove a point, or at least demand the girl give her name and species as he had with Crystal and Arlo. Surprisingly, he didn't.

"Absolutely not!" the king said, his tone laden with disgust. "I chose women of an ancient, *distinguished* magical lineage, hoping my children would be born powerful. In this way, when they were grown, and I called them to Faerie, they could defend themselves against Queen Pari."

He paused and a softer look flashed across his face as he took us all in. Then he sighed.

"You may have never known the love of a father, but be assured, I cherished you from afar. I only stayed away so you might *remain* safe. However, as of late, my kingdom has taken a turn for the worse. I can no longer think only of myself and selfishly keep my progeny safe. I must consider my people." His arms gestured to the windows. I assumed a kingdom was out there, somewhere.

"I called you here not only to get to know you but also to *beg* your help. I hope that with your strong magical blood—and the human-like ingenuity most fae are not known for—you will help defeat Queen Pari. That you will save the land of your forefathers. A land you can rightfully call your birthright as children of royal blood." The king's eyes landed on Finn, who stiffened.

Then he opened his bloody mouth.

"There's been a mistake. I only came through the portal because I was holding the white rock when Lana touched it."

My shoulders loosened only when Finn stopped short of telling the king why he was with me. If Finn hadn't helped, there was *no way* I'd be here meeting my father . . . and a dozen half-siblings . . . and learning all this. That I was royalty, and my father, a king, needed my help to save his kingdom.

"Name and magic?" King Oberon asked.

Finn tilted his head. "Finnegan Fairchild. And nothing?"

"Impossible."

"But I assure you it is, Your Majesty. Lana and I

have been friends for years. She's an amazing witch and has pointed out supernaturals in the past. She'd have told me if I were magic."

I cringed at Finn's description of me as an "amazing witch" and then cringed again as King Oberon took my chin between his fingers. He steered my face upward, his gaze boring through me as if he were memorizing every line and angle of my face.

"I had wondered who would look most like me out of the bunch," King Oberon said, releasing my face. "Pity about the dark hair marring the Fullfeather coloring, but these things happen."

My hand flew through my short, brown hair—hair I'd always liked. My cheeks burned as the others stared.

But Oberon's attention was already back on Finn.

"Your friend, my daughter, is indeed a witch. Still, it is *not* possible you survived the bonekey portal with no magic in your blood. Bonekeys were created long ago as portable means of bringing the various species of fae into Faerie after the Great Sinking. In this specific scenario, I commanded the bonekeys spelled further to recognize only my bloodline."

The king brushed Finn's blond curls back. "Your magical legacy may have been lost and never activated, yet you still had enough magical Fullfeather blood to hitch a ride. That is evident now, is it not . . . Lana? Have a look. Tell me what you think."

I blinked, surprised that he remembered my

name, even if Finn had just said it. Cheeks warming, I turned toward the pair. My hands flew to my mouth as a gasp escaped me.

Oberon's mouth twisted into a smug smile. "It seems I was right."

"What is it?" Finn asked, his hand tightening around mine.

"Your ears," I whispered through trembling lips. "They're pointed. Finn . . . you're part elf!"

Two familiar screeches cut through my epiphany. My eyes caught sight of flashes of gray and brown in the dimming evening light, flying outside straight for the throne room window.

"Watch out!" I cried.

Everyone scrambled back. Finn and I flung out our arms as our hawks soared through the glassless windows to land in a rush of wind and fury. Naela was clicking her beak and ruffling her feathers, while Kane emitted a low keening sound I'd rarely heard from the submissive hawk.

I was grateful I'd worn my leather jacket last night. Though it was no falconer's glove, it protected my skin as Naela's talons dug into my arm.

The group kept their distance. Especially Crystal, who had jumped back a considerable distance and was now eyeing Naela warily. King Oberon, however, ignored my hawk's warning signs and stepped closer.

To my surprise, both hawks fell silent.

"There's no longer any doubt in my mind that you

are *both* of my blood. The Fullfeather line has always had an affinity for winged creatures. Some even had the power to control them as I do my phoenix, Xerxes."

His *phoenix*. My gaze traveled to the large black bird perching behind the throne. It was watching Naela and Kane. Even though it was a bird, I could sense its disdain. I gulped. While I was confident of Naela's ability to take care of herself, a fire-conjuring phoenix could pose problems. I pulled my arm in closer to my side.

King Oberon tracked my movement and nodded at the wisdom in it. "That your familiars found you here, made the journey to a different dimension of Earth, is astonishing. They must stay. I will have cages put in your rooms," King Oberon said before returning his attention to Finn.

"Your magical legacy may be lost to you, but you're a Fullfeather son all the same." The king's gaze fell to Finn's and my hands still clasped. His eyebrows lifted. "It seems your *friend* is also your *sister*. How lucky that you found each other early on." His tone held an edge of insinuation to it, and Finn let go of my hand.

Bodies fidgeted around us, and my face burned. I knew what everyone must be thinking. Although Finn's and my relationship had never been like that, it was still mortifying. I opened my mouth to clarify but stopped short as King Oberon glided to the side of the room, escorted by guards following his every movement.

"If you please, follow me into the council room." The king's hand waved lazily through the air for us to follow. "We have many more things to discuss."

CHAPTER TEN

Finn and I hung back until the others entered so our hawks would have the benefit of knowing who was in the room. Naela and Kane were already on edge, and I didn't need Naela flying at someone's face to defend me.

As we entered behind the others, I saw that someone had anticipated our needs. Two perches wrought in intricate gold and steel sat behind two high-backed wood chairs. Aside from the perches, the council room was quite plain compared to the throne room. Unfamiliar maps lined its walls, and a single gleaming wood table dominated the space.

Naela hopped off my arm to rest on to the perch. Sensation returned as blood rushed back into the limb. I sat only to find Prince Casimir had descended from his throne after the king. And I'd been placed right next to him.

"Sister," the prince said, inclining his head crowned with a mane of glorious silver-blond hair.

Close up, Casimir appeared to be in his late-twenties. I wondered if he was the spitting image of what my father had looked like when he had courted Mam. My father had claimed to be around thirty when he'd met Mam—an age he didn't look much older than now. Then again, Gran taught me that fae aged slower than other magical creatures.

What was more intriguing was how my father had hidden his fae essence from Mam. I suspected that he'd been glamoured. I'd heard some fae, and even demon born witches, could perform glamours to alter their appearance and hide their magical essences. Surely a king would be able to perform one. The prince shifted in his seat, and I snapped back to the present with a hard blink.

"Prince Casimir," I blurted, realizing he was waiting for me to respond.

"Please, just call me Casimir. We are siblings, are we not?"

"Thank you, Casimir. I'm Lana."

"Lana, as in light? How fitting for a witch of your talents."

I gawked. It was easy to tell that I was a witch—if you knew what to look for. But the prince could tell how I wielded my power? That was atypical and an indicator that he was powerful.

"It was at this table where my great-grandfather,

the first ruler of Lyonesse, helped draw the lines of Faerie, creating the realms," King Oberon stated without preamble. "Today, it is where I intend to follow in my great-grandfather's footsteps and change Faerie for the better." The white finery he wore swished as he paced behind Xerxes' perch.

"All royals must put emotion aside when ruling for the best of their kingdom. I say this because what I ask of you will be great. It is my intent that one of you becomes my general and second in line for the throne—the prince or princess general."

A collective gasp rose from the table. Just the idea of being in the military, fighting, didn't seem to be *me*, but I could see that others liked the idea. Crystal had a gleam in her eye that told me she didn't have a problem with leading armed forces.

"For the good of my loyal subjects, however, I must remain impartial to choosing. I cannot allow favoritism or my admiration of other qualities you might possess to blind me to what is best for my people. A king has a duty to those he rules over."

"Here! Here!" Casimir spoke up, and for the first time since I'd met them, the king gave him an indulgent smile.

"Already, you have proven yourselves better equipped than many, for you are not the only children I sired in the Old Land. You are the top echelon, the cunning, the strong, and most intrigued by your bloodline. However, to become prince or princess general, you must be *the best of the best.*"

He stroked Xerxes, their eyes locking in a way familiar to me from years spent with Naela. Was the phoenix calming my father as Naela often calmed me?

"Fae have a time-honored ritual for kingdoms blessed with an abundance of heirs. It is called the Successional and is a tournament of strength, cunning, and power. If you wish to remain in Lyonesse, you *will* partake. The winner will become the general of Lyonesse and the second heir to the crown. Both are pivotal roles that no one should take lightly. I will spend most of the coming months with this person, training them for the role."

"Sire?" A young man as pale as the king, with unattractive fishy lips and a weak chin, leaned over the table. "By tournament, do you mean we will battle in the old ways? By swords and hoof?"

His voice held a distinct note of English aristocracy, as did the way he held himself—too at ease in these alien surroundings. Clearly, he was posh. It was easy enough to picture him at a manor house, riding a stallion through the woods around his family home, or studying at Oxford.

"Those are the old ways according to humans; and *no one* in this room is pure human," King Oberon said. "The Successional will be settled in the old ways according to the fae—with magic."

Magic.

My stomach sank. No doubt most of the people around this table were more powerful than me. Was it even worth it to compete? My father had just said he'd spend the next few months training the winner. Would it be months before I could form a relationship and get answers? Questions clawed their way up my throat. Unable to hold them back, I went for it.

"Sire. I have no personal experience, but I suppose kings are . . . busy." I blushed at how thick I sounded, my voice meek, my wordage underwhelming in such grand surroundings. "I wonder, even if we don't win, will you have time to get to know us all? That's what I came here for."

My face burned. I sounded so bloody *needy*, especially considering the incredible things all around that should intrigue me. But I couldn't help it. To me, being in a magical land meant *nothing* if I couldn't fulfill my lifelong dream of getting to know my father. Risking further embarrassment, I glanced down the table and was surprised to find that no one scorned me.

Most looked interested in King Oberon's answer —a couple bit their lips, others fidgeted. Clearly, I wasn't the only one with daddy issues here. That made sense. If the others had solved similar clues to get into Faerie, they too had put themselves at risk. Yes, we were all desperate in one way or another.

For the first time, the king's grandiosity wavered,

and his eyes softened. "I will get to know my general and two additional majors well, but I fear the rest of our relationships will take longer to develop."

I slumped in my chair.

Unlike the posh Englishman and myself, who had spoken out of turn, the albino man politely raised his hand.

Oberon's eyes shifted to him. "Name and power?"

It was a weird way to get to know us, but I guessed in this situation it fit. Apparently, the king had to make the most of his time getting acquainted. Being efficient would help.

"Dakarai, but I go by Dak. Shifter, my animal aspect is a white lion."

Oberon lifted a brow, impressed. "Your question, my son?"

Dakarai cleared his throat. "What will we do if we don't win the Successional but want to remain here? I'll miss my family, but living in a castle in Faerie *has* to be better than working with tourists who only talk about going on safari. As long as we get to visit our homes occasionally, I'd like to stay."

His accent sounded a bit Australian but emphasized the consonants of his words differently. However, it was his words, not the way he said them, which struck me most.

I'd been so caught up with discovering that I was a royal, that I was in Faerie, and that Finn was my brother, I hadn't even considered Mam. If I stayed, which I was certain I wanted to, would I ever see her again? And how often?

The king nodded understandingly. "You are invited to stay in Lyonesse for as long as you like. Once you earn a title, you may travel throughout the realms and even to the Old Land. It will take work and planning to get you through another kingdom's bonegate, but with the right incentive anything is possible."

"So, those who rank lower have titles, too?" Crystal, the brazen redhead, folded her arms over her chest.

"There will be a title for each and opportunities which would have likely been out of your reach in the Old Land. Diplomatic and military missions will be given to fill your time and broaden your horizons. Additionally, there are currently many eligible princes and princesses of age to marry in Faerie. Others might become explorers or warriors. Here, there are *no* limits."

A girl with glowing black skin, sapphire blue eyes, and full lips sat up straight at the mention of princes. She could have been pulled from a swimsuit model catalog, and it wasn't hard to imagine she'd been dreaming of a prince her entire life.

Crystal, however, leaned forward and placed her elbows on the long table. "Was this all necessary? I don't know about the rest of these people, but I've had a hard life. My mom worked for everything she had, and I learned to do the same. Why couldn't you have helped all the women you impregnated? Why did you spread your seed and then just vanish?"

Casimir shot up, his face pulled tight.

"Son," Oberon warned.

"I will have no one dishonor you, Father." The prince turned his sharp gaze to Crystal. "You speak of work? Of suffering? The fae of Lyonesse have suffered more than any of you could *ever* imagine." Casimir's hand swept toward the window, toward his kingdom.

"You complain of work, but what of those instances in which you got what you wanted?" Casimir spat the words out, obviously disgusted. "When something brilliant came your way, you did not deserve? Perhaps you chalked it up to your skill, your magic, even luck, but I know better. Our father interfered as much as possible on your behalf to make your lives more comfortable."

Crystal's mouth dropped open. "I—"

"Spare us your ungrateful excuses," the prince cut her off. "Just know, our father has done the best he could from beneath the shadows of Queen Pari. For both the fae of Lyonesse *and* you in the Old Land." Casimir reclaimed his seat. He was vibrating with fury.

Our father *had* been watching us then. I wondered if my getting into Trinity had anything to do with him? I was smart enough to get by and do well in the world, but not nearly as bright as the rest of the students at Trinners, and I bloody knew it. Or had my acceptance been a miracle born of Finn's stepfather? That was what I'd always suspected . . .

Finn. Had King Oberon been gathering information on Finn? Finn was only here by chance—not by invite. His mother had never told him he was magic. Perhaps she hadn't even known it herself? From what I knew of conservative Mrs. Fairchild, that seemed a better fit.

"But some of your children didn't get clues on how to get here." I didn't say Finn's name, though I reached for his hand beneath the table.

He pulled it away.

Way to put your foot in your mouth, I chided myself.

"That is true," Oberon said. "The Feathered Fae are the only citizens of Lyonesse able to access the bonegate that Queen Pari stole from my kingdom."

I blinked, realizing that Ellette must be one of these Feathered Fae my father spoke about. I tucked that information away for later, determined to learn more.

"They watched my children over the years, helped them along, and noted the ones who showed magical prowess and extraordinary abilities." The king nodded down the table, indicating the lot of us. "Demonstrating your magic was the first hurdle to claiming an invitation into Faerie. Those who did not exhibit magic when the Feathered Fae were present did not receive a notice. It would have been pointless to bring them here when they could never truly be a part of this world."

My lips parted in surprise. "But I'm not great—"

"I did what I thought best for my kingdom and my line." King Oberon cut me off.

A wave of relief that I didn't have to admit my power had been slow to bloom and lacking since washed through me. No one wanted to admit weakness, including me.

"If you cannot abide by what I've done," my father continued, "I will not hold you here against your will. Just know, all of you are here for a reason, and that you belong here."

The king placed a gentle hand on his phoenix before continuing. "You will have the night to decide whether to take part in the Successional. Those who stay, expect to train every afternoon—save two—for a fortnight. Training is mandatory, so you may discover any latent elf magic. This land may also change your existing magic." He scanned the table, gauging our reactions.

Arlo, the lumberjack ginger, cleared his throat. "What about the free days, sire?"

"On one of your free days, *I* have a surprise in store. The other is a ritual day of rest before the tournament. Your morning hours are free for you to explore as you wish. I suggest taking advantage of the royal library to familiarize yourself with Faerie through literature. Use your time well and understand you will see little of me."

A few people scowled, and the king gave them a kindly smile.

"Traditionally, once a sibling challenges the others to the Successional, their parents are forbidden from interaction so as not to show favoritism. Though this scenario is unique, I will abide by the traditions of my land."

"We won't see you at all?" Crystal looked pissed at the idea. Not that she'd looked anything but sour and frustrated since I'd met her.

"You will see me only in groups, mostly at meals, but do *not* seek me out. It is offensive to one of Faerie's most important royal rituals. I am adamant that the title of general and second heir will be based on skill alone, for it is skill you will need to succeed, not my favor. Prince Casimir will be my eyes and ears among you."

The king paused for a beat, and those haunting gold eyes seemed to level us all. "Now, I bid you good-night, children. Let it be known, I do hope you'll stay."

He swept from the room without looking back. My chest loosened. That had been intense.

Now that the king was gone, I was curious to see how others felt. My gaze scanned the table. I was relieved to see that I wasn't the only one who was stunned. But I barely had time to consider the emotions running through me before the guards herded us out of the council room. I trailed at the back, observing the strangers who were now my new siblings.

A hawk screeched. I lifted my gaze from the cold marble to find Naela, playing the role of my protector, flying above me in small circles. Kane, however, was at the head of the group, his wings flapping wildly as he rode on Finn's arm. Even from meters away, I heard Finn's heavy steps, his muttered curses. He was angry and sending Kane into distress.

I rushed forward. A distressed hawk could be dangerous.

"It's all right, Kane," I cooed, hoping my voice would calm the Harris' hawk.

My method worked like a charm. He took in my voice and Naela's familiar, non-threatening presence above and stilled. His wings tucked in at his sides. I exhaled, glad the danger a scared hawk posed had passed.

"Finn, you need to calm down." I took care to keep my tone light, so as not to trigger Kane again. "Kane is sensing erratic energy from you. Maybe this place is freaking him out too. Wouldn't surprise me."

"Did you know?" Finn whirled about to face me, his usual playful eyes were narrow slits. Kane released another anxious screech.

"What? About this?" I gestured to the castle, my voice echoing off the white walls. "Of course not!"

"Don't be thick!" Finn roared. "I don't care about any of this . . . this royalty stuff. Did you know I had *magic*?"

The tension grew too much for Finn's hawk. Kane took flight, flapping up and down the hallway and making a hideous ruckus. My gaze sought Naela, and I motioned for her to join Kane. She complied, flying up next to Kane gently, trying to soothe him. The rest of Oberon's children glanced up, their faces filled with worry over the frantic screeching.

"Keep moving," I said. "They won't hurt you."

Everyone obeyed, rushing down the hall away from the hawks. Even Arlo, a self-proclaimed eagle shifter, looked worried as hell. Then again, maybe he should be the most worried. He knew what a bird of prey could do first hand. Still, I was sure everyone would be fine.

Though most hawkers could not guarantee such a thing, I was positive Naela would eventually calm Kane. Neither of them would lash out. Naela knew what I wanted her to do, and she rarely failed me.

A familiar, Ellette's words rushed back. For the first time, I believed them.

"Answer me, Lana." Finn's face was close to mine, his tone low, laden with ill-concealed anger.

"About your magic? Course not! I had no idea."

My words seemed to act like a slap in the face,

and Finn recoiled before turning on his heel and stalking away.

I jogged behind him. "I've *never* felt magic off you. You must be a species I've never met before. I don't know what you could be, maybe a really rare fae, but I promise I wouldn't—"

"Don't. Just don't. You've pointed out other supernaturals before. Even an *elf* once. I remember you said elves were rare. If that's part of what I am, why couldn't you feel it?" His eyes snapped to meet mine.

He didn't believe me. And he was pissed at me. The realizations hit me like a fist to the gut. Then the shame steamrolled over me. I felt horrible for hiding what a mediocre witch I was from my best friend. I'd basically been lying about it for years. I was completely in the wrong and needed to come clean.

"Finn, I know I led you to think I'm some powerful witch, but I'm really not. We saw that elf from *so* far away, and I'd never been close to one before that. I only knew what he was because I saw him do magic. Magic a witch couldn't do. There might have been a hundred supernaturals I missed. I swear it! Plus . . . I didn't even know *I am* part elf! How could you expect me to know you were?"

Ryker appeared out of nowhere, a crease between his unruly brows. "Is there a problem?"

"We're fine." I blurted out, but Finn took longer. His eyes were still hard as they leveled me, trying to decide what I was. A liar? Shite for a witch? Oblivious? The truth was, I was a bit of all of them. Finally, he shook his head.

"Good," Ryker said, though he looked unconvinced. "We've arranged for you two to take the larger rooms on your floors to accommodate your birds. I'll show you to your quarters now."

It was only then that I realized we'd reached the end of the hall and were at the bottom of a staircase. The rest of the group was climbing the stairs, stealing wary glances back at Finn and me.

"Kane!" Finn barked.

Kane soared down. The second the hawk landed on Finn's outstretched arm, he turned his back on me and climbed the stairs after Ryker.

A lump formed in my throat. Finn and I had just had our first fight.

CHAPTER ELEVEN

A shriek of laughter pulled me from my fitful sleep, tightening every muscle in my body for a moment. A feminine voice caught my ear, and I sighed, annoyed. It appeared that some of the girls— my new sisters—were early risers. I stretched and lifted myself from the plush feather bed, taking in my new surroundings with fresh eyes.

My room was as lovely as the night before. With its marble floors, canopied bed, and fireplace, all decorated in shades of red, white, and gold, I truly felt I was somewhere I could relax. If only I could erase the extra doorway that bypassed the hall and funneled into the common area, a large, round room at the end of the hall that adjoined two rooms—mine and Crystal's.

While I'd received one of the two larger rooms to accommodate a cage for Naela, Crystal had to lobby hard for the mirror image of my space. That room had originally been reserved for our night guards. They required a space in which to rest and relax as we slept, and that room was ideal since it was bigger than the others on our floor. Now all seven guards—one for each girl—shared a smaller room off the stairwell. The poor things.

I wiped the tears that crusted my eyes. They were puffy. I'd stained my pillows with tears for hours after my fight with Finn.

Maybe he'd calmed down a little overnight? I ambled to my private bath and splashed cold water on my face, knowing my wishes were fruitless. In all our years together Finn had never been mad at me, but I *had* seen him rage at others.

The boy could hold a serious grudge. I wouldn't get him to talk for days. Maybe weeks. Still, a girl could hope, right?

I was just out of the clawfoot-tub when I heard a soft knock at my door. Wrapping a towel tight around my torso, I rushed out of the bath and to the door, hoping to find Finn on the other side.

Instead, I found the handsome, stormy-eyed guard I'd noticed the night before.

"Oh! Umm, hi." I pulled the towel tighter, and the guard looked away, a pink stain spreading across his chiseled cheekbones.

"Good morning, my lady. My name is Garret. I'm one of the captains of the fae guard. King Oberon has assigned me to be your day guardian until after the Successional. I'm sure Sai—your night guard— explained this already, but each contender in the Successional gets two guardians: one for the day, the other for the night."

"Seems to be a lot of guards," I muttered. I remained faintly annoyed that I'd be followed every-where. This girl liked her privacy.

"It's one of the rituals leading up to the tourna-ment," Garret replied. "However, unlike other rituals, this one stems from historical events and is meant to stave off sabotage." He cocked his head. "Did Sai tell you any of this? Did she check your room for mali-cious items too?"

Sai, the same ebony goddess with violet eyes and snow white hair whom I'd spotted in the throne room, had in fact, explained this all to me. She'd done so while she stalked around my bedroom, searching for items that would cause me harm. I hadn't liked the explanation then either, but that wasn't his fault.

"Yes, she already informed me. And did a sweep of the room."

Garret's shoulders dropped as if he was relieved things had gone to plan. Twisting behind him, he picked something up and offered it to me. I peered at the item, a basket containing clothes and things that looked like toiletries.

"Splendid. I'm meant to give you this," Garret said, still holding the basket out. "Also to mention that your hawk may fly wherever she pleases, even when you're training. The forest outside the castle is sparse, but I assure you, there is still small prey to hunt." Garret spoke to the floor, unable to meet my eyes.

"Please, call me Lana," I said, taking the basket and placing it in front of my towel-clad body self-consciously. "Thanks for telling me about the forest. I'll admit, I was a little concerned. It looks so empty."

Last night we took dinner in our rooms, so I'd eaten gazing out upon the bleak landscape. Though it was depressing, it was also a way to distract myself. I couldn't consider Finn's anger while wondering how a foreign queen's actions had caused the trees to look burnt and leafless, the soil black and dry. It was so very different from the greenery I'd grown up with that I'd wondered if the dirt would even feel the same running through my fingers. It didn't seem likely. The forest just outside the castle didn't have that full, earthy scent Ireland was famous for.

"I'll leave you to prepare for your day," the guard said, not commenting on the forest at all. "You will take breakfast and the evening meal in the great hall from now on. The king requests your presence this morning at your convenience. I shall be by the stairs to accompany you at your ready. Please, take your time, my lady Lana." He turned on his heel and marched down the hall.

"Just Lana!" I called after him. Things were

already weird enough around here without people calling me "my lady" all the time.

<hr>

I CRINGED AS I STEPPED INSIDE THE GREAT HALL AND A dozen pairs of eyes swung toward me. Glancing every which way, I tried to deflect the stares by acting mesmerized by my surroundings. It wasn't too difficult to pull off. The myriad scents—roasted meats, vegetables, something sweet, bread, and wine—would have distracted anyone, but then there was the great hall itself.

The cavernous room resembled a massive mess hall, only the tables and benches were made of shining, white wood decorated with greenery and candles that radiated more light than should have been possible. Chandeliers dripping with crystals hung from the ceiling, tinkling in the faint breeze coming from the open windows.

The most extravagant table was at the front of the hall, the head table. Decorated with tall pillar candles and flowers, it ran perpendicular to the rest of the tables, making it stand out more than it already did. Not that it really needed any of the decoration to do so.

My father and Prince Casimir sat alone at the head table, which could have sat a dozen more. Their manes of white-blond gleamed, catching every beam of light in the room. A hooded figure in a black cloak stood behind them and two others—one male, one female—in less shiny black cloaks flanked the imposing center figure. A flag hung behind the head table. The banner was emblazoned with a black and gold phoenix rising from red flames that burst on a field of white. Beautiful and stark.

Among the crowds, a dozen different types of fae sat, stealing my attention. Some appeared to be rich. Perhaps visiting nobles? Others were of the working class, scurrying around and dressed in simple clothes. Many watched me with undisguised interest.

Despite my overwhelm at the surroundings and being stared at, I did my best to give off an aura of confidence as I sought Finn's familiar sandy hair. Finally, I spotted him, his gaze resolutely on his plate.

As usual, he had company.

One of his companions was the curvy girl with dark curly hair. The other was the copper-skinned boy with bushy eyebrows who gave off shifter energy. I couldn't recall either of their names. Or if they'd even given them last night.

A part of me wanted to hold back, to wait until Finn was alone, but I was determined to get over this rough patch as soon as possible. Even if it meant making a fool of myself. At my approach, the girl and shifter scooted over so I could sit across from Finn. I sighed, grateful someone was trying to make this easier for us. I'd just settled myself on the bench when, without a word, my best friend stood and made his way to the other side of the room.

The apples of my cheeks grew hot. From the corner of my eye, I saw the others stiffen, unsure what to say.

"Wicked burn," an imperious voice I already recognized as belonging to Crystal, hissed behind me. A chorus of high-pitched giggles followed. Wonderful—a clique had already formed. My favorite.

Thankfully, at that moment a fae—a dryad, I guessed, recalling Gran's description of their brown bark-like skin—offered me an assortment of food. The girls' laughter quieted as the dryad prattled on, explaining what the food was.

I grabbed a bowl and listened to the dryad describe cockatrice eggs as I shoveled spoonfuls of porridge into my mouth, hoping it would help push back the tears that threatened to fall. When it was clear I wasn't going to respond, the dryad settled for placing a few plates beside me and traipsed off.

"He'll get over it," the curvy young woman I'd sat next to said after the dryad's absence left an awkward lull.

"I agree," the shifter said. "It's a big change for all of us. Imagine not knowing you had magic in the first place and then ending up *here*?" The man's voice came out as an ethereal hiss, unlike anything I'd heard before.

I stopped shoving food in my mouth and stared at

him. His eyes were an unexpected vivid green with strange, slitted pupils.

"What are you?" I asked.

"Kumar Rao. Naga."

My face flushed again as I realized I hadn't asked him his name, only what he was. But Kumar had the good grace not to point that out.

"Naga are chimera of sorts, half snake, half human shifters," Kumar continued, clearly intent on smoothing over my roughness. "We're found in India, where I was born. My guard informed me there are many here in Faerie, though in a different realm. Beast Realm, I believe Ronan called it." Kumar's nose wrinkled, displaying his distaste for the name.

"And I'm Maria Mendoza-Lopez, earth rumbler." My gaze shifted, catching sight of the woman's ears as she tried to push her wild, black curls behind her shoulders for a second time. They were ever so slightly pointed.

"Did your ears become pointed when you arrived here?" I asked, thinking about Finn, and how the gray of my eyes had transmuted to gold.

"Si. Thank God they weren't like this before," Maria said. "I can't imagine walking around Mexico City with these odd points! I'd have to change my hairstyle! What about your eyes?"

"Same. There's always been a ring of gold around my pupil, but not this much. I'm an illuminator, so I figured it has something to do with light." I shrugged.

"An illuminator. I've never——"

The sound of a bell filled the room, cutting Maria's words short. I looked around. Garret, who had situated himself a respectable distance down the table from me, stood alongside the other guards.

"Good morning, my loyal subjects, members of the guard, my children." The king rose from his seat and bowed at every class of person he indicated. He wore an immaculate, tailored, white suit accented with gold. His sleek white hair was pulled back, emphasizing his cutting cheekbones. Prince Casimir remained seated at the king's side, looking well rested and every bit the prince.

I bet I looked like dog meat in comparison.

"Children, thank you for gathering to break our fast. I see everyone has made it, which pleases me greatly. Our first family meal!" King Oberon's face lit up with joy.

My lips turned up a smidgen. Last night, when he'd been explaining what happened—what could happen—my father had been charismatic, but not as joyous. Though I couldn't relate at that moment, it was nice to see someone was happy.

"I realize you have had little time to consider your future. Still, I must know where you stand. Those of you who are undecided about remaining and participating in the Successional, please raise your hand."

No hands went up.

Oberon's eyebrows lifted. "No one? I fear to ask,

then," his tone dropped. "Has anyone opted to forgo their birthright? Dismiss the land their ancestors founded?"

Once again, no hands went up.

King Oberon's face split into a jubilant smile, lighting up the room. "Excellent!" He clapped his hands like a boy before lifting his glass, red liquid sloshing within it.

Wine for breakfast? My brows furrowed, but I caught myself before I hopped on the judgment train. I was in Faerie—eating cockatrice eggs. I would have to expand my mind while I was here. Whatever was in that glass could be anything. Juice, some magical concoction . . . unicorn blood, though I hoped it wasn't the last one. I got shivers just thinking about it.

"I'd like to inform you of how we shall be proceeding. The Successional for rank of general of Lyonesse and second heir will take place in a fortnight—the ritual time allotted once the challenge is issued and accepted as you've just done by opting to remain here. That should give you plenty of time to train and for your magic to acclimatize to Faerie. Be aware, it's not only the magic you possess *now* that could change. New magic might crop up as your latent elven blood becomes enriched by the land and magic of Faerie."

New magic? An old wish to become an elemental, whether it be a rumbler, scorcher, weaver, or diviner, resurfaced.

Maria stood up. "Sire, Maria Mendoza-Lopez, rumbler."

Oberon looked taken aback at the interruption, but nodded for Maria to proceed.

"I must ask, what about our families? Will you tell them where we are? I want to stay here—at least for a bit. But I have a family who cares for me at home, not to mention a job. I need to know what I should tell them."

A look of understanding dawned on the king's face as the logistics of normal life were presented. "You're right. I will send my Feathered Fae to your mothers today with a note from each of you explaining where you are and what you intend to do. Many of them did not know *exactly* who I was all those years ago. It was a necessary precaution to keep my offspring safe from Queen Pari's malevolence."

My stomach clenched at the thought of Mam, how much she had hurt and struggled all those years my father hadn't been around. I wondered how the other mothers had felt?

Finn's mother.

My hand flew to rub the back of my neck. His entire life he'd thought his biological father was dead. To discover here—on a different plane of Earth—that his mother had lied must be terrible.

My instinct told me Mrs. Fairchild was oblivious to her family history and likely embarrassed to tell Finn that his father had left them. It was the only explanation. Mrs. Fairchild was a proper lady, never one to miss a mass or step a toe outside societal norms. So unlike her son.

"Sire?" The weak-chinned boy who looked as if he belonged hunting and birding in the English countryside stood up. "Who are your Feathered Fae and what do they do?"

Oberon grinned. "From your inquiries last night and today I can tell you have a knack for isolating important topics and no fear of asking about them. Both are important qualities for a prince. What is your name, my son?"

"Thank you, Sire. It would please my mother to hear that. My name is Nigel Burger."

One of the cloaked fae, a male with long, dark hair who stood behind Oberon, moved forward to whisper something in his ear.

"Ah. Your mother is a Burger of the landed gentry in Yorkshire?"

Nigel nodded, looking pleased.

"I'm delighted you found your bonekey. Your line was always known for their superior witches. Now, as for your question. My Feathered Fae are my closest advisors. Second only to Prince Casimir and whoever among you wins the title of general and second heir. Feathered Fae are important as they all have the power to shift into birds and hence can sneak through the bonegates of Faerie into the Old Land, should I need them to."

"The bonegates are that small?" Nigel asked.

"Not small, but extremely well-guarded by adversaries of my court," our father answered. "The Feathered Fae also perform much of the scouting around Lyonesse. They keep me informed as to Queen Pari's movements and the health of our land. They are indispensable advisors."

Nigel nodded as if he'd understood everything the king had said. "Thank you, Sire. That was illuminating."

My head spun. Though Oberon had spoken of such things as bonegates the night before, I'd had little time to absorb them. The only thing I was sure of was I'd already met a Feathered Fae—Ellette.

Oberon nodded. "Does anyone else have questions?"

None of my other siblings spoke up. I wondered if most were like me, too scared to be the one to ask a stupid question in front of a large crowd.

"Very well. I have set aside rooms for you to practice your magic and prepare for the Successional. Your training starts at midday."

CHAPTER TWELVE

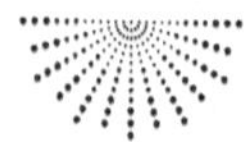

"My lady Lana, you'll be late for training if we don't leave now. The Master Feathered Fae will be displeased."

Garret's voice traveled through the door to my room as I gave a final tug on my pants. They were a spandex-like material that did *not* give like spandex and clung too tight around my thighs and calves.

I yanked the door open before Garret could knock again. "Could you *please* stop pounding? These pants took me *ages* to get into." Garret blanched, and I regretted taking my frustrations out on him. "I'm sorry. I feel like I'm swimming through mud. Is it *really* going to matter if I'm a few minutes late?"

"Unfortunately, yes, my lady Lana. The Master Feathered Fae does not tolerate lateness. If it were a guard-run training, I'd not be so stringent." He gestured down the hall with his hand as if to say, "now can we please get going?"

I sighed. "Fine. And it's just Lana. Drop the 'my lady,' it's weird."

"Until the tournament is complete, it is your title, my la—"

I shot him a glare.

"As you wish, Lana."

I said a quick goodbye to Naela, reiterating that she could fly out the window whenever she liked, and shut the door to my room. We'd only reached the end of the hall when one of the many questions swirling in my head since breakfast took hold. "What do you mean when you say 'my lady' is my title until after the tournament?"

"You are of royal blood. Hence, the guards and servants of Phoenix Castle will be compelled to call you something other than your name. Your ranking in the Successional will determine your lasting title. If you win, you will become Princess General Lana. From there, King Oberon will award each of his children with military ranks depending on their placing in the tournament. If King Oberon is true to his fair nature, they will be in accordance with what kings awarded previous generations of full fae heirs after their Successional."

"You like him, then. The king, my father?"

Garret stopped, his foot hovered above a stair.

My hand flew to my mouth as I realized how tactless that sounded. "I'm sorry. You don't have to answer. That was an inappropriate question."

"Not at all," Garret said, placing his foot down. "For the record, your father is as dear to me as my own—Sinkers be with his soul. I've lived in the castle and served the king since I was young. It's an honor to have been chosen as your private guard, for I would not be where I am today without His Majesty's good grace."

"Oh . . . That's good," I said. I'd not expected such a thorough answer.

We'd just reached the bottom of the stairs when laughter boomed not far behind us. I twisted to find two of my male siblings appear on the floor above, both grinning from ear to ear. Ebba and Ryker, the guards I'd first met when appearing in Faerie, followed close behind.

"I see you're running late, too," Garret said. Anxiety crept over his face, pulling his sharp angles even tighter.

Ebba frowned, annoyed. "These two were more interested in joking around than getting to training on time."

"Just trying to lighten the mood, Ebba! Come on, after everything we've learned, can you blame us?" The man with raven-dark hair, brown eyes, and an obvious Italian accent extended his hand to me. "Giovanni Ricci, water diviner, as our dear father would have us introduce ourselves. Please just call me Gio. My head will explode if another person calls me 'my lord.'" Gio's eyes shot playfully to Ebba.

"Dakarai Adisa. But I go by Dak, lion shifter." The albino man inclined his head, a small smile curving his lips. I suspected he was from South Africa, based on his safari comment and accent.

"Lana Shea, illuminator witch."

"We should really move on—" Garret tried to insert himself into the conversation, but Gio's long whistle drowned out his words.

"An illuminator, huh?" Gio asked, looking impressed. "That makes two. I bet our father will be proud when he finds out. If he doesn't already know."

"Uh, maybe. I'm not well-trained. Who else is an illuminator?"

"Nigel of the landed gentry," Gio answered, imitating Nigel's posh tone, but adding in a stereotypical Italian flair by twisting his hands in the air.

I couldn't help it. I rolled my eyes. Not only was I a crap illuminator, but now I had to compete with someone who undoubtedly had received more instruction than me.

"Our thoughts exactly," Dak said, his presence soft compared to Gio's audacious tone and wild hand gestures.

"We should really get moving." Ebba pushed her way between us. "We're already five minutes late."

"Sinkers," Ryker said, his tone panicked so that it sounded like a curse.

Without warning, Garret seized me by the elbow and guided me down the hallway.

I shot a glance over my shoulder to see Dak spurred into motion by the hulking mass of Ryker's body. Ebba had simply grabbed Gio's hand, pulled, and he'd followed like a puppy at her heels, a huge grin on his face.

***

A WOMAN WHO COULDN'T BE ANY OLDER THAN THIRTY stood before a group when the guards rushed us into the training room. Swathed in a black cloak that fluttered in the faint breeze trickling in from the windows, the woman glared at us.

"You're late." Her voice was sharp as steel. I pulled myself up, sensing that this woman would take no bullshit.

"My apologies, Master Meegra," Garret said. "Ebba and I take the blame. We stopped to converse in the hall and lost track of time."

I stared at Garret. *This woman* was the Master Feathered Fae? But she looked so young! Younger by decades than the male fae standing behind my father at breakfast. I'd been expecting a wizened old warrior. And Gio, Dak, and I had been the ones chatting it up . . . why was Garret lying for us?

The displeasure rolling off Meegra was palpable from across the room. This was no small feat as the training room was the width of three running tracks laid side by side.

"Don't let it happen again," the Master Feathered Fae snapped. "King Oberon wants his heirs in peak condition before the Successional to suss out the most powerful among them. Witches, shifter—fall in line."

My lips pursed, but at Garret's gentle nudge, I crossed the room quietly. He'd already saved me from trouble once. There was no need to test my luck. I queued up next to the Asian woman I'd noticed last night. My eyes caught on the tattoos decorating her arms all the way up to her shoulder. They were so intricate, so beautiful. The sleeve must have taken forever.

"Hey. I'm Himari Ohno, weaver witch," she said, pulling my attention from her tats to her face. She smiled, as if everyone became mesmerized by her ink, and pushed a chunk of lush, black hair behind her shoulder.

"Lana Shea, illuminator."

Himari lifted an eyebrow. "I—"

But Meegra's hard voice rang through the room, cutting Himari short. "Quiet. Guards, wait over there with the others." Meegra gestured to the far wall where a grouping of guards was watching.

The next instant, Meegra was levitating toward us, her black cape rippling behind her. The garment was more than just a cape woven of cloth. It was made of individual black feathers, each fluttering with her motion. It was astounding, as was the ease with which she manipulated air to carry her.

"As for the rest of you, let's get one thing straight." Meegra's cutting gaze moved down the line. "I don't *care* that you're His Majesty's children. All I care about is that you know how to fight, and to do it well. King Oberon did not elaborate much on the tournament and has requested I fill in the blanks—and answer questions you may have."

Meegra unfastened her cloak and allowed it to drop to the white marble floor. I stifled a gasp. Beneath that cape of ebony feathers was a suit of armor unlike the plain armor our guards wore. Made of black metal with feathers etched on its surface in silver, Meegra's armor gave off an otherworldly glow.

With a flourish of her hand, an onyx-hilted dagger flew from her scabbard. Meegra caught it in her opposite hand without even looking. She was power embodied, and she knew it.

"The Successional is nothing less than a gladiator-style competition. You might surrender when the going gets tough, or you will fight to prove yourself. *Nothing* is off limits. Not even death. Few royal children have died in the Successional, but that does not mean it is outside the bounds of the tournament. Until you are lifted from the arena's grounds, I repeat, *nothing* is off limits."

A few children had died?! Ice ran through my veins. Himari stiffened, and on my other side, Gio's mouth fell open. But Meegra plowed forth as if she'd said nothing more than sometimes people come out of the Successional with splinters.

"While you are in Faerie, your power will change and evolve. A fortnight will be only enough time to learn the most superficial of these changes. If you cannot cope with your magic's continued evolution, or if it never awakens,"—Meegra's eyes latched onto Finn—"there is still hope. One weapon per participant is allowed in the tournament. Be grateful His Majesty granted you that much. Had I been in charge of the Successional, I'd not have allowed such a handicap to defile our sacred rite. Lastly, the Successional provides amusement for the kingdom. It is—"

Maria, the rumbler witch I'd taken breakfast with, stepped forward. "I don't get it. Why didn't our father—?"

Meegra hurled her dagger, forcing Maria to jump back. The blade landed where her feet had just been. Meegra's eyes glittered with annoyance. "*You* are only a glorified soldier until after the Successional. *I,* however, am the head of King Oberon's army until the prince or princess general is titled. You *will not* interrupt me again. Is that clear? State your name and species when you answer me."

I could hear Maria's loud gulp even with ten

bodies between us. "Maria Mendoza-Lopez, rumbler."

Meegra sneered. "Humans of the Old Land and their names. In this room, you are only Maria. All of King Oberon's guards have but one name, and you will too until you're titled. Some may call you my lord or my lady, but do not expect that pleasure from me until you've earned it. Is that clear, rumbler-elf?"

"Clear," Maria said, though the scrunch of her nose revealed she did not agree.

"Good. Your question?"

"Why did our father not tell us this himself? Dying isn't really my thing. I might have changed my mind about the Successional had I known." Maria's voice shook, like the earth she could no doubt make tremble beneath her.

Meegra's sneer grew. Apparently, Maria's unwillingness to kill was a sign of weakness. "Like any father, it pains our dear King Oberon to think of his children fighting and in pain. Why would he want to mention death? Better to leave that to someone like me, who has no such qualms. Just so we're clear, our king *fully* expects most of you to surrender. That is what occurs historically in Successionals, as traditionally siblings have grown up together and already formed attachments." She rolled her eyes. Apparently the Master Feathered Fae thought little of weaknesses like forming attachments to one's family. She was bloody terrifying.

"However, I thought it pertinent that everyone knew there have been cases where one sibling desired to eliminate his or her competition. Permanently. It is not against the rules."

I looked up and down the line at my new siblings. Although I barely knew them, none looked like killers. In fact, Kumar the naga looked like he may vomit. I took that as a good sign.

My shoulders loosened. We weren't *expected* to kill, and I was okay with a little fighting to prove myself. Especially when the chance to spend time with my father on the line.

"Himari, weaver witch," Himari said after tentatively raising her hand, and getting the go-ahead from Meegra. "So this tournament is not unique because we're from the Old Land?" She rubbed her inked arms self-consciously.

Meegra scoffed. "The Successional has been held during every royal generation save for your father's. That is only because his siblings died when they were young, leaving him the single heir to Lyonesse. Fae law states that if the younger heirs request it, the older ones must fight. It establishes that the strongest fae rules over the kingdom."

"Nigel, illuminator. Why is Prince Casimir not with us then?" Nigel asked, bravely not bothering for Meegra to call on him.

Meegra nearly choked. "Because, illuminator-elf, Prince Casimir's rank is indisputable. He is the only full fae child of King Oberon. While we fae do not fear bastards as was common hundreds of years ago in the Old Land, we are not stupid enough to place a foreigner's rank before a full-blooded fae heir."

Nigel's face fell.

Gio sniggered and Dak nudged him, trying to calm the water diviner before Meegra noticed.

Nigel glared at the pair.

"Now." Meegra twirled a second dagger between her fingers. "If no one else has any stupid questions, let's get to work."

CHAPTER THIRTEEN

"Five-minute break!" Meegra shouted.

The dagger I'd been sparring with fell from my hand and I groaned. My opponent, Victoria Lam—the gorgeous black Barbie with dark blue eyes—smirked. She wasn't much better than I was with a blade, but that didn't stop her from acting superior during our match.

Must be the vila blood in her veins, I thought. Blood that could bring down the most barbaric of men with a seductive song would give her an elevated sense of confidence.

"I thought illuminators were supposed to be impressive," Victoria snapped, sheathing her dagger in its scabbard. Then, she turned on her heel and sashayed off to join Crystal, our bold, red-haired sister, and Wikolia, who could transform into a vicious white wolf.

And I thought Canadians were supposed to be nice.

I retrieved my dagger from the ground and returned it to its scabbard. The motion was still alien, but I was getting used to the blade. Meegra had given us each a dagger to practice with after her introductory speech. While I wasn't a fan of weapons, I had to admit mine was pretty. It bore a pearly white handle and a swirling pattern etched into the metal.

When I glanced up again, I noticed a few social groups had already formed. The giggles I'd heard coming from the girls' common area that morning and all the faces staring at me as I entered the great hall for breakfast came rushing back at me.

Making friends had never been my forte, and it was even more difficult without Finn by my side. Finn, the person who always smoothed over my awful intro-ductions. The mate who dragged me to parties and made me feel brilliant, or at the very least *normal*, instead of awkward. But Finn wasn't in the training room.

He was the only one who didn't know the magic of his mother's blood. As such, he couldn't be trained right away. A Feathered Fae, recognizable from regular guards by their black cloaks, had whisked him away to test his magic earlier that day.

A sigh parted my lips. I would just have to put myself out there without his help and reassuring smile. After all, my fellow trainees should be more than friends or acquaintances—they were family.

"Did you really not know?"

I turned to find a pretty girl with auburn hair and soft blue eyes. Her accent was American, though not obnoxious like Crystal's.

"Know?"

"About Finn? I talked to him this morning. He's a nice guy and seemed certain you must have known he was part elf. He didn't like it much when I said if that was true, you must be a good actress."

I cracked a smile, the first one in what felt like hours. Finn always commented on how terrible I was at hiding my feelings. "I had no idea. This whole debacle is my fault, though. We've known each other since we were young. I led Finn to believe I was a much better witch than I really am. It's the only way I could impress him because . . . well, he's Finn."

"He does seem to be the impressive type. Handsome and confident, even here his confidence shows and he's completely out of his element. Wish I felt the same." The girl stuck out her hand. "I'm Kate Gilbert, healer. That's what we're supposed to say, isn't it? And for the record, I believe you."

My smile grew. "Thank you. I'm Lana Shea, illuminator, but like I said, a shite one."

Kate shrugged. "Being a crappy illuminator is better than being an excellent healer. Or at least here it is. Unlike a lot of our siblings, I'm interested in actually spending time with our father, but I doubt a healer will win a gladiator-style tournament. I mean, did you *see* me sparring against Himari with my dagger? She nearly gutted me three times. Says it must be a translatable skill from working at a sushi restaurant in Tokyo. Obviously, she was being kind, but it didn't make me feel any better."

She released a sigh. "I hope my elven magic will crop up fast, or that I learn to use a weapon better. Otherwise, I figure I'll play along for a while during the Successional and surrender when I have no other options."

"I'm considering a similar situation. Or just hiding behind an illusion until everyone surrenders, jumping on the back of the last person standing, and holding their nostrils until they pass out."

A tinkle of laughter flew from Kate. "Hopefully the last person standing isn't a shifter. It'd be hard to hold a lion's nostrils."

"Seriously." I shot a glance at Dak. "Wikolia wouldn't be a party either." I now knew that the girl I'd imagined dancing on the Hawaiian islands last night could transform into an enormous, snow-white wolf.

Then again, I doubted I would stand a chance against most of my siblings—shifter or not. Crystal and Nigel wielded their daggers as if they had been born with blades in their hands. Others, like Arlo and

Maria, were learning fast. I shook my head, trying to fling out the self-doubt blossoming there.

"Did you say a few of our siblings aren't interested in getting to know our father? Why did they go through that whole scavenger hunt charade to get here if they didn't care to meet him?"

"Some—Himari and Victoria, in particular—came to chew him out for leaving their mothers. They decided against it when he presented us with a life of royal luxury." Kate said the vila's name so regally that I bit back a laugh. Kate, too, must have made the mistake of asking our vila-elf sister if she went by Vikki. The answer was decidedly, no.

"Yeah, what's the deal with Victoria?" I asked, recalling the vila-elf's snide remark.

"You mean her charming personality?" Kate rolled her eyes. "Apparently, Victoria's mom is a legend in Toronto. She's married four times, to richer and richer men. Must be the vila blood. Anyway, Victoria recently got kicked out of the house and I quote 'was forced to wait tables for a while.' Real work isn't her thing, but if she can snag a prince out of this, she will. She's sniped at a few people; I bet intimidation is part of her strategy to rank higher."

A whistle blew, and I jumped.

"Pair up with someone new and resume the fighting position," Meegra barked. "Be quick about it. We have two more dagger sessions before we break again. On my whistle."

"Wanna pair up? We can go easy on each other as long as Meegra doesn't notice," Kate whispered conspiratorially.

"Now you're speaking my language." I grinned.

KATE SHOVED HER DAGGER IN ITS SCABBARD AND groaned as she approached me.

Compared to her, I had no room to complain. We'd sneaked in a single half-hearted sparring session against each other before Meegra separated us. The Master Feathered Fae then paired Kate with Crystal, and me with Wikolia. While sparring with the strong wolf had been murder, she had nothing on her fellow girl gang member Crystal.

The redhead was ferocious, super fit, and capable of learning skills Meegra had shown us only minutes before with remarkable ease. Her hair whipped around her head like a crimson tornado as she twirled and leapt at whoever was unlucky enough to be her opponent.

During training, Meegra had expressed how impressed she was with the dwarf-elf. She even asked Crystal to demonstrate a few fighting tactics before the group with her. Meegra dominated, but Crystal's natural strength and agility strung the demonstration out longer than anyone expected.

I wouldn't have lasted ten seconds. Maybe not even five.

"I'm going to put so much lavender and salt in my bath tonight," Kate said as we limped our way out of the training room.

"Same, after I eat *all* the food at dinner." My stomach rumbled at the thought.

They'd served us a late lunch in the training facility. The meal was a meager affair of bread, cheese, and cold cuts. A "soldier's meal", which Meegra informed us was the meal we'd receive when we traveled in the name of the Crown after the Successional.

"Did she ever let up on you?" I asked Kate.

"Crystal? When has she ever let up on anything?" Kate's tone held a note of familiarity that sparked my interest.

"You knew her before coming here?"

Kate rolled her eyes. "Oh right, you missed the breakfast debacle. Yeah, Crystal and I attended the same college in Idaho, both pre-med, though she graduated a year ahead of me. She just finished her first year at Harvard Medical School."

"What?" Little about Crystal said doctor to me. "She's so buff and . . . brutal. Not at all how I picture most medical students."

Kate laughed. "Be prepared to have your mind blown, then. She was also an Olympic gymnast. She went when she was fourteen or something. She's probably been working her ass off ever since to make up for the fact that she didn't medal."

My face fell. I was up against someone who had the tenacity to become an Olympian and a doctor before they were twenty-five? Who could compete with that?

"That's how I felt, too, when I first met her," Kate said, reading my expression. "But then her winning personality wore on me and I realized not everyone is perfect."

"What happened at breakfast?"

"Oh, just typical Crystal using mind games. Once she found out I was a healer in undergrad, she asked if it was ethical that I become a licensed doctor. What if I couldn't resist using magic on my patients? I told her I had no intention of working as a Western doctor. I would take none of their vows. I only wanted to deepen my knowledge of healing. She thought working so hard for no gain in status was the most ridiculous thing she'd ever heard and never ceases to bring it up."

"There are lots of medically trained healers where I live," I quipped. Mam wasn't one of them, but a witch she went to nursing school had her own apothecary a few towns away.

"It's not that weird where I live either," Kate said. "Anyway, this morning I walked in on her telling Victoria and Wikolia my story. Her tone was *not* flattering. I actually heard her assure them they'd be able to beat a healer with so little ambition easily."

I pressed my lips together, not wanting to admit that when Kate told me she was a healer, I'd thought her an easy mark, too.

"It pissed me off, but I have to admit that she's got a point," Kate sighed. "My magical powers are basically useless in this tournament. While I'm not opposed to fighting, I probably won't learn fast enough to come close to winning. Especially when compared to naturals like Crystal or predators like the shifters."

"No magic is useless. I have faith that you'll figure it out." Without thinking, I threw an arm over Kate's shoulder.

The closeness of the gesture startled both of us, and for a moment, our gazes dropped to the ground. Suddenly, I realized I was touching *my sister*. A person I never thought I'd have and a relationship I'd always craved. Warmth rushed through me, and with improbable ease I relaxed into the touch of a relative stranger and dragged my eyes up to meet her's.

Kate responded in kind, her lips turning up at the corners as she threw her arm over my shoulder, claiming me as kin.

I'D JUST EMERGED FROM THE BEST BATH OF MY LIFE when someone knocked on my door.

My spine straightened. Maybe it was Finn? I still hadn't seen him since the Feathered Fae took him away for testing.

"Hold on a second! I need to dress," I called, not willing to risk running into a guard in my towel again. Quickly, I dried off and threw on a pair of loose black pants and a soft, knit sweater, both of which had appeared in my room during training. My heart was beating wildly, as it always did when I had to admit I was wrong about something. After one last scrunch of my damp hair and a calming inhale, I opened the door.

Kate stood before me with Kumar at her side. Both looked elated.

"Hey?" The word came out as a question. I'd just sat with them at dinner, and everyone had left the table yawning, talking about how they couldn't wait to relax. Jet lag, or Faerie lag, whatever you wanted to call it, was hitting most of us hard.

"Come with us!" Kate said, grabbing my hand and pulling me toward the stairs.

Garret jumped up from a chair at the end of the corridor, and his scent of leather and metal pulsed down the hall toward us. "You said you were just having a word."

"If I had said anything else, would you let me interrupt her?" Kate turned. "Seriously, Lana, I think you have the most protective guard. He barely let us near your door! Said you were talking about going to bed as soon as possible. Like you may die or something without ten hours of sleep."

My cheeks flushed. I had actually told Garret something along those lines.

My guard shot me a concerned glance, and I realized he was trying to save me from peer pressure.

"It's fine, Garret. They want to show me something."

Garret nodded and, ever the shadow, followed me as Kate led us down the stairs.

Ebba, at her limit with Gio's flirting, had made use of her high rank in the fae guard and reassigned herself to Kate late in the afternoon. We found her gossiping with other guards as we exited the stairwell. The look Garret gave their grouping was one of utter contempt.

"Chill, Garret, my man! We don't need to stare at their doors every minute." Ryker, the muscular god amongst guards, laughed when he caught Garret's glare.

"We're supposed to stay within earshot of our charges, Ryker. Until their rank is established, they're vulnerable."

Ryker was not deterred. "I know, man. That's why I'm standing here, guarding Dak's door like a good little peon. But seriously, you were already up there, so

Ebba and Ronan stopped to talk. There was no need to crowd the hall. Am I right?"

"For Sinker's sake," Garret mumbled, which only made Ryker grin wider.

"It's cool, bro. I doubt any of the new royals will battle it out in the stairwell. You should relax a little," Ryker assured his friend.

Battle it out in the stairwell? Yeesh. So our father thought someone—a competing sibling—would strike us dead in the hall before the tournament? That seemed unlikely. Magic and weapons weren't allowed outside the training rooms, and would anyone risk breaking the rules only to be tossed out of Faerie? Or did something else compel our father to station guards at our side day and night?

My father's speech about Queen Pari came rushing back. Could she have agents in Oberon's castle? Is that why he thought we needed guarding at all hours? I shivered at the thought.

A door cracked open and Dak peeked outside. Just beyond him, Gio could be seen moving water through the air as if it were leaves blowing in the wind.

A pang of jealousy shot through me. Only a diviner witch could manage moving water with such grace. In my experience, nothing about magic came that easy.

Ryker stiffened at Gio's show of power. "Yo, man! You know you're not supposed to do magic in your room! Don't make me be like Garret and implement checks every two minutes."

I pressed my lips together, trying not to laugh as Garret mumbled something under his breath that sounded like: "Every two hours and only when she's awake."

However, the next instant my mirth evaporated when the door opened wider. Finn was in there too, gazing out at the group, his eyes ignoring me. My stomach sank at his deliberate disregard.

"Sorry, Ryk!" Gio said, and the water vanished as if it had never been there. "What's going on out here, anyway?" Gio joined Dak and leaned out the door. His bottomless brown eyes locked on Ebba, who looked away.

"I wanted to show Lana something cool. You can join, if you want," Kate said, pulling me down the hall, not willing to waste another minute.

There was a flurry of words and a door shutting behind me. I cast a glance over my shoulder. Kumar, Dak, and Gio were twenty paces behind us, guards in tow.

Finn, on the other hand, was nowhere in sight.

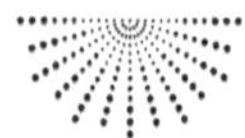

"Where are we going and how on earth did you find it?" I asked as I followed Kate through the castle.

"I asked Ebba if there was a healer aspect of Faerie. She said there was and showed me where the healers worked. On the way there, I found this." Kate stopped at a window, really more of a wide opening in the white stone of the castle as there was no glass, and gestured outside.

Dak, Kumar, Gio, and I moved forward. A collective gasp rose from the group when we caught sight of what Kate wanted to show us.

"It's magnificent," Kumar whispered a slight hiss at the end of his words, reminding me that as a naga he might share a little DNA with the majestic creature before us.

A dragon, ten meters tall and black as night,

paced in a massive courtyard below. Fae milled about the dragon's cage. The enclosure was magically enhanced and weak wisps of fire disappeared against its boundary every time the beast released flame.

"And I thought I was the biggest predator around," Dak murmured.

"I'd say third biggest," Gio piped up. "The dragon and Meegra have you beat. I'm not one to fear the ladies, especially the *gorgeous* ones around here," Gio shot a glance at Ebba, who appeared bored. "But I can't be the only one terrified of the Master Meegra."

Meegra certainly was terrifying, and we all knew it. Still, she was nothing compared to the creature before us. My eyes ran along the dragon's hide, taking in how its black scales glinted and gleamed in the early moonlight. Its claws scratched at the earth, leaving deep divots, and its tail swished from side to side, creating grooves. This creature reeked of danger and magic. Yet, there was something else there, too.

Like the unicorn, this dragon had a sickly appearance and a faint stench of decay emanated from it. Its eyes were clouded, and its chest heaved as though breathing was work. The spikes running down the beast's spine drooped to either side, reminding me of a killer whale kept in captivity for too long.

"It *is* astonishing, but why does it look ill?" I turned to the guards.

"King Oberon and Prince Casimir found her like that while on a diplomatic mission with the Feathered

Fae," Garret explained. "They brought the dragon here so she may heal. It hasn't been going well. As the king mentioned, the land around Lyonesse is dying—being depleted of magic. The slow death of the land affects every creature in it. Pari's evil affects the health of every being in our kingdom."

"You all seem healthy," Kate countered. "Everyone I've met so far appears vibrant."

"We're protected by the power the Feathered Fae bring back to us," Ebba said.

"But—what does that mean?" Kumar asked, his bushy eyebrows furrowed.

"In addition to advising the king, the Feathered Fae supply magic to the king and his army. *Us*." Ebba gestured to herself and the other guards.

"What does supplying magic entail?" Kumar pressed.

"The land still retains some power, and that is accessible to all, but there is precious little surplus in and around the city," Ebba explained. "What makes its way inside the city walls gets used right away. The Feathered Fae are essential for harvesting magic from farther afield and bringing it to the castle. That's why the king prizes his Feathered Fae above all others, and why most children of Lyonesse wish to become a member of their elite group." Ebba's mouth twisted into one of the first unattractive facial expressions I'd seen grace her face.

A sore subject, perhaps? Wanting to give her

privacy, I turned back to the dragon, who had laid down and closed her eyes. She looked shattered, and my heart broke for the wild beast. The land was dying because of Queen Pari. She must be a true monster.

"Why didn't anyone invite us?" An imperious voice barked from down the hallway. I groaned as the group turned to find Crystal, Victoria, and Wikolia in wolf form striding toward us.

"Why is she in wolf aspect?" Dak asked, rightfully. If magic was forbidden outside the training room, shifting should be off limits, too.

"We had to find you somehow, didn't we?" Crystal shot back. "Wik sniffed you out. We heard the commotion you guys made in the hallway all the way from our rooms. Our guards didn't know where you'd gone off to, but Wik said she could find you. She's an excellent tracker." She beamed at the wolf, one-third of her girl gang.

"Where are your guards?" Garret asked as he peered behind the newcomers. "They're to be with you at all times and should have denied her shift. Transform." Beneath the command, there was worry in Garret's tone.

I wondered if he was anxious about Wikolia seeing the dragon in her wolf form. A shifter's animal aspect was more primal and could take over within the shifter if instigated, as they would be if a larger predator was present. It was what happened in shifter fighting rings the world over. Fighters who could slip in and out of their animal psyche with the greatest ease were always the best. But surely sighting something as huge and dangerous as a dragon would be enough to send even the most controlled shifters into attack mode.

Fortunately, Wikolia did not challenge Garret's authority. She shifted back to human aspect.

Crystal, however, sneered at Garret's command. "I won't allow a bunch of guards to tell me what to do. Let alone be followed around by them. *I commanded* them to leave us alone, said if they didn't I'd make their lives hell after I win the Successional." Crystal's brown eyes bore into Garret's.

His face grew red with frustration and his lips had just parted when Crystal broke their connection and pushed her way past him.

"What's so amazing that everyone had to come see?"

Commanded them. After I win the Successional. My eyes widened at the language Crystal had used and how she'd treated Garret—who, while a touch uptight, was kind and fair. I whirled about, a reprimand climbing up my throat, but stopped short when I took in her smirk.

"That's it? That's what you guys came scurrying down here for?" Crystal scoffed and shook her head as if we were children.

"Oh, shut it, Crystal," Kate said. "Don't act like you're not impressed."

She was right. Though Crystal was doing her best to act unimpressed, her gaze betrayed her, remaining transfixed on the dragon's gleaming scales.

Crystal bristled and their familiarity showed in the sneer she shot at Kate. "I *guess* it's impressive, but didn't you assume these creatures were everywhere here?"

"It is pretty, though," Victoria murmured, entranced.

I bit back a laugh at the look of mingled exasperation and disgust that Crystal gave her minion.

"I'm ready to head back," Kumar said, crossing his arms over his chest, uncomfortable with the tension building in the air.

"Me, too," I agreed, already feeling my eyelids droop.

"We're done here, too," Crystal announced for her lot.

Dak and Gio agreed it was time to turn in. I suspected that the fear of reprimand we might get for under-performing was greater than the thrill of remaining to gape at the beast. We left as a herd, the guards a dozen steps ahead.

Thoughts of reading by the fire, then sinking into my soft bed, were clouding my brain when Crystal strode up next to me.

"Lana, right? I hope you don't mind, but I just *have to* ask," she said loud enough for my siblings to hear, but not so loud to garner the guard's notice.

"What's that?" I was not in the mood to pretend that I didn't know her name. By now, if we hadn't introduced ourselves to each other, we knew everyone's names by how often Meegra had screamed them during training.

"Should we find a counselor here to help you?"

"Excuse me?"

"You were screwing our half-brother, right? That would warrant seeing a therapist. I, for one, would prefer to not share a living space with someone who's bound to become mentally unstable because of their past actions. I say this as a medical professional, not out of an irrational fear."

Heat raced across my cheeks.

"No one would blame you. He's handsome, that's for sure. Obviously you didn't *know* you're related, but still," she leaned closer as if telling a secret, "incest is incest."

"N-n-no!" I stammered. "Nothing like that happened. Finn and I are best friends! We have been since we were kids."

My eyes widened, and I looked around, taking in Kumar's apologetic look. On the other side of Crystal I heard a delicate snigger: Victoria, barely holding in her mirth. Kate, too, looked uncomfortable. Apparently, everyone had been wondering about Finn and me. It was only Crystal who was ballsy and cruel enough to ask. Only Crystal who wanted, as Kate had said, to play mind games.

"*Sure,*" Crystal said, her tone that of a doctor who didn't quite believe what her patient was saying. "Still, if anything ever happened—even once—I think you should talk to someone. As I said, it's understandable, but still disgusting."

"And like *I said,* there's no need. Nothing has ever happened between us. Finn and I aren't like that. We're just really good friends."

"Such good friends that he won't talk to you?"

I recoiled, her words cutting through me as harshly as a physical stab to the gut. Still, I didn't want her to think that she got to me, so I held eye contact and my face hardened. "Are you sure your mother was part dwarf and not a demon born witch? Because you seem to have a nasty streak."

Crystal laughed, loud and raucous. My face burned. She was delighted by my humiliation.

"Lay off her, Crystal," Gio said. "We all know why Finn is mad. It was obvious that he wasn't aware of his heritage. Not saying I agree with him, but the guy has every right to be upset. Lana is his best friend, and we often lash out at those we're closest to. She's an easy target. Something you've obviously discovered."

"You wound me! I was just trying to help my sister out," Crystal replied, her tone artificially high. She shook her head as if she couldn't believe what she'd just heard. "But I can see that my expertise as a healthcare professional is not wanted. Pity. I'd hate to see you spin into psychological distress, sis. Especially before the Successional. That would really dampen your chances, wouldn't it?"

My mouth opened to retort, but I didn't get the chance because Crystal kept right on yammering.

"Well, I did my best. See you around." With that Crystal pulled ahead of me, taking Victoria and Wikolia with her.

I blinked. Had all of that really just happened?

Gio grabbed my hand. His callouses dug into my smoother skin as he squeezed. "She was out of line. Sorry, she said that to you."

"Thank you for sticking up for me," I said and quickened my pace. My face burned and more than ever I wanted privacy. I couldn't get to the privacy of my room fast enough.

CHAPTER FIFTEEN

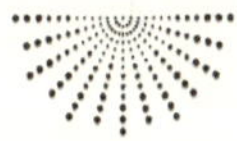

Ten more days.

I was the sorest I'd ever been, barely able to lift the swords Meegra supplied us with once she was sure we wouldn't slice off our heads. Others were having trouble, too—Kumar and Kate among them.

According to Kumar, though naga looked ferocious when transformed, with their snake-like lower body and muscular human torso, they had not had to fight for many centuries.

As for Kate, she tried. But as her powers lay in building something up and strengthening rather than destruction, she was at a disadvantage. To make matters worse, none of our fae powers had cropped up. Although, that didn't mean some of our siblings weren't excelling.

Of course, bloody Crystal was one of them.

The haughty redhead often appeared indistinguishable from a missile as she used her athletic prowess to launch her body at an opponent, sword slashing like an extension of her arm. And that wasn't even considering magic.

In the human dimension, dwarves didn't have much magic compared to witches. They relied on what other supernaturals in the Old Land considered a ridiculously lucky allotment of strength and cunning. But Crystal wasn't just a dwarf. Nor was she in the human world. She was a half-elf in Faerie. Her traditional elven powers could pop up at any time, and that prospect was beyond intimidating.

During our training sessions, a handful of guards had appeared twice to help us coax out our fae powers or to demonstrate advanced fighting techniques against Meegra. It was a welcome change of pace from Meegra's sole instruction, for the guards were *much* kinder than Master Meegra.

These sessions were the only times I saw Sai, my night guard, in the light of day. As Meegra required only the most powerful guards present, Sai got no sleep. However, one glance at her animated violet eyes and you knew Sai didn't mind the missed sleep. She relished being included with the guard elite, among them Garret, Ebba, and Ryker, who I'd since learned was also Sai's cousin.

Sometimes their family relation was hard to believe. They were so very different. Where Sai was almost as serious about her position as Garret, Ryker often laughed off the stricter duties of a personal guard.

Though everyone liked Ryker—Dak and Gio constantly milled about him, cracking jokes—I was glad to have Sai and Garret as my guardians. I didn't think Ryker would have taken it upon himself to console me for hours the night Crystal had humiliated me by asking if Finn and I had slept together. Sai, however, called for a maid to bring me a fragrant tea made of chamomile and some unnamable herb and sat on the edge of my bed as I cried my eyes out.

That night I'd learned Sai had her share of troubles too. Being part hobgoblin, she and Ryker often felt looked down upon at court, especially by uppity visiting nobles who considered their species of fae unfit for military duty.

I found it comforting that while prejudice existed in Faerie, my father kept an open mind. That despite what some nobles in his kingdom said, he'd seen talent in Ryker and Sai. So much talent that he'd offered his home to them. It was nuggets of his character like this that I clung to as I tried to convince myself that the training days, pain, and humiliation were worth it. And nuggets of goodness, no matter how small, were *everything* when Finn continued to avoid me like the plague.

A now-familiar knock sounded on my bedroom door. *Garret.* He always knocked the same way.

"Are you ready?" Garret asked as I opened the

door, a slight smile on his face replacing the reverent glances that had dominated our first couple days together. He was loosening up a little.

Today's smile was the tenth he'd given me.

"Just a minute. I have to let Naela out," I said, leaving the door open and rushing over to my hawk, who'd been resting in her cage.

"Here you go, Boss." I opened her door wide and did the same with the window, allowing the fresh air to billow inside. "Leave whenever you want. I'll see you tonight."

Naela cracked open a haughty eye before shutting it once more.

I should have been happy to get that much acknowledgment. Naela had been less than pleased these last few days. The forests around the castle, while not barren of rodents, were not of the caliber Naela preferred. That I'd had no time to fly with her ruffled her feathers, too. I found it strange that since arriving in Faerie, I could sense my hawk's emotions with greater ease.

Apparently, Ellette and my father had been right about our relationship—witch and familiar. I wondered if Finn and Kane were experiencing the same changes?

"Maybe you should have a word with Kane and ask? We both know Finn won't even look at me," I said to Naela as I walked back to the door.

She didn't reply. The stubborn bird. I rolled my eyes. "I'll make it up to you later, Boss. I promise."

Again she ignored me. I huffed and let myself out of the room. It seemed that lately I could do nothing right.

Garret escorted me to the training hall. When I got there, I scanned the room. Immediately, I found Finn chatting with Arlo. Veering in the opposite direction, I joined Maria and Kate in a chat. The girls seemed sore too, and in Maria's case, slightly hungover. Though I felt bad for her, I was also relieved not to be the only one hurting. Misery loved company. I'd never really understood that saying until now, but there was certainly a truth to it.

"Today, you level up," Meegra proclaimed, halting all conversations as she swept into the training room.

Level up? What does she do, spy on gamers when she goes to the Old Land? I wondered, falling into line seamlessly next to Kate while trying not to notice Finn at the end of the line.

After many failed tries to corner him and explain myself, I'd decided it was best to give him space. It had only been four days, not nearly enough time to come to terms with the life-changing circumstances of learning he was a magical being.

Meegra donned her usual attire, a mix of black leather and metal etched with intricate, silver feathered markings. I'd learned that black metal, leather, and cloaks were the standard Feathered Fae garb.

However, Meegra's uniform was special, particularly her cape, which was created from feathers plucked from a wild black phoenix. Passed down from one Master Feathered Fae to the next, the cape was analogous to a crown. Rumor had it, the cape possessed magical qualities. As for the rest of the Feathered Fae, they wore luxurious cloaks of black velvet.

I felt a searing gaze and snapped to attention just as Meegra marched in front of me. Her eyes blazed like she was trying to see through me.

"You have ten days," Meegra barked. "Whether you surrender in the first seconds of the Successional or fight until the end is not my concern. However, now that we've covered the basics and everyone has at least *some grasp* on weaponry or magic, I should impress upon you one thing. The king would much rather see a little action, a little *initiative* from his heirs."

She paused for a single, dramatic breath. "The king respects those who *fight* for what they want." Her narrowed eyes shifted to Kumar, who as a pacifist had refused to fight during his sparring sessions.

"The entire kingdom will be watching, assessing who is to be the new leader of their army. They will want spectacle, and the king loves nothing more than to please his subjects. Therefore, to add a little fuel to the proverbial fire, today you will spar two on one against a guard. Pair up with someone you have not challenged yet. I shall assign you a guard to practice with." She gestured to Crystal. "You will spar with me. The rest of you, move."

A rush to find a partner ensued. Crystal strode to stand by Meegra, a glint of pride in her eyes at being singled out. A minute later I was alone. As was Finn.

Days ago I would have been ecstatic over our pairing, but now that he could barely look at me, my stomach dropped.

Meegra's fingers motioned us together, and I inched toward him. Trying to make the best of the situation, I flashed Finn a tentative smile. He looked away pointedly.

Heat flamed in my cheeks. I dropped my gaze to the floor as Meegra assigned each duo a fae opponent. Ebba was assigned as our guard.

I smiled as Ebba marched toward us, her usually serious expression breaking into a grin of excitement. She was itching for a fight.

Finn, uncharacteristically, colored. If we were on good terms, I would have chuckled.

"Hey, Lana. Finn," Ebba nodded to each of us. "An illuminator, a trained elf, and a mystery species. Maybe today we'll get your secret out of you, Finn." Her eyes sparkled with the challenge. "Either way, this should be fun."

I hoped Ebba was right. Finn had been closed-lipped about what the Feathered Fae who had assessed him deemed his lineage to be. Perhaps they hadn't found anything. No one knew. Since his evaluation, Finn had opted to use a blade in all his sparring matches, revealing not a sprinkle of power.

"Those from the Old Land will work together to defeat the fae I assigned you," Meegra said. "You have five minutes to discuss strategy."

The factions spread out to claim a sparring circle, an enclosure about ten meters in diameter drawn upon the marble floor and charmed to absorb magic trying to escape the circle.

"How do you want to do this?" I asked, turning to Finn. "Ebba is a good fighter." Though we hadn't actually sparred against guards yet, Meegra had used Ebba for demonstrations more often than any other guard.

"Make that an *excellent* one," Ebba shouted a few paces in front of us. "I'm equally strong in all four elements."

"Whatever you want. You're the one who actually knows magic," Finn mumbled, still refusing to look at me. Ugh. When would this surly attitude end?

"You have magic too, Finn," I said, my voice soothing. One of us had to make an effort. Meegra had paired us. If I knew one thing about Faerie, it was that there would be no arguing with the Master Feathered Fae. "It's just new. Have you felt an inclination toward any of the elements? Or maybe being around the shifters has awoken a primal nature you didn't realize before?"

"I don't care what we do, but let's make one thing

clear." Finn's tone was cold as his eyes met mine for the first time in days. "I don't need anyone trying to make me feel better about any of this right now. Especially you, okay?"

"Ah, good, a divided front. This will be easier than I thought." Ebba strolled the outer rim of our sparring circle.

My face was on fire and my mind cast about wildly for words. But words and people had never been my strong suits. So I stood there, shuffling my feet and waiting for Meegra's signal to start.

Today didn't start off promising, and so far, it didn't seem like that was going to change.

CHAPTER SIXTEEN

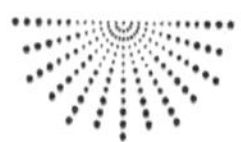

"On your toes!" Ebba yelled, glee evident in her voice as a gale of air knocked me against the boundary of our sparring circle.

Finn darted out of the way of Ebba's next onslaught, a geyser of water, just in time. Water splashed the periphery of the circle.

I shot a beam of light into Ebba's eyes. Unlike my non-existent fae powers, my illusions and manipulations of visible light had actually gotten better since I'd been in Faerie. It was remarkable, seeing as before coming here I hadn't improved in years.

Capitalizing on Ebba's momentary visual impairment, I leapt up and rushed toward Finn. I was halfway there when Ebba regained her senses, and Finn went down as the ground shook beneath our feet. His head hit the white marble, emitting a loud thwack.

I winced at the sound, and my frustrations with him vanished as blood seeped through his blond curls. Finn tried to play it cool, shooting back up and stumbling, but it was no good. He needed a moment to steady.

I tried to give him one, bending light to form an illusion. The light molded to my will. With more angling, it would snap right into place, making Finn invisible. I shot another beam of visible light at Ebba so she wouldn't see her prey disappearing before her eyes—nullifying my efforts.

"Ahhhh! Okay! Enough with the bright lights. What if you actually blind me?" Ebba screamed as my stream of light sent her reeling backward.

Seizing my moment, I bent the light just the right amount and wrapped Finn and me in a cloak of invisibility. I put a finger to my lips and pulled Finn to the opposite side of the circle where Ebba wouldn't expect to find him. There was a cut on his forehead from where he'd fallen and he was still bleeding a little, but otherwise, he'd recovered. Or at least he no longer looked dazed.

Good, he could help then.

I brought my fingers to my lips, mimed being invisible, and gestured at Ebba with my dukes up.

Finn sighed, understanding my infantile communication but clearly not wanting to work with me. This desire of his to go at it with only a blade frustrated me. It was the reason why out of *all* the sparring teams, we most resembled rabbits trying to outwit a group of hawks hunting overhead. We were everywhere and weren't working together at all.

Well, too bad for him. I'd gone to the trouble of creating an illusion to save his butt. The least he could do was work with me on a surprise attack. I was about to mime as much when an uncomfortable heat fanned against my cheeks.

I twisted and gasped. A wall of flames barreling toward us. We leapt apart, outside the confines of my illusion, which flickered with my fear.

"Ha!" Ebba screeched and the fire split, one branch reaching out for each, as we scampered away and pressed our backs into the shield.

"Surrender!" Finn and I cried in unison, both out of tricks, cornered, and neither willing to risk a burn for practice sparring. An injury had to be *really* bad for Meegra to allow us a trip to the healer's wing.

"And that, my half-elf friends," Ebba's flames fell as if they'd never been there, and she pumped her fist in the air, "is how it's done! Now if you'll excuse me, winning has me parched. I need a drink of water before Meegra starts the next round." Ebba called Oren over to release the circle and skipped away, a smug grin on her face.

I stood and surveyed the rest of the sparring circles. At least our battle, while short-lived, had lasted longer than Kate's and Maria's against Ronan. Still, as I watched Gio and Arlo tag team Ryker, I couldn't help but feel a little distraught. They were working together and actually *winning*. Dak and Himari, too, were holding their own against Garret, using communication and coordinated movements.

Jealousy bloomed within me. If Finn and I weren't fighting, we could be that good, even with him not knowing magic yet. We'd always been a great team. I rubbed the back of my neck, trying to quell my rising frustration.

We'd worked out hard things before; why should this be any different? Why were we relegated to sucking because of one stupid fight? Despite the resolution I made just that morning to let Finn approach me on his own, I turned to face him, determined to set our relationship to right.

"Can we *please* have a chat?" I asked.

Finn, who was still seated, shook his head vehemently and stared at the ground. "No. I don't want to hear anything you have to say to me. Or hear what I could have done better. *Please*, just let me be."

"But we need to——"

Finn slammed his hand on the white marble floor. I reared back, startled.

"You don't get it, do you, Lana? You never got it. I suppose I should thank you for it now." Finn's voice cracked as if it had been under pressure, and with obvious reluctance, he met my eyes.

My mouth dropped open.

Tears filled his eyes.

"What don't I get? We're both in a new place, Finn. Are you really willing to hate me for not knowing what you are? If so, I'm sorry I was thick. It must have been terrible for you to be around someone so oblivious—"

"Just stop with all that, Lan." Finn sighed as if the conversation was already wearing him out and dropped his gaze to the ground again. It wasn't like him not to make eye contact. He was usually more confident than that. "You know, a part of me wishes we'd never come here. Mostly, though, I'm relieved because it saved me from making a huge mistake. From acting on my feelings for you and there being the slightest chance you'd reciprocate."

I froze. His *feelings* for me?

"Coming through that portal tore my world apart," Finn continued. "My vision of you and me raising a family, growing old together, us loving each other . . . it was all forced to vanish. Not to mention it made me disgusted with myself." The words fell from him as if it pained him to say them.

Loving each other? Our relationship had *never* been like that. Even in the Old Land, I thought of Finn as my brother. Someone I could always turn to. I shook my head.

"B—but—I don't understand," I stammered. "You never said anything."

Finn shook his head, and droplets of blood flung to the floor. "I did, Lan. Since we were little, I've been trying to win your attention. You just never saw my actions, my words that way. You never saw *me* that way." He pressed his lips together for a moment, inhaling deeply. "As I said, I should be thankful for your disinterest. But forgetting what I held onto for so many years—a fantasy life—isn't easy. I lost a big part of myself coming here and gained a massive amount of shame. I'd rather just deal with this on my own."

Finn's blue eyes met mine. "I also gained something I'm grappling with, and I'm not ready to talk about it yet. Honestly, I believe you didn't know what I was. You've always been a shite actress, but I still need to stay away from you for now—perhaps for good—I don't know. Just give me time to deal with all this stuff. It's too painful for me to include you right now."

Finn pushed himself up off the floor and stormed off.

My lip trembled. Finn, my best friend and half-brother, had just told me he'd been in love with me. Memories came racing back. Finn, always there when I went through my many emotional difficulties. Finn, offering to be my constant date to any dance or social I dared venture into. Finn, holding my hand as we walked through campus on our first day at Trinity. Finn, asking no questions when I showed up with a ludicrous scavenger hunt to find my father.

Finn, the one person who was always there for me when I needed him—waiting, loving me from afar.

The wave of shame and repulsion he must have felt when he realized the truth must have been enormous.

So, he lied and said it was because I didn't tell him what he was to hide his shame. My heart cracked in half for my friend, for myself, for finally understanding why our relationship may never recover.

LATER THAT EVENING I HOBBLED BACK TO HALF-ELF Tower—the name Ryker had dubbed the tower that my siblings and I lived in.

As if things weren't going bad enough with training and Finn admitting he loved me, near the end of the day I'd gone and gotten myself injured. My Achilles tendon had been sliced in half by Arlo in golden eagle aspect. It was now mending, held together by the combined benefits of a slow-working, *vile-tasting* but potent elixir and a magical surgery.

Garret walked beside me, at the ready to catch me should I fall. He'd already offered his shoulder to lean on, but I'd declined. The healer had ordered me to keep weight on my foot. Increased load meant increased blood flow, which meant my tendon would have a better chance of healing while I slept if I pushed it now.

Even if I wanted nothing more than to hide in bed the next day, there was no way Meegra would let me out of training, so I was trying my best to heal overnight. Finally, we reached the door to my room. I waved goodnight to Garret and closed the door—ready for some time alone to sort out my tumultuous day before the elixir took effect and made me crash. I closed my eyes, pressed my back against the door, and inhaled deeply.

What the—? My eyes flew open as my heart began to race. It smelled different in my room. Kind of . . . savory. I glanced about and found several plates filled with an assortment of foods on the table by the fireplace, which someone had lit for me. Slowly, my heart rate returned to normal. I hobbled across the room and found a note with the food. I opened it and smiled. Kate had been here.

Lana,

I AM SO SORRY ABOUT YOUR ACHILLES! I HOPE IT HEALS lickity-split!

IF THE FAE HEALERS DIDN'T GIVE YOU A REGENERATION elixir (black, smells like feet, tastes worse, but will work wonders restructuring your tendon and give you the best night's sleep you've ever had), come to my room. I have some stashed away for moments such as these.

. . .

IF THEY DID, EAT A TON (THE ELIXIR WORKS BEST WHEN the patient fuels up) and rest! Meegra hinted that training tomorrow will be even crazier than today. I think maybe she's trying to weed a few of us out before the Successional even starts?

NO NEED TO WORRY ABOUT THE FOOD BEING POISONED or anything (Sai mentioned Garret may freak out about that, so we had to get his blessing to bring you food). I brought it so you wouldn't have to go to the kitchens to eat. I tried to get all your favorites, but Garret made me put that mushy green stuff on there, too. No idea what it is, but he says it's good for you.

SLEEP WELL, SIS (I ALWAYS WANTED TO SAY THAT!),
  Kate

Kate had drawn a large heart around her signature, which made me smile.

Naela was there too, returned from her day of flying. Kate had probably nestled her in her cage to keep her away from the food. Though my hawk had only known Kate a few days, she seemed to trust her as I did.

After I inhaled the first plate, I stood, wobbled a bit on my bad ankle, and made my way over to Naela. I gave her the fat I'd cut off my meat before inhaling a second round of food. Once finished, I set my plates outside the door as if I lived in a fancy hotel and performed my nighttime routine. Experience taught me that if I kept moving, it was easier not to think about the things that were upsetting me. I only needed to keep moving until the elixir kicked in.

I washed my face with a dreamy cream made by mermaids that smelled of salt and sun. Sai had provided it when the cream in my toiletries basket proved too harsh. My night guardian swore by it, and as her skin was the most luminescent I'd ever seen, that was enough for me to give it a go. I followed the cleanser with a moisturizer, also made by mermaids, though less pleasant smelling. I suspected the active ingredient was some sort of seaweed. Lastly, I brushed my teeth with the strange powder the fae patted on their teeth and rinsed off. I was just slipping beneath the covers when a shrill scream, followed by wild laughter, sounded from the common room next door.

Are you kidding me? I rolled my eyes.

It had become a routine for Crystal, Wikolia, and Victoria to have drinks and gossip for hours after dinner. Most nights they did so in Crystal's room, which was the mirror to mine, sharing a wall with the common room. On those nights the hallway deadened the noise to a softer din that I could sleep through, unlike the shrill laughter piercing my wall now. I ripped myself from the bed, fiddled clumsily with the lock on my door, and burst into the common room.

It was a right party in there. Crystal, Victoria,

Wikolia, and Arlo were gathered around the fireplace playing a card game and laughing their arses off. Five night guards surrounded them, instructing the game, which was from Faerie. Himari sat in the corner, knitting.

"Would you mind keeping it down in here? The healer said I need to get rest if I want to heal properly."

"Hey, Lana! Sorry about your injury," Arlo called out. "I knew you'd be prepared for normal bird of prey activity, so . . ." He shrugged.

Clearly he wasn't that remorseful that his talon had sliced my tendon. I wouldn't expect him to be. We'd been training and almost anything went in training.

"Lana!" Himari stood from her seat. "Kate and I were wondering when you'd get back. She went to sleep ten minutes ago." She gestured to the seat next to her.

I didn't want to talk to anyone after the emotional day I'd had. All I wanted was for the elixir to kick in and to go to bed. But Himari looked so eager that I limped across the room to join her. Once I felt the elixir working, I'd excuse myself.

"What are you making?" I asked, taking a seat by the fire and nodding at the mess of yarn.

"A scarf," she said, as if being able to knit was nothing. I wasn't fooled. I tried to knit once and ended up accomplishing a single solid line before giving up.

There was a pause, and my eyes dropped and ran up her tattoos. What did they mean? Besides the fact that Himari was from Tokyo and a weaver witch, I didn't know much about her.

While I tried to be friendly with everyone since arriving in Faerie, it had never been in my nature to put myself out there. And if I was being honest, the Successional had been a deterrent to get too close to the other participants.

We would fight each other in a few days. Fighting for a dream made real and plopped before us like we were in a fairytale. The competition had me keeping my distance from everyone except Kate and Kumar, who seemed like the only safe ones to bond with. Both were so pacifist, already admitting they'd likely surrender straight away. The threat that they'd steal my dream of meeting my father was low.

Still, couldn't there be a balance? Unlike most people, I had an intrinsic connection with these near strangers—my siblings. Suddenly, it felt wrong not to interact more. My gaze lifted to meet my sister's eyes.

"What are your plans for after the tournament?" I asked the first question that came to mind.

A small grin spread across Himari's face and she put down her knitting. "That's everyone's question, isn't it? A few of us have it figured out, but I'm not sure. It's not like I have a lot to go back to in Tokyo. My mother works in the red-light district and has for all my life. I'm a bartender with an English degree. There's not a lot of advancement in that line of work, and to be honest, I'm not sure my degree is something I want to use." She looked a little sheepish, as if it were uncommon to allow your degree to go unused. I was fairly certain it was the exact opposite. At least, that's what I'd heard.

"But here I'm *royalty*," Himari sighed out the last word. "I could marry a prince, or depending on Faerie's openness to such things, a princess, once I earn a rank. I could build a life of *dreams*." She paused and a half snort-half laugh blew out her nostrils.

"It's kind of funny. I came here to yell at our father for putting my mother and me in such a shitty situation. Once I got here, though, and saw I had opportunities, I didn't want to get kicked out. What about you?"

I nodded. Though marrying was the furthest thing from my mind, I couldn't judge her for it. We all had our own motivations for being here. I doubted any of them were the exact same. "I'll stay here a bit, too. I want to get to know our father."

We chatted about our lives before Faerie, until a loud yawn broke from me, interrupting our bonding. The elixir was finally taking effect. "I think it's time for me to go to bed. The healers gave me a regeneration elixir that's supposed to knock me out. I can feel it coming on."

"I'll hit the bed soon, too," Himari said, giving me a small smile. "Night, Lana. It was good getting to know you a little better."

"Same to you," I said, and I meant it. I was glad I'd put myself out there for once. Himari was cool. "Good night."

CHAPTER SEVENTEEN

The next morning I woke to Garret pounding on my door.

"Lana!" he called out. "You've missed breakfast and would soon be late for training!"

I sighed and peeled back the covers. Once I was dressed, I went to say goodbye to Naela. Instead, I discovered she'd already let herself out the window for a day of flying. I questioned if I'd locked the cage after feeding her, or if this was yet *another* contraption Naela had figured out how to escape from. I suspected the latter. My hawk was a ninja like that.

Shockingly, my Achilles tendon had healed overnight. If the fae had one thing down, it was a regeneration elixir. It was a good thing they did too, because Garret and I had to sprint through the castle halls to make it to training on time, or I'd face

Meegra's wrath. As we ran, he handed me hunks of bread to eat so I'd have enough energy for the day.

"Lana, so good of you to join us today," Meegra said as I burst into the training room with seconds to spare.

Crystal coughed, hiding a few mumbled words as I joined the lineup. Victoria sniggered. Did I have crumbs on my face? I wiped my cheeks.

"Today you will spar two-on-one, rotating the role of the attacker," Meegra said, ignoring their outburst. "Because of the numbers, one group will be one-on-one. No weapons today, just your bodies and magic. The teams are as follows . . ."

I held my breath and then let out an audible groan as Meegra read my name off with Crystal's and Finn's. The only explanation was that she was *trying* to torture me. There was no way the Master Feathered Fae could have failed to sense the tension between Finn and me yesterday.

My training partners were already together and claiming a sparring circle when I dallied over to them. Crystal was talking animatedly, and Finn was listening, his chest pointed away from me. The moment I entered the circle, Meegra and the wardmaker Feathered Fae appeared. Their black cloaks flapped as they walked around the circle, sealing us inside for safety. Now there was no escape.

"Who wants to be the opponent first?" Finn directed his question at Crystal.

"Me," Crystal replied, placing her hands on her hips and radiating annoying confidence.

Crystal moved to one side of the circle while Finn and I made our way to the other side. We stood there, as awkward as you please, while the seconds ticked by. I stared at the floor, not having a clue what to say. Finally, blessedly, Meegra's whistle blew.

The next thing I knew, Crystal was flying toward me. She'd covered half the distance of the circle already, her compact gymnast body like an unstoppable projectile. I braced myself to shoot a beam of light into her eyes and dart out of the way at the last minute. Hopefully she would hit the ward and knock herself out.

A split second later, my eyes widened as something slithered up my leg. I glanced down. Tendrils of wind, visible only by the dust they collected off the floor, were winding up my calves, pulling me to the ground.

Shite, when had Crystal gained access to air?

Whack! Crystal's body slammed into mine, knocking me to the ground and banging my head on stone. I groaned and then groaned again as Crystal kicked me in the stomach before moving on to Finn.

"Don't you love it when your elf powers materialize in your sleep?" Crystal's voice was high, though her stance was low, fists up, preparing to take down a gaping Finn next. She threw a punch.

Finn dodged it and lunged out of Crystal's range.

I grunted as I tried to pull myself free of the air

ropes, which were freakishly strong for being made of air. Instead, the ropes persisted, winding their way up my body.

Crystal kicked at me as she zoomed by, but this time I was ready for her. I wrenched one arm free from the ropes of air and pushed against the floor as hard as I could. Just in time, my body rolled out of the way of her foot and I shot a beam of light straight at her face. Crystal fell back onto Finn, blinded. Being the idiot gentleman he was, Finn caught her, which gave Crystal the opening she needed to make her move. Pirouetting in Finn's arms, she launched a punch that sank into his gut, knocking him to the floor next to me. Our skin touched, and unable to stop my discomfort or my instinctive reaction, I flinched away.

Hurt flashed across Finn's face before he concealed it with a stony mask. The moment of distraction was all our opponent needed to make her move. Dusty air ropes wrapped around my partner's torso, knocking him out of the match too.

I cursed my body's reaction as Crystal twisted her hands midair so that the rope cinched tighter. Why couldn't I have kept that to myself? We didn't need more salt poured in our wounds.

Crystal approached. "Obviously, you two are going through tough times, but you should work more on your communication. That was *way* too easy."

My teeth ground together.

"Which is saying something, considering I'm brand new at controlling air," she continued. "Damn, I love the sound of that. There's so much I can learn to do with air, like steal the breath from people's lungs."

"Right," I grumbled. "What do you say you let us up and we start round two? I'll go next; you guys can discuss strategy for a few minutes."

The air ropes disappeared, and I glanced up, surprised. I'd expected Crystal to gloat more. Had everyone's phone not died days ago, I could imagine her snapping a selfie with each of us lying on the ground. At the very least, I figured she'd keep us on the floor and place her foot on us or something.

I narrowed my eyes as Crystal helped Finn up and began whispering to him. No doubt she was already concocting a plan I'd hate. I turned, not wanting to witness her scheming or Finn's frustration at my reaction.

Kate and Maria sparred closest to us, and their match was going as expected. Maria was on the offense, tossing vines from her hands to lasso Kate, who dodged and wove around the small bushes and trees Maria grew from the ground as obstacles. It was only a matter of time before Maria caught Kate, whose elven elemental powers had yet to materialize.

Still, I had to hand it to Kate. She wasn't accepting defeat, no matter how likely. In addition to growing more skilled with her blades, she spent hours in the library learning about pressure points and other mechanisms to force people to pass out. Of course, knowing all the pressure points was useless if you couldn't get close enough to a person. Still, maybe she'd catch a break during the Successional. Stranger things had happened.

My focus shifted to a circle that could be mistaken for a circus show. In the shifter circle, Dak in lion aspect and Wikolia in wolf aspect charged at each other—canines bared, claws out—as Arlo circled above, waiting for his chance to strike whichever of the shifters wasn't on his side during this round. Though his talons were sharp enough to slice through my tendon just the day before, Arlo's hesitancy was smart. An eagle may do damage, but I wouldn't bet on one against a lion or wolf.

An eerie hiss tickled my ears. My spine straightened, and I whirled about. My mouth dropped open.

A massive, vivid green serpent's tail unfurled behind Kumar as a hood of scales grew from a human torso and rose over his head. For the first time, he was transforming into his naga aspect.

I watched, stunned, as fangs replaced Kumar's canines, morphing his shy, kind smile into a terrifying sight. But it was his eyes that made me shiver the most. Their usual bright green shade intensified to a poisonous neon that chilled my blood.

What had happened? Kumar had always been an

insistent pacifist, refusing to shift and fight until now. My attention darted to Kumar's opponent.

Nigel's weak chin wobbled, but he was still fighting despite the terrifying naga before him. Flashes of red light—visible light and hot infrared mixed—flew from his hands to rebound off Kumar's magically imbued scales. The briefest of pauses followed as Nigel, clearly perplexed by how to defeat a naga, considered how to proceed.

In that second Kumar took control of the sparring ring. He struck, shooting forward with the speed and accuracy of a serpent. His fangs sunk into Nigel's arm, and the illuminator went down with a bloodcurdling scream. Kumar slithered forward, ready to attack again, and I gasped as the reason why he'd transformed became clear.

Himari was lying on the ground, lifeless. Kumar's giant snake tail had hidden her from view before, but now she was unprotected. A red slash stained her face —a superficial burn—one that was an artifact of infrared light. But that injury wasn't what horrified me most. All along her arms and chest, Himari's skin bubbled and smoked. Also, I could just discern a faint halo of green light clinging to her, almost dissipated into the atmosphere, but not quite.

I sucked in a breath, recognizing the signs, though I'd never seen them first-hand. While infrared light burned skin and could even cut through it when formed into laser beams, that wasn't the worst thing light could do to a person. There were higher energy radiations on the light spectrum—smaller wavelengths —and they were increasingly damaging to flesh.

From the green halo of light, I could tell Nigel had woven ultraviolet radiation with white light. By using ultraviolet radiation, he'd chanced mutating Himari's DNA on a *molecular* level. And judging by the many slashes on her skin, he'd used it more than once.

That fecking bastard.

My heart rate thudded ever faster as I considered the severe ramifications of Nigel's attack. Cancer. Deep mutations in genetic material. Damage that if not attended to right away could lead to real issues down the line or if she had children. I was about to call for help when Meegra blew her whistle and shot over to the circle enclosing Kumar, Nigel, and Himari.

Kumar responded to the whistle: his deadly tail withering into his legs, his fangs shrinking, his reptilian scales smoothing into skin. As soon as he was human, he joined Meegra at Himari's side. He looked shattered.

For the first time, the Master Feathered Fae did not sneer at him as Kumar relayed what had happened. I noticed he gripped at his head oddly as he spoke. Had he been hurt too?

Meegra motioned for Himari's guard and Ryker to carry the wisp of a witch to the healer's ward. Once Himari left, Meegra moved on to Nigel, who was making such a ruckus that those in the throne room could probably hear him. I rolled my eyes. I had no pity for him.

"I need an antidote!" Nigel howled. "That bloody snake bit me! He cheated!"

Kumar's hands formed tight fists. "I didn't cheat. My partner needed help. How else would you expect me to fight against someone who can do magic?" He stopped then, placing his hand on his temple again, said, "Plus, my mind felt funny; transforming cleared it."

A satisfied smirk crossed Nigel's face, pushing me to my limit.

"Kumar wouldn't have bitten you if you hadn't used unnecessarily dangerous radiation on her!" I yelled, pressed up against the sparring circle. "Why didn't you just stick with infrared, huh?"

He was out of line. Though there were no rules as to how dangerous sparring could get, what Nigel had done was the most dangerous magic I'd seen so far. Definitely more dangerous than a chomp on the leg or laceration from a blade.

Nigel glowered at me. "Just because I'm more skilled than you doesn't mean I should limit my magic to the base spectrum." I was about to retort when he broke our connection and pointed his finger at Kumar. "As for your snake, I'm warning you. Watch your back. I've gutted beasts bigger than you in Mozambique—kings of the jungle—and I won't hesitate to cut you open if you ever flash your fangs at me again."

A rumble vibrated through me and I gasped at Nigel's stupidity and lack of compassion.

Dak, still in lion aspect, growled, the sound low and dangerous. He had not taken kindly to Nigel's talk of hunting lions for game near his country of birth. I thought Nigel should be quite glad that Dak was still enclosed within his circle.

"All of you, quiet *at once!*" Meegra commanded and everyone froze. Without another word, Meegra bent down to examine Nigel's bite. After a brief examination, she beckoned two more guards over. "The bite is superficial, but he still needs an antivenin. Take him to the healer's ward. Once they give you the antivenin, return immediately."

The guards escorted Nigel out, but not before he shot a final glare at Kumar, who stood alone in the center of his circle, victorious for the first time.

"Naga, join the healer and rumbler in the next round," Meegra commanded. She wasn't one to allow us to stand around long. "The rest of you, stop staring and pick your next opponent. We start on my whistle."

Why had Nigel sparred so hard? From what I'd read, one ultraviolet slash was so painful it brought most people to their knees. Himari's arms had been completely covered in smoking skin and a green hue, telling that he'd hit her more than once. My fists clenched. This was just practice, not the actual Successional. It made me wonder if something else had transpired.

A flash of red caught my eye, yanking me from my thoughts. I twisted to face my opponents and tensed. Again, Crystal was nearly upon me, with Finn just behind her. Meegra must have blown her whistle.

Reflexively, I pulled light from the air and shot it at Crystal, blinding her and stopping her in her tracks.

"Is that the only trick you've got?" Crystal snarled, continuing her charge forward with super-human speed even as she blinked rapidly to regain her vision. "I thought witches were supposed to be powerful? You can't even take on a new air worker?"

Partially blinded, she collided with me. However, unlike earlier, I didn't go down. Visible light pooled in my hands, willing me to throw it at her, begging me to act. Instead, I punched her in the jaw.

"Argh!" Crystal growled, shocked. Even though I had the element of surprise, it didn't take her long to retaliate, landing a hard slap across my face.

Behind her Finn stood motionless, his jaw working, his blue eyes bearing down on me. He was clearly still upset from when I'd flinched away from him. An unintentional insult that—after all that had transpired between Nigel and Kumar—felt like it happened years ago. Or perhaps Finn figured his partner was doing well enough on her own. I couldn't argue with that.

Crystal and I duked it out like a pair of sorority girls from American programs for a few minutes more before her physical strength prevailed, and I found myself pinned to the ground.

"Seriously," Crystal grunted as she hoisted herself on top of me, straddling my torso. She flicked her wrist and bound me with invisible shackles of air, leaving me incapacitated. Then, she leaned in, hovering her nose inches from my own. "You're pathetic. I doubt you stand a chance in the Successional."

My body trembled with anger. "Save it. You won, now let me up." Though I hated saying the words, I hated being beneath Crystal more.

"Why? Meegra hasn't blown her whistle, and this is a perfect demonstration of my new powers." Crystal trailed her finger over my jawline, and the sensation of a blanket, but far more crushing, rushed up my body.

She lifted her hands. And yet, I remained immobile. The air Crystal controlled smothered me to the ground in place of muscle and might. In fact, it was probably stronger and more effective than most people, simultaneously crushing my ribcage and constricting my airways.

"You may as well get used to being under me anyhow." Crystal smirked. "That's how it will be after the Successional. Didn't you say you came to meet our father? Perhaps I'll allow that when you fill my royal cup as I sit beside him on a throne. If you're a good little cupbearer."

I needed air. Fueled by anger and fear, I scrambled to free myself, calling light to my aid more frantically than ever. My mind was flailing, so what happened next—*how* it happened—I wasn't sure.

All I knew was the light I'd called to my aid warmed. My eyes bulged. It was *infrared* light! I pushed my power and called for visible light. Effortlessly, the light from the infrared spectrum mixed with visible light. The product glowed a brilliant crimson. Amazed and elated, I shot the red orb toward Crystal's face.

She yelped and leapt off me as heat seared her skin.

I drew in a ragged breath as the crushing wall on my chest let up. Crystal's concentration had broken. I was free.

Not wasting a second, I jumped up and shot another beam of infrared woven with white light. Freedom pulsed through me. Red light stampeded toward me as it never had before and allowed me to use it as though I owned it. Infrared light and I were one.

"Stop! Stop it!" Crystal screamed as another beam landed on her butt with a sizzle.

But her refusal to let me up and her joy during the

many times she'd humiliated me were too fresh in my mind. I unleashed another shower of rays, all of them infrared. The light pelted Crystal everywhere it could, and I watched as her face, arms, and hands turned the same color as her hair, burning with the rage of my light.

It felt good; the high was so potent that I let it fly again. I'd accessed a new spectrum. Or perhaps the new spectrum had accessed me? It certainly felt as though it had taken me over. My next shower of infrared light grazed Crystal's neck and seared off a chunk of her hair. She screamed in agony. Another, the most scorching yet, was sitting in my palm ready to be unleashed, when suddenly *I* was thrown backward by a wall, a *storm* of heat and wind. I collided into the hard boundary dictating our training circle, confused as to what had just happened. My confusion only grew when I glanced up.

Finn stood between Crystal and me, balls of fire in his hands, a wall of flame before him, and a funnel of wind blowing his blond curls high. He looked scared and defiant, even ashamed.

I looked about, taking in the destruction, the fire and air magic being used. Someone must be helping him because it didn't make sense. No new magic worker could cause this amount of chaos. But the sparring circle was still up, wasn't it?

And then I saw it. Finn's eyes were flashing red.

In a rush, all my air left me, and fear shot through

my heart as I came face-to-face with a being I'd always been taught to fear.

Finn wasn't just embarrassed that he'd loved me. He was ashamed of his powers. He'd wanted to hide them from *me* because I'd never spoken highly of the unholy sect of witches and their cursed blood.

Demon blood.

Finn was a demon born.

CHAPTER EIGHTEEN

"Another cider," I snapped when a brownie servant asked if I required anything else at dinner.

"Is that a good idea?" Kate asked. "You've already had three drinks. Remember, Meegra said we have training earlier than usual tomorrow."

"It's a fine idea," I grumbled hotly.

"Yes, my lady," the brownie squeaked. "Right away."

Kumar shot me an understanding look. After his debut naga performance, he'd received his fair share of wary glances, too. It was only when Himari joined us at dinner and thanked him for protecting her that people relaxed around him.

The same had not happened to me. Quite the opposite, actually.

Crystal and her entourage had been glaring at me all night, despite the fact that the red welts on Crystal's arms were fading thanks to the castle healers. By morning she'd be as good as new.

It's not like I used ultraviolet light on her or anything. Infrared burned but it couldn't cause the serious damage ultraviolet light did unless focused into a laser, which took immense concentration.

Although what Nigel had done was worse, no one besides Kumar was looking at him like he was a monster. Not even Himari, who claimed the sparring session was all one fuzzy memory. Apparently, she'd experienced too much pain to recall much of it.

The cider arrived, and I hefted the mug to my lips, only to see Kate raise her brow.

"Let me be, Kate." I sighed. "It's been a long couple days."

Learning Finn had loved me and being treated like a pariah after my sparring session with Crystal was more than enough. But discovering Finn was a demon born—the one type of witch I'd been taught to fear—was simply awful.

Kate opened her mouth to protest, but Kumar placed a hand on her arm and shook his head.

Nodding at him, I raised my cider to him. "Sláinte," I said, filling the uncomfortable silence that had crept over our table with the loud glugging of cider slipping down my throat.

My head pounded when I woke the next morning and I buried my face in the pillow, hoping for some respite before training began again. Burrowing as deep as I could, my face created a valley between the feather-down mountains. I relished the softness, the lovely quiet. Thank goodness my sisters weren't awake making a ruckus in the common area. I only wished it was easier to breathe in my cocooned position. Tilting my head to the side, I inhaled the cool morning air. A strange tang filled my nostrils. I sniffed.

Was that . . . metal?

I cracked my eyes open and froze. A dagger was perched atop the mountain of my pillow, pointed straight at the tip of my nose. A scream ripped from me, shattering the morning calm.

Garret barreled into my room from the hallway door, his sword unsheathed, his eyes combing the room. "What happened?"

My hand shook as I pointed to the dagger covered in blood and staining my pillowcase red. "S—s—someone was in here." I looked around my room for the first time. The room was enveloped in a deafening silence that prickled against my skin in warning.

Silence. My jaw clenched.

What moments before had seemed like a treasure now registered as dangerous. My room was *never* completely silent unless Naela was asleep or out flying. But there was no way she was asleep after a scream like mine.

My eyes flew to her perch and my heart stopped. A lifeless body lay at the bottom of the cage, blood smeared across its feathers. I scrambled out of bed and darted across the room, my breath tight in my chest, constricting me from the inside, jacking me up higher. It was only when I clutched the sides of the aviary that air filled my lungs once more.

It was not Naela who was dead at the bottom of the large metal cage, but another bird—a fat pigeon-like creature meant to scare me into believing someone had broken in and killed my beloved hawk.

I was sure Naela had been here when I'd gone to bed last night, more than a little drunk and conflicted as hell over the events of the day. From what I remembered, I had spent a good hour running my fingers through her feathers, trying to calm myself. Thank goodness I'd left the window open; clearly, Naela had let herself out during the night. Perhaps she'd sensed the approaching danger and had fled to safety? I cursed myself for dulling my senses so much that I hadn't roused when the killer had arrived.

"Who would do such a thing?" Garret's eyes bulged out of their sockets as he hurried closer. "And how did they get into your room? Sai was in the hall the whole night."

I checked the door that exited into the common room, a direct access point that bypassed the hall—and hence Sai. The handle turned, unhindered. In my drunken stupor, I'd forgotten to lock it as I normally did.

My face hardened and all the muscles around my eyes and in my cheeks throbbed as one name clarified in my head. I knew one person who would do such a thing, one person petty enough. One person who liked to play mind games, which this *surely* was. She wouldn't even have had to go through the hallway and encounter Sai, because like mine, her room exited into the common space.

"*Crystal.*" Her name ground out of me. I twisted toward my wardrobe and yanked out clothes. I'd barely undone my pants when Garret sputtered and turned around. Oh right. Probably shouldn't change in front of my guard. "Sorry. I'll be done in a sec."

I quelled my temper long enough to change, wash my face, and brush my teeth before running from my room and toward the training hall. Garret trailed me, still red in the face from when I'd almost stripped in front of him. I arrived in the hall and zeroed in on my red-haired sister.

"What the hell kind of game are you playing!" I stormed over to Crystal.

My fists clenched when it registered that she was talking to Finn. Were they becoming new best friends or something? A fresh wave of anger rose in me, and unable to think straight, I launched myself at her. I got in only one hard shove before her guard pulled me back. I let out a frustrated growl, unable to believe this was happening. They would let us fight each other all day, every day, but heaven forbid we have a go at each other out of the confines of our training circles.

Screw the training circles, I thought, wriggling free of the guard and calling light to protect myself, and by extension Naela, from this psycho.

"Why did you try to hurt her?"

"What the hell are you talking about?" Crystal snapped, her red hair wild.

"Don't act like you don't know," I snarled. "Go after me all you want. I *invite* it now, but don't you *dare* try to touch my hawk ever again."

Crystal's eyes narrowed. "I didn't touch your damn bird, didn't even get near it. I hate birds, and *yours* is terrifying. In fact, when I win the Successional, expect her free-flying powers to be revoked."

"Naela?" Finn's eyes widened. "What happened to her?"

"None of your business," I shot back.

It wasn't fair, nor did my jumble of emotions concerning Finn make any sense, but at that moment, I didn't care. I was focused on one thing: sussing out Crystal's lie. I glared at her—wishing I had mind magic, willing a confession—but Crystal just stared right back at me, her gaze unflinching. Her words ran through my head again and again as I sought the waver, the underpinnings of deceit there.

After a minute, however, my stance loosened a smidgen. No matter how much I wanted to duke it out with Crystal for humiliating me, something told me she was telling the truth. Her past actions agreed with her words.

The night Naela and Kane had flown into the throne room, Crystal had leapt far away. And while Crystal liked Arlo enough in his human form, I'd seen the way she shied away from him in his bird form. The only time I recalled her engaging with him as an eagle was when Meegra paired them together to spar. I let out a furious huff. I believed *she* hadn't been in my room, but that didn't mean I thought she was innocent. Far from it.

Crystal was pushy and manipulative and was *certainly* still pissed at me for yesterday. She could have persuaded someone to do her dirty work for her. Her guard, maybe? She wasn't lying outright, but there was no way in hell I trusted her. Unable to come up with a retort and not willing to give an apology, I whirled about and stomped to the far side of the room to join Kate and Maria.

"What was that about?" Maria asked, running her hand through her wavy black hair.

"Nothing," I mumbled, no longer sure who I could trust.

Out of the corner of my eye, I noticed Garret

waving me over. I excused myself and went to meet him.

As soon as I was close enough, he pointed behind me. "I saw Naela out that window. She was looking in here. I think she may have felt your distress and come to check on you."

"Oh, thank goodness. Thank you for telling me." I exhaled, the worry in my heart dissipating. Though I'd guessed my hawk was still alive, a sighting was a welcome confirmation.

"You're welcome." He paused for a beat, as if considering his words carefully. "Listen, I know this morning was—distressing, and believe me, I will have a talk with Sai. She must have poked her head into the guard's room at just the right time—"

"No!" I exclaimed. "I'm not mad at Sai. I'm pissed at myself for getting so drunk I didn't hear anyone sneak in."

"It's not just that," Garret blurted. "There's not much time left until the Successional, so you must keep your head on straight. Rushing in here after someone threatened your familiar was a normal reaction, I think you need to keep your feelings closer to your chest." Garret nodded his head to the side of the training room we'd entered from.

I followed the gesture, my throat closing when I caught sight of what he was alluding to. Above the door we'd entered by was a balcony on which the king and Prince Casimir stood, looking down on us all.

Bloody hell. Had they seen my outburst?

"They walked in as you were storming over to Kate and Maria," Garret said, his tone soft, consoling. "I wanted you to know so you could control your reactions as you saw fit."

When had my guard become so in tune to me? I supposed we had been spending a lot of time together. It struck me as miraculous that I felt comfortable around Garret. Amazingly enough, he wasn't the only one. I felt comfortable with Kate and Kumar, too. I'd been in Faerie only six days, and somehow I'd found more people verging on friends than I'd ever had before.

"Good." My eyes latched onto my father, who I'd seen only at meals since our first night. "Do you think he'll reach out to us today?" Even to my own ears, my voice sounded wistful.

Garret frowned, but it was a soft frown, full of understanding. "It's said King Oberon lost many children before Prince Casimir was born. That's why he held the prince at arm's length for so long. He was sure his son would die at any minute and could not handle the pain of losing another child he'd grown attached to. Only in recent years did he feel the prince strong enough to train to succeed him. I'm sorry to say this, because I know you want more, but your father will remain true to his word. He'll wait until after the Successional to get to know any of you—in case something happens."

A sigh escaped me.

Garret inched closer, compassion clear in his gray eyes. "If it makes you feel better, it is common for parents to remain detached from their children in Faerie. At least until after the children have been through their mandatory testing. And the Successional is more rigorous than that. His Majesty is not trying to be cruel; he is only protecting himself as all fae parents do."

My brows furrowed. "Why? What happens during testing? Is it dangerous?"

"No, not dangerous per se. Just life-changing," Garret assured me. He straightened his spine and his chest expanded with pride.

"We call the testing to be chosen as a guard or Feathered Fae the Harvest. It happens when we're five. Until that age most families do their best to train their children, like you're doing now, but with an emphasis on athletics and the fundamentals of magic rather than fighting. Other bonding is limited. Many parents keep their children at an emotional distance because they hope they may be given over to the king's service. If that happens, they may not see their children for years. It's a way of protecting their hearts."

Five years old? My heart clenched. That was so young.

"Didn't your parents miss you, though? Don't you miss them?" I asked, trying to imagine myself being taken from Mam or Gran at such a young age. At present, not being able to ring up Mam was hard enough, and I was an adult. As a child, never seeing her would have shattered me.

"Yes, but eventually we earned visitation privileges once a month. When we graduate to the guard, we have the freedom to leave the castle. We can even stay with them on our days off."

"That doesn't seem like enough."

Garret raised his brows. "It's not much, *but* there are other compensations that make it worth our while to stay. Like the payoff. It's far more than most fae can afford. Our families receive food and fuel to keep their homes warm. Parents of a Feathered Fae receive even more, such as stipends to purchase frivolous goods. Or if they are wealthy already, as Master Meegra's family is, they often request personal audiences with the king. A family can achieve a higher social rank if they have a child in service of the crown." He stopped and swept a hand around the room.

"You've only seen inside the palace walls, but in the wider kingdom of Lyonesse, people live different lives. Because of less magic in our kingdom, most are poor and work hard every day to make a living. Many fae reach their maximum magical potential by the time they hit puberty, which is why the testing is done so young. Find a student younger, especially one with raw magical talent, and you can push him or her further than imagined. I doubt I'd be half as strong if

I wasn't picked to be a guard for the Fullfeather dynasty."

"Yo. Are you telling her about Harvest?" Ryker came up beside us.

"I am."

"Did you mention the most important part?"

Garret tilted his head. "What would that be?"

"Who holds the records for all the tests! Throughout guard training, too. Most of which still stand today." Ryker flexed his muscles ludicrously.

Garret closed his eyes and shook his head.

"In our guard training graduation, I beat Garret in a footrace by a full minute," Ryker continued, a grin growing on his face.

"Ah, yes," Garret's face twisted into a smirk. "The race in which your younger cousin smashed your record the next year, correct?"

Ryker's grin flattened. "At least she's family. No one can say Sai and I don't belong here."

"Why didn't you get chosen to be a Feathered Fae, then?" I asked before the teasing could continue. "If you broke so many records, surely you'd be a shoo-in, right? Was your magic not strong enough when you were younger? Or was it the shifting criteria?"

Both guards fell silent, their eyes traveling all around the room, anywhere but at me.

Had I said something wrong?

"Sorry if I—"

"Don't apologize. It's just the system," Ryker said.

"What do you mean?"

"My elf ancestors were warriors, but hobgoblin blood runs through me, too." His lips twisted slightly, as if he himself was conflicted about his lineage.

"I'm sorry, I don't really know much about hobgoblins." In truth, I knew next to nothing. I felt like a fool, but it was better to admit that I didn't know than pretend I did. If I was to stay here, I needed to understand this new realm.

"It's okay. I wouldn't expect you to understand what I meant," Ryker said, his irritation lifting slightly as he smiled at me. "Hobs are a species of fae the Fullfeathers traditionally considered undesirable. Even if I could shift, our commander in training made it abundantly clear I would not have been chosen to become a Feathered Fae. It took years longer for me to earn the rank of captain than it did Garret or Ebba, despite my abilities and us all being in the same Harvest year. Still, His Majesty would never pass over a soldier of superior strength and magic because of a little hob blood."

I glanced at Garret, who nodded. "There are prejudices in every realm. For instance, many fae look down upon the giants. But in Lyonesse it's well known the Fullfeathers are not fond of hobgoblins."

Ryker snorted. "A tradition that seems as if it will continue. The prince—"

"However," Garret lifted his voice in warning. "Ryker and Sai are excellent citizens and warriors.

Perhaps they will change the crown's perception and the royal line will come around. The chances are good that with the arrival of you and your siblings, things will change around here."

Ryker snorted again. "Only time will tell, but I hope you're right, brother."

CHAPTER NINETEEN

The next morning I awoke earlier than usual to take Naela on a walk. After my scare yesterday, I wanted to put in the effort to spend more time with her. Once we'd had our time, I'd check out the castle library as my father had suggested.

I probably should have visited the library sooner. Other people frequented it often. In fact, Kate and Kumar had invited me to join them in the library every day. They claimed it was one of the best libraries they'd ever seen, filled with books on fae medicine, history, and religion. Their obsession hadn't resonated with me until yesterday, when I realized I didn't want Crystal lording over me—or threatening Naela again. To avoid that, I'd have to win the Successional—or at least beat Crystal, who was a serious contender for first place. With my new access to infrared light, I finally had a real shot at winning. I hoped that if I studied, I could find information to sharpen my competitive edge.

Opening the door to my room, I heard a frantic shuffle and peered down the hall just in time to see Garret fall out of his chair, pick himself up, and run toward my door.

"Everything all right, Lana?" Garret asked, sword already drawn from its scabbard.

"Fine, just taking Naela on a stroll."

Garret stopped mid-stride, confusion washing over his face. "But . . . the sun just rose."

I couldn't help it, I burst out laughing, which only deepened Garret's puzzlement. The fae were creatures of the afternoon and night. Every day in the castle started slowly. Or, if you glanced outside, one would think it never started at all. Here the sun's apex resembled something more akin to a bright twilight rather than high noon in the Old Land.

Between the odd sun cycle and my general exhaustion since arriving, poor Garret had served as my alarm clock every day. He probably hadn't realized I could even wake up so early on my own accord.

"What's so funny?" he asked when giggles continued to trickle from my lips.

"I'm sorry, Garret," I said once I composed myself. "I'm not laughing at you. More *with* you, if you know what I mean?"

He cocked his head.

"Never mind," I said. "It's just that I had an

epiphany last night. I want to maximize my training. You know, put more effort in. I only have a week left to do so. I figured I'd take Naela for a stroll on the grounds, so she doesn't claw my eyes out for neglecting her, and then hit the library. Wanna come?"

It was a stupid question. Garret was my guard. He had to come, no matter what. Still, the invitation lit up his face, and he nodded.

"It'd be a pleasure to get out of the castle for a while," he said, his stance loosening.

I cocked my head to the side, taking in Garret's uncharacteristically relaxed posture. Being one of our guards must be pretty boring. Especially if you were Garret, who seemed to take his job more seriously than the rest of them, sitting in a straight-backed chair at the end of the hall instead of congregating in the room reserved for guards to take a kip or play cards when Oberon's children were in their rooms. I bet Garret had been going crazy, wishing I'd wake up and explore a bit while I slept in.

"What are we waiting for, then?" I asked, gesturing for Naela to follow as I strode down the hall.

I breathed deeply, savoring the fresh air as I stepped outside. The castle grounds looked so different in the early morning. Or perhaps it was that I was walking through them, not merely catching glimpses out of windows.

Naela let out an excited screech that made me smile. "Go on, Boss. Fly free."

She soared away, allowing me to take in the morning at my leisure. Unlike the black, barren landscape outside the castle walls, the courtyards were lush, filled with green trees, bushes, and even colorful flowers despite the chill in the air. Had I been in Ireland still, winter would be fast approaching. The insistent cold made me think Faerie was on a similar schedule. As Garret and I walked together, I marveled at all I hadn't explored yet.

We chatted about little things and shared stories as Naela soared above us. Occasionally, my hawk would dive to land on my arm for a bite of meat or swooped between our shoulders. She liked the attention that got her.

After our discussion about the Harvest, I felt closer to all the guards—even the ones I didn't know by name yet. They weren't just people protecting us. They had their own stories and lives. Although Garret grew up behind the walls of Phoenix Castle, he had plenty to tell of his mother, who lived in the heart of Lyonesse.

"So, you, Ryker, Ebba, and Sai have always been close?" I asked after Garret concluded an amusing story involving a game of hide and seek. The tale was so in character with what I knew of the guards. I could practically see a mini-Ryker popping out of a closet near the kitchens, terrifying his friend. Garret swore he'd checked that same closet numerous times, but Ryker swore he'd been there the whole time.

"Ryker, Ebba, and I arrived at the castle the same year." Warmth filled Garret's voice, as it always did when he spoke of his friends. It was there even when he chastised them, which in Ryker's case was often.

"We'd outperformed the rest of the children in our Harvest year by a long shot. The rest saw us as a threat, so we clung to one another. Once it was clear shifting wasn't a skill we'd master, and therefore we were ineligible to become Feathered Fae, the others from our year included us more often."

"When you say you arrived in the same year . . . how long ago was that?" Garret gave me a curious look, and I blushed. "It's just that most fae I've met look so young. Even my father looks thirty-five! It throws me off. Gran mentioned that the fae age more slowly, but didn't go into much detail. And to be honest, I never asked."

Understanding dawned in Garret's eyes and he chuckled. "Yes, I suppose that would confuse someone from the Old Land. Ryker, Ebba, Sai and I are all as old as we look—in our late twenties. Fae age as humans do until they hit about thirty, then the process slows. For every fifty years we appear to age only a year after our thirtieth birthday."

"Holy hell," I whispered. That meant my father was around three or four hundred years old.

Garret shrugged. "For us, it's normal. Your father

assigned younger guards to you and your siblings because he thought we'd be able to relate better. The Feathered Fae bring back novels from the Old Land when they can. The younger fae like myself find them to be quite entertaining. Though we've never been there, certain cultures from the Old Land have influenced us."

"So how are you, Ebba, and Ryker all captains of the fae guard if you're so young? Is that the highest rank?"

"Lyonesse has been at war with Buyan, Queen Pari's kingdom, for years. Much of the older command perished before their time." Momentarily, his gaze dropped to the ground.

"Their deaths were a great loss, but they allowed Ebba, Ryker, and me to work our way up the ranks quickly. Captain is a high rank, but not the highest. The only ranks higher are that of the majors and the general. The Feathered Fae are a specialized sector of the king's forces, with Meegra as the highest rank. However, majors and generals of the fae guard would outrank her. We all believe the king is saving those positions for his children."

"And what about Sai?" I'd noticed Sai hung around the trio when her schedule permitted.

"Sai arrived at the castle a year after me. She's not a captain, although most expect her to become one soon."

Naela dove. I felt a pull between us, a familiarity

that was becoming stronger the longer I remained in Faerie. She wanted me to provide a perch. I flung out my arm seconds before her weight landed, her talons digging into the thick, leather gauntlets that covered my forearm. She shook her feathers and made a cooing sound that told me she was pleased.

"It's amazing, the bond you two have," Garret commented as we strolled closer to the castle, skirting its walls to avoid having to pass through a robust garden bordering a turret.

"Finn and I used to think it was because we found our hawks as wee eyas—tiny chicks—all alone in a field. I suppose it was stupid to think so, but who could have imagined all this?" My voice thickened with emotion.

Would Finn and I ever be able to return normal? Though I was embarrassed by his romantic love for me and distrustful of the demon blood I'd been taught to fear, I hoped so. We both needed time, but our relationship was too important to lose.

A gentle, warm hand landed on my shoulder. I lifted my gaze to find Garret watching me, his storm-gray eyes understanding. "You two will make up and have a better bond for it. All friends fight. You wouldn't believe the quarrels Ryker and I have gotten into over the years. Blood has been shed. Unkind words said."

"Sinkers know we never went through half of what you two are going through." He shook his head as if he couldn't fathom it, which I found slightly amusing, considering all he'd been through. "Put yourself in Finn's shoes. His entire world flipped the day he learned of his heritage. Finn may need more time than you wish, but he'll come around. That he's still here speaks volumes."

Though Garret didn't know the whole truth of why Finn was upset or that he was a demon born, his words soothed me and gave me hope. Tears pricked in my eyes. Without thinking, I flung Naela off my arm and launched myself at Garret. My arms wrapped around his torso, and I pressed my cheek against his armor.

The steady heartbeat of the fae I'd come to depend on this past week beat in my ear, muffled by the metal and leather separating our skin. In the castle's shadow, his body radiated heat and strength. Only vaguely was I aware of how Garret stiffened and his sharp inhalation. Then, slowly, he stroked my hair comfortingly.

His touch brought me back to my senses. My cheeks burned as I realized what I'd just done. I'd acted on impulse, needing a comfortable connection like I'd once had with Finn. But now, with Garret's arms wrapped around me, it felt like something more, something unexpected. Like butterflies and tingles— with my guard.

Shite. How inappropriate. I pulled away. A chill

swooped in and stole Garret's warmth, the scent of him that hovered on my skin.

"I'm so sorry," I said, my tone tight, embarrassed. "It's just that—what you said was so beautiful. We have a lot to work through, but it gave me hope."

Gray eyes bore down on me, unyielding and . . . something else I couldn't quite place. Garret opened his mouth to speak but was cut off by a body, careening around the blind corner, straight into him.

"Bloody hell!" Nigel yelped as he jumped back, straight into his guard, who followed a meter behind. My brother wore training gear, and his face was flushed. Catching his breath, Nigel glanced back and forth between Garret and me. "First time I've seen you out here, Shea."

Nigel addressed everyone as if we were at an all-boys boarding school, where last names reigned. It was yet another of his elitist habits that I found highly annoying.

"I'm flying Naela," I replied, inching away from Garret.

Nigel's pale blue eyes shot up, searching for my hawk in the sky. Finding her far away, his shoulders relaxed. "A walk . . . right. I thought for a moment you may be putting in extra hours training. Should have known better."

"What exactly is *that* supposed to mean?"

Nigel shrugged. "Just haven't seen you putting in an

extraordinary effort, now have I? You're more the sleeping-in, lag-about type than the leader type. It's fine. Some of us are born to lead while others follow. It's the natural order and all that. Anyway, I've set myself a rigorous routine this morning. See you around." With that, Nigel took off, leaving me clench-jawed in his wake.

***

THE DINING HALL WAS PACKED WHEN I TOOK A SEAT next to Kumar and across from Kate.

"Did you sleep well?" Kate asked, her blue eyes taking in my tense muscles with concern.

After saying a brief hello in the library, I'd avoided them both, preferring to sit in my own corner and stew over what Nigel had said. I remained silent until a brownie served my tea and a variety of breakfast foods and left.

"I'm fine," I replied. "Sorry I was being stand-offish earlier. I went for a walk with Naela and ran into Nigel. He said things that ruffled my feathers."

Kumar grunted at my side. "Seems to be his specialty."

He was right. Nigel had a knack for frustrating his siblings. Besides Prince Casimir, he'd made no close friends. I was Miss Socialite by comparison.

Kate, bless her good heart, changed the subject straight away, launching into an engrossing story Ebba had told her of the Water Realm. It wasn't until the trumpets blared, the signal announcing that the king was about to say something, that I became aware Prince Casimir and my father had joined us.

Silence fell as the trumpets died and the king stood, a glass of wine, his usual breakfast beverage, in his hand.

"Sinkers be praised! I'm pleased to see everyone is present this fine morning!" His charismatic voice boomed over the long, narrow hall, and sent shivers down my spine.

I smiled. Though I hadn't had one-on-one time with him, I already felt connected to him in a way I never would have imagined.

"On this beautiful morn, I have a surprise. Will my children taking part in the Successional please stand?" My father's grin widened as we rose, one by one.

My face heated as well-dressed nobles invited to breakfast with the king, soldiers, and Feathered Fae stared at us. One pointed at me. I looked away. I despised being the center of attention.

"I mentioned you were to have two days free from training," my father continued. "Today is one of those days."

Kate's shoulders softened and Kumar sighed, but I frowned. I'd just resolved to up my game and now we were getting a day off? Figured.

"However, today will not be full of hours lazing about your royal chambers. No, no, no." King

Oberon raised a finger, wagging it in the air. The nobles in the crowd chuckled. "Instead, today we celebrate! We show the kingdom what you are made of. Dazzle them with the spectacle that the Successional is known for! Endear the common fae to you so they might support you! Does anyone know of what I speak?"

No one answered, which judging by the size of my father's maniacal grin was what he wanted.

"In just a few hours' time, we are to have a parade!" He roared the last three words, spreading his arms wide in triumph.

Murmurs rose with the king's excitement. Before they could get out of hand, my father commanded everyone's attention once more by tapping a fork against his wine glass.

"And that's not all. The parade will be followed by a game of faeball! I know my heirs have been quarantined, but the match will be their opportunity to sit among my subjects and get to know them."

There was no holding back the excitement any longer. Nobles, who'd been present at each of our meals but were prevented from talking to us, pointed and whispered. Their eyes scanned our table, already planning whom they'd approach. Brownies' helpful hands flew over their mouths. Soldiers spoke softly amongst themselves. My siblings and I remained still, our eyes wide.

A parade—an exhibition to show off our magic

—*and* networking with fae nobles?! I closed my eyes, battling back the distress that surged within me at the thought of hundreds, if not thousands, of eyes on me. Judging me.

Fight it, Lana, fight it. No one wants an anxiety-ridden head of their army . . . or daughter, I thought, breathing to force my rolling stomach under control. It worked—kind of like a miracle.

I opened my eyes, took another deep breath, and straightened my spine to project confidence. It wasn't what I'd been hoping for when I woke up that morning, but that couldn't be helped. Shit changed. I needed to be more adaptable.

And if the fae of Lyonesse wanted a parade full of spectacle and a charming princess, well, I'd do my best to give them one.

CHAPTER TWENTY

For having been raised in a magical household, I'd grown up fairly sheltered from the wider world of magical beings. In lieu of attending coven gatherings, Gran and Mam preferred a solitary practice and only occasionally invited friends over. All of them, save one shifter friend of Mam's, were witches. Whatever other supernaturals I'd seen had mostly been by chance; walking down the street or twice, in my favorite coffee shop.

Phoenix Castle had been a huge change. As in Faerie, most species were mixed, I was never sure what people were. Regular goblin? Hobgoblin? Pixie? What was the etiquette for asking? Or did most mixed-species prefer the generic term fae? How many fae races were there that I had no idea about? This, and much more, ran through my mind as we lined up just inside the castle wall for the parade and prepared to meet the subjects of Lyonesse.

When the castle gate opened, one thing became clear: The diversity in the castle was *nothing* compared to what we were about to encounter.

Fae of every skin color, hair color, eye color, shape and size imaginable lined the streets. Some were winged, like the sprite acrobats I'd watched perform during dinners, and some had scales instead of skin. Many acted as if they were about to view a show, settling into chairs and munching on food, the scent of which was making my mouth water. Others stood stoically waiting for the parade to start, so they could assess their king's strange heirs. No matter where I looked, there was something new to see, smell, hear, and yearn to touch.

Kumar came up beside me, his green, curious eyes taking everything in around him in awe. "It's amazing, isn't it? Most of the books in the library are illustrated in black and white. They don't do the fae justice."

Gio joined us, his mouth spread in a wide smile. "I hope the parade goes to the water. I'd love to get a sneak peek at Water Realm and meet the mermaids. Maybe feel my feet in the ocean again." A wistful look rippled across his face, dampening the joy there. No doubt he was thinking of his days fishing with his family off the coast of Italy, performing magic while nestled in their small boat.

The queue, led by my father with Meegra at his side, and surrounded by every single one of his heir's guards plus some, stopped just outside the castle walls.

"My subjects!" King Oberon called out once the castle gates closed behind us. "I have a special treat for you! Today you meet my heirs!"

The crowd lining the road into the city roared. A few winged fae shot up in the air and performed a dozen joyous backflips. One fae, a gruff-looking male with a long white beard, shook his hat, stained reddish-brown at the tip, as he bellowed his pleasure. Fae children, all too skinny and mangy with dirt covering every inch of their skin, ran in ecstatic circles around their parents.

"My children, as a gift to your people, I ask you to exhibit your powers as we proceed through the king-dom," King Oberon said, his eyes sweeping the parade line.

Dak was the first to oblige, transforming into an enormous white lion and sending gasps through the crowd. Arlo and Wikolia followed in quick succession. The golden eagle soared high in the sky as the white wolf loped from one end of the parade queue to the other.

Those with elemental powers went next. Crystal whipped up tiny tornados that circled in her palms. Maria levitated the small boulders lining the street. Gio summoned a ring of water to dance around him.

A flash of light followed, and I turned to see Nigel

had called two massive balls of light to hover before him. Straightforward and easy, so unlike my fellow illuminator's usual showy fashion. Perhaps he was keeping his cards close to his chest.

Whatever Nigel's motivation, we seemed to have switched places because simple was *not* what I had in mind. This parade was about getting subjects to like and cheer for you during the Successional. Their opinion may have an impact on my father's. Which meant my goal was to make the best first impression possible.

Unthinkingly, I glanced to my right and caught sight of Garret and Sai at the edge of the queue, helping to separate the heirs from the crowd. Garret winked, and Sai gave me an encouraging smile.

I straightened my shoulders, hoping I appeared confident, and crossing my fingers, I called infrared light. The air pulsed with heat as infrared light rushed toward me. Despite the thrill that ran through me, threatening to derail me, I wove the red light with visible light as if I'd been doing so for years. Finally, I released it.

The crowd released a gasp. Dozens of fae pointed at the halo of red light that hovered over me, tinting my skin with a faint red glow—like a saint.

I'd be exhausted and overly hot after the parade, but it would be worth it to impress the fae of Lyonesse. I chanced a glance at my father. He wore a proud smile on his face. I beamed back. This would be totally worth it.

Kate stepped forward, straight-backed and proud, and pulled her decorative blade from her scabbard. Meegra had insisted we all wear one during the parade, mostly for show, but for Kate it would be used for more. She still hadn't materialized elven magic, and healing would hardly be impressive in this situation. Still, my healer sister excelled at working with what she had. Twirling and thrusting the blade into an imaginary foe, Kate put on a show that had the crowd bursting into applause.

"That was fantastic," I whispered when she returned to stand by me. Between Kate's new skill with a weapon and the research she'd been doing on pressure points, she might stand a chance in the Successional after all.

Victoria, another sibling who had yet to exhibit any elemental fae powers, went next. Shocking us all, she opened her perfect mouth, and a song spilled out.

The fae men in the crowd inched toward her, entranced. I swore I felt her pull, too, though I knew that was impossible. Vila songs only worked on men. Still, it was so lovely, one couldn't help but be mesmerized.

Victoria had never revealed her song in training. She'd probably been planning to keep it in her back pocket until it would have the most impact. If that had been her plan, she'd chosen her moment well.

"Perhaps only a few notes now and then, daughter? No need to enchant all the male fae of Lyonesse," Oberon yelled over her angelic notes.

I turned to see his hands clapped over his ears, his eyes crinkled with amusement.

Victoria stopped singing. "As you wish, Sire," she beamed.

Only Kumar and Finn remained to exhibit their magic. They stood side by side and from the stiff set of their shoulders, it was obvious that the last thing either of them wanted to do was reveal their powers.

This would be Finn's second time using magic in the open, his first time being when he'd protected Crystal from me. In that instance, I'd been the only one close enough to see the red flash in his eyes, betraying him as a demon born.

When I was younger, I'd constantly been on the lookout for a demon born to show him. We'd never seen one, but Finn was well aware of the signs. He knew the second he used his magic and his eyes flashed red, some people from the Old Land would freak. Especially if they were witches, for it was our culture to be wary of the unholy sect of witches.

Though I, too, felt distrust coiling in my stomach, I didn't want to. I loved Finn like a brother and knew, without a doubt, he wasn't evil at his core. Still, my body rioted at the thought of a demon born in my presence. I hated that about myself and hoped, for Finn's sake, that the fae did not feel the same way.

All around the fae waited, their eyes growing wider with questions as the seconds passed.

Sensing his sons' hesitation, the king strode down the queue until he stood before Kumar and placed a gentle hand on his shoulder.

Jealousy shot through me, unwanted and cruel. Yes, I craved my father's attention, but Kumar and Finn needed it most now—needed his strength and acknowledgment.

You'll have your time. After you win, I thought.

"My sons, there is no need to be nervous. These are your people. They will love and revere you. Your powers are rare and beautiful, no matter what you have heard. You must not be ashamed of the majestic creatures you are."

Apparently bolstered by our father's little speech, Finn presented himself to the crowd. I thought I caught him glance briefly in my direction before lifting his hands. Fire erupted from his palms and as if to make a point of exactly what he was—how powerful he was—Finn conjured a tornado to whip around him and water to rain down on the crowd all at the same time. Though I couldn't see them, I knew his eyes were flashing red—the telltale sign of the demon born working magic.

The fae shrieked with pleasure. Some danced in the rain, while more observant onlookers gasped and pointed at Finn. He was powerful, a demon born capable of wielding multiple elements. He would be a hit during the Successional.

When he decided the crowd had had enough, Finn ceased the waterworks and the tornado but kept the fire in his hands and turned to face his siblings.

Kate gasped when she saw his crimson eyes. "Did you know?"

"Only since that day I fought with Crystal," I said. "His eyes flashed red when he did magic to protect her."

"Does *he* know of demon borns' reputations? That they're cursed?" Kate asked.

I nodded and then glanced around to see how many of my other siblings recognized Finn's maternal ancestry. Maybe he had a chance to start fresh with someone here—someone who had not been raised with the superstitions of a witch.

Maria, Gio, Himari, Nigel, and Victoria all stared at him, shock apparent on their faces. But that still left Dak, Arlo, and Crystal, who appeared normal. Perhaps the shifter community was less aware of demon borns. I had no doubt that Crystal knew exactly what Finn was, but true to her slightly evil nature, she wasn't terrified by it. In fact, she looked a little excited to have a demon born for a brother.

If only I'd worn that expression on my face when I first noticed, then all Finn and I would have to get over was his admission of love. That hill seemed so much smaller now that we had two to climb—his shameful love and my personal prejudice.

The fire evaporated from Finn's palms, and he rejoined the parade queue. Everyone's gaze wrenched from him as it was no longer appropriate to stare.

Only Kumar remained to exhibit his powers. After Finn's showing, he looked incredibly lighter. Like nothing he could reveal would be nearly as taboo or fear inducing. Probably he was right.

I realized Finn had likely chosen to go first, not only to get it over with, but to give Kumar the courage to reveal himself. It was one of the acts of kindness Finn was famous for—those smaller gestures that could be easily overlooked.

Finally, Kumar stepped forward, his stance and face softened. A vivid green tail unfurled behind him; his green eyes brightened and became more poisonous looking.

Fae gasped, pointed, and pulled their children close—all more worried about a naga than a bit of demon blood.

But Kumar did not slink away. Instead, he slithered to the forefront of the queue, where he stopped right between Meegra and our father and stood tall.

THE PARADE WOUND ITS WAY THROUGH THE STREETS of Lyonesse for hours. Most of what we saw were homes inhabited by the aristocracy, with turrets and spires and statues clinging to their brightly painted sides. Here fae celebrated our arrival by dashing out of their homes and offering us meat just off their roasting spit and dripping with juices. Some gave sugar-dusted edible flowers that popped and fizzed in your mouth. A few ladies gave leis made of exotic flowers. It was an easy delight to walk through these neighborhoods and take in the kingdom's vibrancy.

But there was the other side of Lyonesse, and we walked through a bit of that, too.

The homes in the less affluent areas were little more than shacks. They were painted just as brightly as the manors we passed, though patches where the paint had chipped off revealed the bare wood beneath.

The fae who lived in these neighborhoods wore frayed clothes riddled with holes. Their skin looked wan and their wings drooped. Still, no matter how dogged the fae appeared, their smiles were wide, welcoming, full of love for their king and joy over our display of power. It made my heart explode to know that these people, no matter how downtrodden, had hope that my father could return their kingdom to greatness.

We'd just stopped in a large square in an area my father had announced as Hob Hill when a hand gripped my calf. I started. Fae were not supposed to approach us directly, but go through the dozens of guards who surrounded us to give gifts or a good word. And none of the guards would dare to touch my calf. I hoped whoever intruded wasn't a creeper.

Hesitantly, I looked down to see a fae child with dull green skin and large blue eyes holding out a lei of flowers. The blooms resembled dandelions, but much larger. I exhaled, no longer worried over this wee girl.

"Hello," I said.

The language rune tickled on my arm as it worked. Unlike in Phoenix Castle, where the rune was relatively benign because the fae living inside its walls knew English, the rune had been active during the parade. I didn't know what language the fae spoke, couldn't even hear it with the rune, but it wasn't English.

"Thank you for the lovely flowers." I squatted to accept her offering. It would join the dozens of other leis hanging around my neck.

"What's going on here?" Meegra swooped in. Her sharp green eyes darted between me and the girl before narrowing. The girl slunk, so that she stood behind me.

"She's only giving me a flower necklace." Anger welled inside me as I lifted from my crouch to face the Master Feathered Fae.

I was willing to put up with Meegra's superior attitude during training. After all, she was a great fighter and could teach us loads. But on a day we were not training and were supposed to be celebrating? Not bloody likely—even if I was bending the rules a bit.

"She's just a harmless child," I added. "And I want to talk to her. Preferably without *you* lurking over my shoulder."

Meegra's face lit up, an unattractive maroon color. "How dare you speak to me—"

"I think His Majesty is calling you, Master Meegra. Time to stop terrorizing Lana and this young one," Sai said, coming up beside me. Normally she wouldn't be up at this time of day unless Meegra required her for training, but when my father had requested a heavier guard during the parade, Sai had volunteered.

Meegra glanced toward the front of the line to see that, indeed, my father was attempting to catch her eye. A frown flitted across her face, but she caught herself. Throwing back her shoulders, Meegra tried to regain her position as the one who always had the upper hand. "But of course he is. I'm his Master Feathered Fae, indispensable to His Majesty. Unlike—"

"Let's skip whatever cruel thing you were about to say." Sai cut Meegra off again. "I've heard *it all*, and you have a king to attend to. Better scurry to the front of the column, see how you can *service* His Majesty." Sai's violet eyes leveled with the Feathered Fae's. It would take more than Meegra's title to intimidate her.

"Yes," Meegra's eyes narrowed. "I will. And I

believe you are needed at the back of the column. Isn't that where a soldier of your rank stands?"

Sai shifted closer. It dawned on me that she was here, being insulted by Meegra, not because she cared that my father needed Meegra, but to help me. She'd intervened to ensure that *I* was not the one receiving Meegra's insults. I was thankful. After all, Meegra was an intimidating opponent. But if I won the Successional, I'd be ranked above her. At that point, I'd have to stand up to her on my own. May as well start now, I thought, throwing my shoulders back.

"I've got this, Sai."

"As you wish, my lady." My night guard, who normally used my name, spoke my title and bowed her head, making it clear to Meegra whom she was listening to before striding away.

I stood my ground, and Meegra's green eyes bore into mine as she leaned forward, dangerously close to my halo of red light.

"Know this, illuminator-elf," she growled. "Right now, you are *nothing*. Judging by your display of power, you will remain so. The only reason I'm not punishing you right now for such insubordination is because your father wants a good show. And I do only what *my superior* wants. Consider this a warning."

Then, as if trying to recall why she'd gotten so worked up in the first place, Meegra shifted her gaze to the bedraggled girl. Again, her eyes narrowed.

The girl let out a terrified squeak.

"And to think, I thought—but no—not this pitiful, little mouse." She sneered and turned, a whirlwind of black feathers. Without sparing us another glance, she strode to the front of the column.

The girl's crystalline eyes filled with tears that trailed through the film of dirt on her face.

"I'm so sorry you had to see that," I said, bending down to her eye level. "She was cruel. It seems to be her thing."

The girl just nodded, gave a hearty sniff, and held the flower necklace out once again.

I released my halo of infrared light so as not to burn her. Blessedly, cool air blew away the cocoon of heat that had bordered on stifling for the last few hours. I sighed and bowed my head so the girl could reach more easily. She placed the necklace around my neck. The weight of the flowers pressed down on the other leis and the velvet-soft of petals brushed my cheek. A sweet scent of an unnamable Faerie bloom filled my nostrils, and I smiled. I was just about to lift my head when her young voice filled my ear.

"When I'm of age, I want to live in the castle with you," she whispered. "I want to protect you—help you save our bonegate so magic can come back. Will you save a spot for me? I promise to work my hardest."

I bit my lip, unsure. The girl couldn't be older than four. Would I even be in Faerie when she came of age? Or would I have returned to the Old Land?

Deep down, I knew I didn't want to go back. Other than Mam, the Old Land held nothing for me. Although my motivation for coming here—to meet my father—had been selfish, that was changing. Today alone had been an eye-opener. There were so many fae to help. As a princess, I could do more than I ever dreamed possible in Ireland. Plus, I still wanted to beat Crystal—*badly*.

Still, I couldn't get this child's hopes up. Everything in my future depended on the Successional. Although I'd resolved to work harder, I was still far from being the front-runner. Who knew how much influence I'd have if I came in last?

"I'll try my best. If I do well in the Successional, I'll speak to my father about you. What's your name?"

"No. I won't serve the king. *Only you,*" she whispered and pressed her finger emphatically against my shoulder as she spoke. "I only want to work for you. You'll do great things, I've seen it."

Oh. My mouth gaped before I caught myself.

"That's kind—"

"Pardon my daughter, m'lady." I nearly toppled backward as a female fae burst from the crowd, took advantage of a gap in the guard line, and pulled the girl back to lean against her legs. "She's always been a talkative one. I hope she didn't offend you." The woman had the same faint green skin, bright blue eyes, and a look of apprehension her daughter had worn when confronted with Meegra.

"No, it's fine. She was just telling me she saw—"

"Aye," the woman cut me off. Her tone was nervous, as if she couldn't wait to get out of the crowd. "She sees a lot of things, this one. Some of it true, some utter nonsense. Best not fill your head with her dreams. Anyhow, we must be off."

The woman hauled her daughter away, retreating through the crowd.

Young blue eyes flashed back at me, still awaiting my answer, needing to know if she had a spot in my service.

My heart clenched. What the girl wanted me to promise depended on many things outside my control. Even so, I nodded.

I hoped I wouldn't let the mysterious girl down.

CHAPTER TWENTY-ONE

I'd never seen a community so united. It was as obvious as Wikolia's wolf aspect's fur gleamed white that the fae of Lyonesse believed in their king.

Their trust radiated from them every time they looked at my father, in every trembling hand he held, and in the eyes of every mother fae who handed over her babe to kiss. King Oberon's subjects believed he could bring change to his kingdom and make their lives better. And many had extended that belief to us—his children—too.

The moment the castle gates closed behind us, I released the light hovering over my skin. Sweat dripped off my temple from the effort I'd exerted. More than anything I wanted to go to my room, wash, recline on my bed, and think about all I'd seen.

But it seemed our first free day was shaping up to be just as exhausting as if we were sparring against

Meegra herself. Instead of dismissing the parade queue, the king beckoned us to follow him.

Soon enough he'd led us to the great hall where the scent of roasted meats, baked goods, and elven wine assaulted us. While many fae took wine with all of their meals, it had never been as abundant as it was now. Crystal bowls filled with ruby liquid marched down every table. Though I'd never partaken in such an activity, I recognized the ambiance from American programs.

We were about to participate in the fae equivalent of tailgating to prepare for the faeball match.

DINNER AFTER THE PARADE HAD BEEN THE FIRST MEAL in which my father insisted his children sit at a table near the front of the great hall. It was a move that put us on display for the noble fae he'd invited. While it was normal for a few chosen aristocrats, who I assumed were personal friends of my father's to be present during our meals, this meal was different. Hundreds of fae nobles attended the post-parade feast, all sizing us up, pointing at us, and whispering. I wasn't sure why until Dak commented that they seemed to discuss whom they'd bet on.

Of course, the few fae in the city of Lyonesse who had money wouldn't just watch the Successional with wonder. They'd do what people with too much money all over the world do.

They'd gamble it away.

"I think I drank too much of the wine at dinner," Kate said, stumbling a little and catching herself on my arm.

I was in the same boat, my legs wobbling as we traipsed down the hall. We were on our way to a field somewhere on the castle grounds where apparently all the important matches of faeball were played.

"We'll get water when we get into the pitch," I said, and hoped that would be possible. "Where is it anyway—"

My question died in my mouth as we turned a blind corner, and a stadium sprang up. As soon as I saw it, I knew I hadn't yet explored this side of Castle Phoenix, because I couldn't have missed this. Either that or they deconstructed the stadium after each use, which judging by the intricacies of the hoops and stands, I highly doubted.

The faeball pitch was in the shape of an oval, much like a hockey rink but at least three times the size. Stands, or the closest thing I could compare them to, ran the periphery of the field. Unlike stands surrounding football fields, the lower seats didn't start near the ground, but five meters in the air. Scaffolding was absent, leaving me to believe they were supported by magic. The seats at the top were as high as a three-story building. The top box, adorned with lush velvet seats for my father and Prince Casimir, floated above it all in the dead center of the arena.

Without asking, I knew my siblings and I would not be sitting with our father. The box was far too small to accommodate all thirteen of us. Where were we to sit, then?

"You and your siblings are to find spots in the stands and sit amongst the subjects of Lyonesse. No more than three of you may sit together. We want you to spread out. You might be too intimidating otherwise." A guard answered my unspoken seating question as we neared the entrance to the arena.

I didn't recognize him, nor did I recognize any of the guards who were accompanying us to the stadium. It was the first time since they had assigned us guardians that Garret and Sai were not nearby. This was because they were both taking part in the match.

Kate and I veered toward the far end of the field, away from another gathering of our siblings. In the periphery of my vision, I saw Finn and Kumar go the exact opposite direction. Since the reveals of their powers before the parade, Kumar hadn't left Finn's side. It had quickly become clear I wasn't the only sibling wary of Finn's demon born nature. Because of this, I was glad Kumar was sticking with Finn, giving him support, while the rest of us worked out our issues.

We grabbed cups of water, downed them and sighed over the cool liquid that washed away the film of wine on our tongues. Then we refilled our cups before moving on. After choosing our seats, Kate and I contented ourselves with fae watching and taking in the stadium more closely.

There was a lot I'd missed from the outside, like the six hoops, three gold and three black, floating around the field. I assumed these were some sort of goalposts. There was also an odd, isolated cloud hovering just above the top box in the dead center of the stadium. When I'd first noticed it, I'd assumed it was an actual cloud. As it still hadn't moved ten minutes later, I concluded it was something else— something magical.

"Lord Gantar at your pleasure, My Ladies. How is it possible no one has claimed the pair of you?" A portly, well-dressed fae who looked to be part goblin and part sprite appeared. His gossamer wings folded neatly behind him as he plopped down out of midair to sit next to Kate. He lifted a bushy eyebrow. "Pray tell me, what are your powers?"

Now that he mentioned it, it did seem odd. Small crowds had gathered around the groupings of my other siblings—especially around Gio and Dak with another large crowd surrounding Crystal, Victoria, and Wikolia. I wondered who among them was the primary draw? Was it the shifters? From what I'd heard, there were no shifters or chimera subjects in Lyonesse. I could only hope that people weren't seeking Crystal. If it got any bigger, her ego might launch her into space.

Kate had fallen into a quiet discussion with Lord Gantar about healing and earth magic, which I was pleased about. Apparently, we were expected to make small talk during the match, but if I could avoid it, I would.

My hopes were dashed not a minute later when another fae sat down next to me. I recoiled. Her dramatic features of purple skin, a long, needle-like nose, and large protuberant eyes took me by surprise nearly as much as her overwhelming scent of peony. The fae didn't seem to catch my reaction, and without introducing herself launched into many questions.

I answered her, and with each bit of information, she seemed to take a tally on my strengths and weaknesses. Yet another sign betting would occur during the tournament. The nobles of the kingdom were using the match as a chance to see who their prize-winning-heir would be.

The stadium had just reached capacity when a blaze of trumpets sounded and a gleaming, golden door I hadn't noticed before opened. My father and Prince Casimir appeared. As the king and prince filed in, all the fae in the stadium, my purple-skinned inquisitor included, hushed and stood. Kate and I followed suit.

Alongside my father and brother strode two guards

and Meegra. The group strolled to the center of the field to stand before the top box, which had lowered in perfect harmony with their pace, touching down just as the king reached the center. Everything was choreographed, everything was perfectly timed—as it always was when my father wanted to put on the spectacle.

And then the show continued, with my father picking the four fae subjects who would fit in the box with him, his guards, Meegra, and the prince. When he finished, he sat on the largest plush chair in the box and gestured for Prince Casimir to join him.

Instead, Prince Casimir bowed and then glided over to speak with a lovely fae with long blonde hair and an amethyst gown who had been excluded from the top box. Even from so far away, I could make out the lovely fae's shock as her hand flew to her mouth. She shook her head to deny whatever the prince had offered. But my brother was having none of that. Prince Casimir led the blonde fae into the box and bid her to take his seat.

Once she was settled, he strolled out of the top box and made his way toward the stands. He was halfway to where I sat before I realized he was heading straight for us.

"Greetings, sisters. Good day, Lord Gantar. Lady Aurelia." Casimir inclined his head at the pudgy fae who'd been chatting Kate up and the peony-scented lady next to me.

"M-m-my prince!" Lord Gantar blurted, looking flustered. "I'd like to thank you for inviting my household to the game. Our children are sick, and my wife thought it best she remained at home, but I did not dare pass this honor up!"

"I, too, am honored," Lady Aurelia said in a simple manner that belied the myriad questions she'd asked me.

Prince Casimir waved a hand as if it was nothing to him. In all likelihood, he had no idea who received an invitation to the match and who didn't. "I hope you enjoy the game. My father selected the most excellent players among the fae guard. I'm hoping to enjoy the company of my dear siblings. I haven't had much time to speak to them yet."

"I understand, Prince Casimir." Lord Gantar stood. "I shall leave you to them. Many blessings to the royal family."

Lady Aurelia appeared conflicted. Apparently, she'd only gotten a fraction of the information she'd wanted out of me, but realized that she, too, should step aside for Casimir.

Prince Casimir smiled at her. "That was kind of Lord Gantar, but please, Lady Aurelia, do not feel as if you must leave. Although, I have one request."

Lady Aurelia inclined her head. "How may I be of service?"

"Might you allow me to steal your seat? My sister Lana and I have similar powers, and I have been hoping to catch up with her for some time. Perhaps Lady Kate would be amenable to a chat?" Prince Casimir's gaze shifted to Kate, who nodded.

Though Kate had agreed, she looked a little surprised. Perhaps she hadn't thought the prince knew her name. Still, I doubted her surprise could surpass my own. Prince Casimir had come all the way over here to talk to *me*?

He'd been present at a few of our trainings, watching from a distance, high above the training room floor. While I'd hoped to leave an impression, I didn't think I'd done enough to warrant a private audience. Whatever his reason, Prince Casimir settled in next to me, and Lady Aurelia moved next to Kate and began a constant flow of chatter.

"It's unlikely anyone else will approach us now," Prince Casimir said. "I hope you don't mind."

I shook my head, confused, yet pleased with the situation. The fewer people around me, the better. And as Prince Casimir was our father's eyes and ears until after the Successional, this could be a good chance to impress him.

The trumpets blared again, announcing the start of the game. Two teams filed out of the doors at opposite ends of the stadium. My gaze found Garret, dressed in gold that complimented his olive complexion. He was on a team with Sai and a few others I recognized as my siblings' guards. Ryker and Ebba wore black, marking them as members of the opposing team.

Though I knew nothing about faeball, I had a feeling this would be a good game. We'd only seen the guards perform magic a couple times, but it was enough to know that Garret, Ryker, Ebba, and Sai were all extremely talented. Competitive too, particularly the females.

"Ebba and Garret are playing against each other." Kate brushed my arm. Her eyes glinted at the prospect of her guard taking on mine. "This should be *interesting*."

She was trying to egg me on, but it didn't work. The cloud hovering above the top box stole my attention too quickly. It had descended to stop a meter in the air, right by where the two teams faced off.

"Ah, father charmed the elemental sphaerula himself this time." A smile bloomed on Prince Casimir's face. "That's promising for the game."

"What do you mean he charmed it?" I asked, but didn't catch his answer as at that instant the match started, and a roar rose from the crowd. I gasped as players passed the sphaerula and the cloud morphed from fireball, to rock, to a circular vortex of air, to a ball of water and on.

"Wait . . . the ball changes through the elements?" That was wild!

Casimir nodded. "Every time a player touches it, they manipulate it to their strongest element—or the closest opponent's weakest element, depending on their strategy. Once they have a chance, they try to shoot it through the hoops, which are always in motion just to make it more difficult. Every shot that makes it through is five points." He gestured up at the hoops. They'd been static when we entered the stadium, but now they were flying in the aerial space between the top box and the ground on their team's respective sides of the pitch. "They shall play until the first team reaches one hundred points, or until the charmed hoop disappears."

"How do you mean?" The hoops seemed pretty solid to me.

"One of the hoops on each side is charmed, like

the sphaerula. No one, except the fae who charmed them before the game, knows which it is." He wagged his eyebrows. Apparently the question of the disappearing hoop was an exciting event in the game. "They'll eventually disappear at the same time, which signals the end of the match. They'll flicker first to warn the players, but when they're gone, the game is over. Whoever is up in the points wins."

"Huh." I turned my attention to the field.

Not only did the sphaerula change elements, but each player used elements against other players, whether or not they were in possession of the sphaerula. The flinging of elements at one another made faeball quite a violent game, with all sorts of things being hurled across the pitch. Most players focused on the sphaerula, or attacking other players.

Although it seemed one or two on each team were keeping an eye on the hoops. Two of those players were Sai and Ryker. I recalled Garret telling me about the Harvest and how the cousins had dominated their Harvest years. I believed it. Their athletic prowess was on full display during the match.

Before today the Harvest had confounded me, but after the parade the need for it made sense. Not only did the competition allow for the poorer families to feed themselves more easily if the king chose one of their children for the guard, but the timing of the Harvest ensured my father chose children before malnutrition set in. It was still sad to think of kids separated from their parents. How could it not be? And yet, when I took in the strong castle guards and compared them to the fae I'd seen lining the streets of Lyonesse, the Harvest seemed like an excellent idea.

A shriek behind me wrenched my attention back to the game. My eyes landed on Garret rushing down the field. The ball was a blazing fireball floating before him as he dodged and weaved through players on his way to the black team's hoops. His arms pumped back and forth, his biceps bulging to extreme proportions.

Bloody hell. I unbuttoned the top button of my jacket. Despite it being winter, I was getting quite warm. Suddenly, Ebba came out of nowhere, a tornado of blonde hair and air magic propelling her forward to tackle Garret. I shot out of my seat as my guardian flew to the ground, the ball of fire still hovering over him.

It disappeared a moment later, in Ebba's possession as she sped down the field.

"Everything all right, Lana?" Kate asked, her tone teasing.

I glanced down and saw her eyebrows arched.

"I—yeah, I'm fine. Just didn't expect—"

"Ebba to kick Garret's butt? Don't worry, I'm sure he's *just* fine." Kate smirked knowingly.

"I'm not worried about him!" I blustered, unsure I wanted others to know about whatever was going on between Garret and me. "It just startled me!"

"I take it you like this guard—Garret?" Prince Casimir said.

I jumped. I'd been so caught up in the game, I almost forgot he was there.

"What? Yeah. I like him. He's my guard, and he's nice."

"Nice . . . in what way?"

Huh? Why was Casimir asking all these questions?

"In a helpful way." I shrugged, keeping my eyes on the game. "He always makes sure I'm on time and tells me about Faerie when I don't understand things. And a couple times he's brought me food before I even knew I needed it. He's just considerate."

Casimir frowned bemusedly. "I see."

I turned back to the game, not bothering to wonder why he appeared out of sorts. From what I'd seen in the castle, the king and prince did not speak to their guards often as though they were friends. They only gave orders. In my father's case, Meegra was the only exception.

On the field, the two hoops were still flickering madly. To add even more tension, the hoops that had remained solid had soared higher than ever before. Higher than most guards could fling the sphaerula, no doubt. Everyones' focus was on the flickering hoops. And Garret was *so* close to the black one, but Ryker was fast on his heels. If Garret pushed just a little harder, perhaps he could make a goal before the hoop was gone.

Garret, however, was one step ahead of me. He released a great gust of wind and sent it forth, right at the flickering black hoop. Then, in a masterful maneuver, he pulled the air back to him like a boomerang. The flickering hoop was flying closer to *him*, closing the gap.

It zoomed about a quarter of the way across the length of the stadium when Garret took his shot. The sphaerula left his hand in a blazing ball of flame. The hoop was coming closer, clearly still being manipulated by Garret.

But the trajectory was off. I was sure of it. So was the crowd. Fae were already shaking their heads at Garret's miscalculation. Ryker had slowed down in his chase. Obviously, he was sure the shot would miss, and the hoop would die out, causing the game to end in a tie. I leaned forward, hoping that a miracle would happen.

However, it wasn't a miracle that happened. It was Garret's quick thinking. Yet again, he released another burst of air. It flew toward the ball of fire, catching it, and altering its trajectory. My mouth fell open as the sphaerula soared through the flickering black hoop seconds before it disappeared.

Half the crowd jumped to their feet in wild applause, and once I regained my breath, I joined in. Though I hadn't been much for sports in the Old

Land, the excitement in this stadium was contagious. Plus, when your friends were playing, it felt more personal.

"I've been thinking," Casimir said, getting to his feet belatedly and placing a hand on my shoulder. "How would you like a lesson in light magic tomorrow? You recently accessed infrared, correct?"

I gaped and whirled around to face him. "Yes! That sounds amazing! Thank you so much!"

That Prince Casimir was willing to help me after I'd resolved to do all I could to win the Successional felt like a good omen. Perhaps the universe was looking out for me. Hope fluttered in my chest at the thought.

"Wonderful. I'll come to training tomorrow," Casimir said, looking pleased.

I paused, thoughtful. "Can you do that? How will Meegra take it? I've noticed she likes to be in complete control."

Casimir grinned and brushed his long, blond hair over his shoulder. "Probably not well," he admitted. "Unfortunately for her, I outrank her. Even if she is sleeping with our father, that doesn't give her the power of a queen."

Meegra was sleeping with the king?! No wonder she was always so sure of herself. This revelation didn't bode well for me, since Meegra seemed to dislike me on principle. "I didn't know that. It doesn't give me confid—"

"Lana! Look!" Kate cut me off. "Father just asked Garret who he wanted to dedicate the match sphaerula to."

Dedicate the sphaerula? Like in a medieval tourney when a knight gave flowers to a lady after he competed? Was it still in the shape of a cloud? I barely had time to wonder, for when I looked down at the arena, Garret had made his way across the field to stand below us.

He was looking straight at me.

My face burned with the fire of a thousand suns. I had to force myself not to stare at the ground. Trumpets sounded and immediately silence fell in the stadium. I had no idea what was happening, but everyone was staring at me. It was making my mouth go dry and my armpits damp. Then, suddenly, Garret spoke.

"My lady, Lana, it's been my pleasure to serve the kingdom of Lyonesse at your side this past week. I hope you've enjoyed your stay and will remain with us as a bright jewel of the kingdom." He opened his hand.

The sphaerula appeared in his palm, though much smaller than before and seemingly more solid. Garret released it, and the enchanted object zoomed toward me.

I caught it with one hand and stared at it. The second it hit my skin, the cloud evaporated and transformed into a gem about the size of a bottle cap. It was astounding, with a swirl of colors unlike what I'd seen before. There was ruby red, emerald-green, sapphire blue, and shimmering opal, all mixed into one stone. I stood there, my mouth opening and closing like a damned idiot, staring at the breathtaking stone.

Kate nudged me. "Say something."

"Umm, thank you, Captain Garret, for putting on a great match and your friendship. I'll cherish this token." Then, even though I wasn't wearing a dress, I did an odd little curtsey.

Internally, I groaned. Did that sound as lame as I thought it did? I shot a glance at Kate. She was pressing her lips together so hard they'd turned white from trying not to laugh. Yup. I sounded super lame.

The stadium was still silent. Was I supposed to say something else? Give him something in return? Just when I thought I'd die of embarrassment, the king began to clap, and the crowd erupted into applause.

Garret grinned as he bowed again.

I released a breath I hadn't been aware of holding. Thank goodness that's over, I thought, sitting back down as quick as I could. It was only then that I realized Prince Casimir had vanished.

CHAPTER TWENTY-THREE

Over a week had passed since the bonekey sucked me into Faerie.

This meant I'd wasted a week with my half-hearted training and hours of sleeping in instead of studying. My past laziness upset me, but there was no use in dwelling on the past.

At least the parade had been a success. Or at least, I thought it had. I felt like I'd done enough to impress the fae of Lyonesse and endear myself to them. I especially wanted to keep my promise to the green-skinned girl.

After meeting the strange girl and chatting with nobles at the faeball match, I dared to envision a future beyond the Successional. I was driven to catch my father's eye *and* help the fae of Lyonesse. For the first time in my life, I had abundant purpose.

Unfortunately, no one informed my coordination about my new goal of actually winning the Successional, not just surviving it. Unlike Kate, who was excelling with blade-work, my dagger was nearly as awkward in my hand as the first day I held it. Swords were still too large and clunky to be a feasible weapon option. And archery? Forget it.

My magic, however, was another story.

Light was coming more naturally than ever before. I hoped that with Prince Casimir's help, I could progress even further. For the first time in a long time, I was a novel mix of determined and hopeful. I would do all that I could to speed up my growth.

So when Meegra paired me up with Dak, a strong opponent who would normally have me cursing her name, I merely rolled my shoulders back, entered the sparring ring, and got on with it.

"Come on," I urged the coalescing hot light before me for the fifth time. By the way his muscles had tightened, I could tell Dak would pounce at any second. But I nearly had it this time and was determined to succeed. "Just a little more."

As if tired of hearing me beg, a thin, red flash bloomed. Quicker than I would have dreamed possible a week ago, I wove the infrared and visible wavelengths of light together, pulled the weave before me, and expanded it like a sizzling shield. Hell to the yes!

Dak leapt and swiped at the light. The odor of burnt skin and hair filled the ring, and the lion scampered back with a pained roar.

I went for the metaphorical kill.

Expand, I thought, spreading my fingers wide apart, and the light responded—stretching and thinning from a shield into the red-hot walls of a cage. Within seconds it had Dak surrounded. I bid the shield to contract, and it did so, creeping closer to the shifter's full mane.

Dak held up a paw and transformed. "I surrender."

I grinned and released the light, allowing it to dissipate into the surrounding air. "Good set."

"You're advancing a lot," Dak said.

He didn't look upset about losing, probably because he was in the same camp I'd been in only days before. He didn't want to leave Faerie and return to a life of showing tourists around Johannesburg for pennies, but he didn't care about his rank in the Successional. All Dak wanted—or said he wanted—was a life of exploration and adventure.

"Yes, she is," a regal voice said from behind me. "And she's about to get even better. Ready for our lesson, Lana?"

"You bet I am."

Casimir grinned and instructed Oren, the Feathered Fae wardmaker, to draw a massive training circle around us. Meegra's lips pursed as she watched, clearly not liking what was going on one bit. Too bad she didn't have sufficient power to stop us.

The ward finally to his liking, Casimir turned to me. "I noticed you can use white light and infrared light, but the infrared seems to be more difficult for you. Did you only recently access it? And I'm assuming you pull it from the air rather than generating it yourself?"

I nodded. Generating light yourself, with your own life essence rather than pulling it from the atmosphere, was a feat only master illuminators accomplished. Really, when you took in all there was to know to become a proficient illuminator, let alone a *master*, it was no wonder why we were rare.

"Do the fae work the same way?" I asked, unable to hold back my curiosity. "And are there loads of fae who can control light? Do you still work with the elements often, even though you're specialized?"

Casimir gave a little chuckle.

My cheeks flushed with heat as I realized what I'd just laid on him. "Sorry. Guess I have a lot of questions. My Gran educated me, but we didn't study the fae much as there aren't many full fae in the Old Land. You could say being here is a kind of crash course."

He gave me an indulgent smile before answering. "I never work with the elements anymore, not unless I must. The electromagnetic spectrum entices me much more and takes a lot of power to train with. It's usually that way when a fae works to hone their magical essence into a specialty power. We are reluctant to move backward. Light fae are like illuminators in that they are rare. It is why our father was so pleased when he discovered he'd sired three."

Why I'd received a letter that drew me to Faerie suddenly made more sense. Our father prized light-workers. Even though I wasn't a good one, he wanted to see what I could do. Now I only needed to work my butt off to earn my spot here.

"But enough about me," Casimir said, plowing forward. "In your last match, I noticed you worked with large swaths of light. Have you ever considered something more focused?"

Sounds of metal clanging and wind whipping through the training room resumed, distracting me. My shoulders loosened, taking in the flurry of activity around us. Meegra had commanded that the sparring exercises continue; Casimir and I were no longer the center of attention.

"Sorry? What do you mean by more focused?" I asked, forcing myself to stop watching the other matches. Casimir was being kind in helping me. The least I could do was give him my full attention.

"There's a lot going on in here," he patted my shoulder softly. "By focused, I meant forming the light into shapes—weapons you can use. This requires you to manipulate various spectrums into laser beams."

I pulled my eyebrows together. I'd heard of lasers, but I hadn't considered making them—it was another, more advanced skill.

"I'll take that as a no," Casimir said. "Well then, I believe the best way to proceed is for you to *feel* what I'm talking about. Is it common for mentors to engulf a student in their magic in the Old Land? Are you amenable to such a process?"

Now, *this*, I understood. Back home, many elementals found it easier to produce new variants of their magic for the first time after being exposed in a storm of a mentor's power. It was not unheard of for mentors to throw their pupils into tornadoes, tsunamis, infernos, or avalanches for teaching purposes. It was tough love, but the elementals who went through such experiences swore it helped them get to the next level. I'd never been enveloped in another lightworker's power, but my heart rate quickened at the prospect.

"I'm fine with that," I said, trying not to sound too eager.

Prince Casimir's lips turned up slightly and then, without a word, he laid his hand on my shoulder. It was cold and dry and strangely flat, unlike any other magic worker I'd connected with. I frowned, and Casimir grinned, reading my confusion.

"I'm suppressing my magic right now. I wanted to

show you what my blank slate feels like. Especially as there may be differences between our magics, you having half-witch blood and me being an elf. Once I call the light, it will be infrared. I'll swarm us with it, shape it, and hand it to you. Ready?"

I'd barely nodded when heat shot through me—starting at my shoulder, radiating down my arms, and searing the nerves of my spine all the way to my toes. Tingles branched off my nerves, seeking places previously untouched, warming them pleasantly. My fingers swelled before my eyes. A smile bloomed on my face. Casimir was moving infrared light through me.

There was another subtle push, and my body wasn't the only thing on fire any longer. The air I inhaled heated my nostrils, eradicating the cold damp of the castle, lulling me into ease. Suddenly, I jumped as a flash surged almost a meter in front of me.

Casimir reached out with a steady hand and grabbed the flash. The prince had not only called white light and infrared and woven them together—he'd constructed a glowing red sword with a white hilt.

It reminded me of a lightsaber, but completely made of light. I'd never been so close to that kind of power. Nor had I seen anyone pull a weapon out of thin air as Casimir had just done. But what was most surprising was that now that I knew how it felt, I had an *inkling* I could do it, too. For once, magic felt within my reach, and that was exciting.

"Did you sense how I did that? Called both wavelengths to me—to us—allowing you to feel them, wove them together, and then I pushed it a little more?" I nodded, and he continued. "When I pushed the energies further, I was envisioning them as a sword. I also offered the slightest bit more energy to create lasers and thus give the light definition. It is much like when we envision illusions we'd like to construct out of white light, we're just bending and forcing the light to our will, but in different manners. Here we're flattening it, making it rigid, almost solid. Want to try?"

Heck yes, I did.

I did as Casimir said, trying to mimic his steps. I got as far as coalescing red light before me, creating a surge of heat, and then—nothing.

My shoulders slumped at the failure, but I straightened them almost right away. No one ever excelled at anything on their first try.

So I tried again.

And again.

A dozen times more.

After what had to be the twentieth attempt, I lowered myself to the ground. I'd been so confident, so sure I could do this—and I hadn't even come close. I couldn't say I wasn't trying hard either. I'd worked myself to the limit, and it showed in the trembling of my arms and legs.

"It's all right," Casimir said, coming to sit beside me and swinging his arm over my shoulder. "You were close and your arms will steady soon. This reaction happened to me, too, when I accessed ultraviolet radiation." Casimir's words were comforting, though his frown told of his disappointment.

Ultraviolet? That was an energy on the opposite side of the spectrum from infrared—with visible light sandwiched between. "How many wavelengths can you access?"

"Visible, infrared, terahertz, microwave, radio, and recently ultraviolet. The smaller wavelengths are a challenge for me. It took months to get ultraviolet down. Its energy is erratic and excitable, which makes it difficult to harness."

I gaped. The prince had half of the electromagnetic spectrum under his command. A gamut of energies ranging from radio waves—which consisted of harmless, enormous wavelengths—to the devastating, nanoscale ultraviolet rays. Only the X-ray and gamma radiation portions of the spectrum lay outside of his grasp.

"I'll have to take your word for it," I said after a moment's awkward silence. "Obviously, I'm so freaking far behind you, I can't even imagine."

"Not a real surprise though, is it?" A jaunty voice said.

Casimir and I turned to find Nigel, standing just outside the sphere of our sparring circle, watching.

"What's that?" Casimir asked.

"That out of the three of us, King Oberon's children who are lightworkers, she's the weakest. It's not a branch many women excel at, even in the Old Land."

"Is that true?" Casimir asked. Before I could respond that it certainly wasn't, Nigel plowed right over me.

"Yes. It's just like women don't make good generals. Especially when the moon calls. From what I've heard, deciding becomes damn near impossible during that time of the month. Am I right, Lana?" Nigel had a tone of teasing to his voice, but it was clear that he wasn't teasing. He meant what he said.

I scowled.

"Hmm, here female lightworkers are just as strong as males. Just as rare too," Casimir said. "Anyhow, don't be envious I'm sharing secrets, brother. I've seen Lana's guard play faeball and must have some way to impress her." The prince wagged his finger playfully at Nigel.

My eyebrow quirked up. What did Garret have to do with any of this?

"As for women not making good heads of the armed forces, here it is quite the opposite." Casimir gestured to the Master Feathered Fae.

"Take Meegra, for example. She's one of the most formidable soldiers Lyonesse has ever produced.

Though, should Lana not win the tournament, there are other ways she may accomplish greatness in the kingdom." His eyes shifted to me and softened. "Imagine if you were Queen of Lyonesse, Lana! That means that even whoever claimed the top spot in the Successional would have to listen to you."

My lunch swam up my esophagus at the subtext. Queen. As in married to a king. As in *him*. What the bloody hell? Suddenly, all of Casimir's strange questions and probing about Garret during the faeball match made sense. He had a plan for me. One that did not involve me having a crush on a guard.

But Casimir was my *brother*.

While I was trying not to be sick all over the training room floor, Nigel acted as though what the prince said was normal. "Point taken, old boy. Although, to be honest, I didn't come over to debate. I only wanted to request we duel, brother. It's rare that I get to spar with another lightworker since my mentor left."

I nearly sighed with relief when Casimir's spine straightened in interest. My lesson was over, which was perfect. I wanted—no, I *needed*—to put some distance between myself and the prince. Because as much as I wanted to set him straight, I'd learned a thing or two since arriving in Faerie. Fae culture was different from what I was used to. Although I did not intend to marry my brother, delicacy in such matters would be best.

"Do you mind?" Casimir's hand nearly brushed my shoulder before I dodged it.

"Not at all. You two spar," I squeaked. "I'll talk to you later," I added, already striding away as fast as possible.

What in the blazes had I gotten myself into by accepting Prince Casimir's help?

Early the next morning, I was even more thankful for my decision to begin studying seriously. The library was brimming with cozy snugs, perfect for concealing oneself. After my room, it was the best place to hide from Prince Casimir and had the bonus of many distractions.

Now that I knew the prince's motives for helping me stemmed from making me an attractive prospect for marriage, I didn't want to see him again. At least not until I won the Successional, proving I didn't need to be anyone's queen. That I could be powerful on my own.

I sat with Kate and Kumar, breathing in the musty odor of books that seemed universal to libraries in all dimensions. They knew of the comfiest place to sit, because for Kate and Kumar, the library was heaven. They'd been here every morning, piling their arms high with books and reading until it was time to eat. Some days they'd even return to the library after dinner.

Kumar divided his time between the history and the religious beliefs of Faerie. Currently, he was delving into its history, his legs perched on an ottoman and a tome that must have weighed five kilos spread before him.

Kate's passions lay elsewhere. This morning she was studying at a frantic pace, hoping to learn more about her new earth powers. They had popped up unexpectedly, red and gold leaves bursting fantastically from her hands as she sparred. She now had only five days to master her new gift.

Though my magic was coming along nicely, I still felt a twinge of jealousy when Kate told me of this new development. Apparently, my desire to have an elemental power would never go away. Still, I was happy for Kate and couldn't help but admire her as she tore through one earth magic book after another. With her new power and the skill she'd developed with her blade, I thought she might end up doing well in the Successional after all.

Using Kate's fervor as inspiration, I picked up a book titled *A Modern Compilation of Fae and Their Lands*. Written in 1850 A.D., I considered the book anything but modern. No matter what I thought, the goblin librarian had assured me it was my father's favorite and the newest edition he'd permit. It was written by an elf scholar who, after relocating from the Old Land a couple centuries after Faerie's creation, traveled the new dimension of Earth far and wide for decades.

Inside its pages told tales of the different species of fae, what their common attributes were, and where they lived after the Great Sinking—the term used to refer to the creation of Faerie from the islands of the Old Land.

I learned fae could move between Faerie realms but rarely did so. Instead, most remained in the realms of their birth their entire lives. Some of this made sense. An elf could hardly live in the Water Realm with mermaids and sirens, and vice versa. But reading between the lines, I deduced most of these arbitrary divisions were a result of dislike.

A Modern Compilation of Fae and Their Lands flatly stated that no self-respecting fae, whether from Sinkers Realm or Free Realm, would *ever* consider moving to the False Realm. Or, as one author dubbed it, the Slave Realm. The slaves were the giants who'd built the castles and roads of Faerie as payment for their passage into the new plane of existence safe from humans. I wondered if my father was as prejudiced against giants as Ryker claimed he was against hobgoblins. This book didn't paint them in a pleasant light.

I closed the book and sighed. Truth be told, I was uncomfortable with being confronted with prejudice after prejudice—especially my own against demon borns.

"I'm gonna go rest for a bit," I said to Kate and Kumar.

They barely glanced up to say goodbye, they were so engrossed in their books. After I returned the tome to its shelf, I nodded to Garret, who'd been standing nearby, waiting for my studies to end. With my guard in tow, I slipped out of the library.

As we trudged down the corridor, I realized I wouldn't be able to relax in my room. I felt too conflicted. I wanted to explore, to see something new, to take my mind off of what I'd read. Gran had always said when intuition strikes follow it, so I took the next turn.

"Are you lost? The Half-Elf Tower is the other way," Garret said, startled by my sudden change of direction.

I shook my head. "No. I'm not as tired as before and just wanted to check out what's down here. Father said we could explore, and I'm taking him up on the offer."

Garret didn't stop me, though I noticed his shoulders harden. What was down this hall that would make him so tense? I was about to ask when light coming in the window caught on a glint of metal, exposing a guard standing in an alcove ahead. I tilted my head. No, not one guard, but three. That was unusual. I'd never seen a guard simply standing around the castle. They always had somewhere to be.

My step faltered.

That is . . . unless they were waiting for someone, and my father was the only person I'd seen with more than one guard as an escort. My heart started pumping faster. I picked up my pace and soon could distinguish the features of the guards. As I'd suspected, they were ones who routinely followed my father around.

My father was close, meters away, and Garret had known where he would be. He had to have. His face was so tense. Had I stumbled upon the king's personal chambers?

He'd said he didn't want to interact with us before the Successional, had claimed it would be offensive for us to approach him as distancing the parent from the child was a pre-Successional ritual. But what if I didn't win? What if this was my only chance to speak with him for months? Did I dare contradict his wishes and put any future relationship in jeopardy?

My father's guards had noticed me, but none seemed bothered by my hovering, which was a relief. If Meegra was escorting the king, she'd have shooed me away at first sight. I was about to ask the guards where I was when, suddenly, my father's voice boomed into the hallway. I started at the sound, which was direct, imperious even, so unlike my father's usual jovial manner, but his guards took no notice. They simply turned and went through the door.

The moment they were out of sight, I poked my head around the corner and nearly gave myself away with a gasp. A lattice pattern wrought in gold partially obstructed my view, but what I saw was still stunning.

The room my father stood in was not really a room at all, but a small courtyard. The walls were stark white, in line with the general aesthetic of Phoenix castle. The floor, however, was a beautiful, startling lapis blue, dotted with some sort of pattern. I squinted. Were they crescent moons?

My gaze shifted to a fountain unlike any I'd ever seen in the center of the courtyard. Crafted of gleaming gold, the fountain's channel was filled not with water, but hundreds of candles. All lit, the fountain resembled a large torch.

Or a shrine.

It was the most reverent place I'd seen in the palace. I wondered what my father was doing in there, kneeling on the floor, staring into the flames. I'd just gotten up the strength to test my luck and poke my head out further when my father rose to stand. I shot back behind the door, nearly colliding with Garret. Grabbing his hand and squeezing it hard, my eyes traveled up and down the long, white hallway, looking for a spot to hide.

I stilled like a child caught with their hand in the biscuit tin as the sound of heavy boots slapping the marble filled my ears and then—unexpectedly —disappeared.

I stood in the same spot for five minutes, waiting to hear even the smallest sign of life. When I was almost positive no one was still in the courtyard, I peeked around the corner again and released my breath. There, on the other side of the room, was a recessed and unadorned door carved into the marble. No wonder I'd missed it before, with the rest of the splendor in the courtyard intoxicating my senses. My father must have exited through there. My shoulders fell from where they'd been hitched up around my ears. Relieved, and even more curious, I dropped Garret's hand and stepped into the courtyard.

"Sinkers!" Garret hissed and grabbed my wrist. "This room is restricted to the king and prince—or those who have received an invitation."

I yanked my wrist back from him. "My father said I was free to explore. He never mentioned anywhere was off limits. I'm sure if Casimir is allowed, I am, too. As you're with me, I invite you to join," I said, trying to play down my annoyance. Garret was only trying to do his job, which he took very seriously. But I hadn't strayed a toe out of line since coming here. Couldn't he look the other way for once?

Sidestepping the intricate lattice-work, I made my way to the belly of the courtyard and stood before the fountain. I shivered. The energy was different in here —stronger somehow.

Aesthetically, the courtyard was even more stunning than I'd realized from the outside. Natural light streamed down from above to reflect off the gold fountain and create a shimmery haze.

Thuribles, similar to the intricate silver censers Mam used when smoke or incense were needed for rituals, hung along the bottom of the fountain. Their onyx color was slightly camouflaged in the shadow of the fountain.

Trees—green, leafy, and fresh smelling—grew from a bit of dirt at the four corners of the courtyard. Two pools of water rippled between the trees, their lengths running perpendicular to the lattice doors. Elaborate tapestries, similar to the ones in my room, lined the walls. My eyes scanned the works of art but latched onto two in particular. One was a map I was unfamiliar with. On the other, the Old Land, *my world*, stared back at me.

I made my way across the room to the map, zeroing in on Ireland, and placing my finger where I lived. Where Mam was.

Sinkers, I miss her, I thought, surprising myself by using the fae turn of phrase that could mean anything from praise to a curse. Had the slip happened anywhere else, I'd have been pleased. I would have felt it brought me closer to my father and deeper into this new world I was determined to be a part of. Now it only made me feel even further away from Mam.

"What is this place?" I whispered.

"It's a place where King Oberon and Prince Casimir come to be alone and think. A place of reverence," Garret explained, his voice strained from being pulled into a place he thought he shouldn't be. "It's said that this courtyard was the first built in Faerie. Where the giants laid the first stones, claiming this land for all fae. There are rumors that His Majesty placed his wife's bones here after she died, though no one except the king and Prince Casimir knows for sure. King Oberon comes here often, I believe, to contemplate in the open and commune with the elements."

I'd compared it to a shrine and hadn't been far off. Garret's theory made sense. This room radiated power. The elements, so close; the worlds; even closer. It would be the perfect place to center oneself—to revere a loved one lost.

Once again, I turned to the fountain of fire in the room's center. This time something new caught my eye. It was a discreet, extremely lifelike painting of a woman. I moved closer, something drawing me to the painting.

Had she been human, I would have guessed she was of Indian descent. However, her pointed ears told me this woman would claim no country of the Old Land. She was fae. Her portrait was placed carefully between the candles so as not to burn it. Though, upon careful observation, I noticed its edges were black anyhow.

"Who's that?" I asked, wondering if perhaps I was seeing Casimir's mother. If that was the case, Casimir had inherited none of his mother's dark, smoldering features.

I turned to see Garret, no longer looking nervous, but stern.

My eyebrows lifted. "Do you know?"

He nodded. "*That,* is Queen Pari of Buyan."

"What? Why would my father have a painting of her if they hate each other? Especially in a place like this?"

"The king does not like to speak of this, but it is said King Oberon and Queen Pari grew up as playmates and used to be great friends."

I gasped. "What? Well, what happened? Please tell me you know!"

He shrugged. "Supposedly, they had a falling out right before she took control of his bonegate. I do not know for sure, but believe the king keeps the photo here as a reminder of that betrayal. You saw the weakness, the hunger, the sorrow of our kingdom during the parade?"

I nodded. I would have been blind to miss it.

"Our misery is all Queen Pari's doing," Garret frowned. "It was a despicable act. If I had to guess, I'd say King Oberon keeps her photo to remember what he is striving for."

CHAPTER TWENTY-FIVE

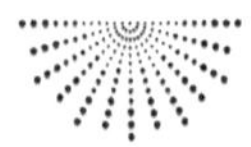

The next day, I strolled through a courtyard dotted with thickets of trees, shrubs, and gardens, happy not to be training. Many of my siblings clearly felt the same and had opted to spend the unseasonably warm morning outside, too.

Gio and Dak slept nearby, hats over their eyes and post-brunch snores sneaking from their lips. I envied their peaceful states.

I'd spent half the night thinking about Queen Pari and the mysterious courtyard I'd come across the day before. Now, I regretted my restlessness. Perhaps after I flew Naela, I would sneak in a wee kip before training.

I strode past Wikolia, Victoria, Arlo, and Crystal, sitting in a group gossiping. Far away, in a garden at the front of the castle filled with rose bushes, paths, and fountains, the pale forms of Nigel and Prince

Casimir strolled. While before Nigel's sucking up to the prince had annoyed me, now I was grateful for it. If Nigel monopolized Casimir's time, maybe I could avoid another awkward conversation.

Finn was outside flying Kane too. His brown sickle form soared on the winds in the distance. I put space between us and roamed about the opposite end of the vast courtyard. As Finn could still barely look at me, I assumed he felt mortified. I was uneasy around him, too. Best to let things settle between us and within us a bit before we spoke.

Naela and I veered toward a copse of trees. It was far less impressive than those in our woods back home, even so, it would do the trick.

"Ready to fly, Boss?"

Naela did a little head bob, and I swung my arm forward, releasing her. She soared high above the castle turrets, bobbing and weaving in the wind before diving toward me to claim a prize. I flung a bit of meat in the air. Naela caught it, did a single flip, and dove to land on my arm.

"Someone's showing off!" I grinned and released her again. We went on like this for some time, Naela soaring high and then screaming back in a rush of wind and wing. Twice, she detoured for what I assumed was a mouse in some far-off corner of the courtyard. I had to work to hold back a smirk when she returned, clearly peeved that the tiny animal had escaped her clutches. On the third time this happened, I burst into loud giggles. Naela responded by flying away in a huff, which only made me laugh harder.

"Your familiar is as well-trained as Xerxes." Prince Casimir's smooth voice cut through my laughter. I let out a yelp of surprise as I whirled about to find him and Nigel.

His eyes were wide, sincere. "My apologies, sister. I figured you noticed our approach."

It was not a totally unreasonable assumption. The courtyard was mostly open space. Although I was pretty sure that they came around the back of the copse, the one direction that would provide them cover. Did Casimir know I was avoiding him?

"It's all right," I replied, taking a step back. "I haven't gotten to watch her fly much lately, so we were in our own little world."

A piercing shriek, followed by raucous laughter, rang across the courtyard, prompting us to turn around and see what was so funny. Crystal had left her lot to talk to Ryker. Crystal let out another laugh, more animated this time, and brought her hands to her mouth in surprise. What the hell? I tilted my head and then my mouth dropped open as the realization struck.

Crystal—competitive, brazen, and bossy Crystal, was *flirting*.

"It is a sight, is it not?" Casimir wrinkled his nose. "A soon to be titled royal princess of Lyonesse flirting with a mere guard! And a part hobgoblin at that." He spoke with such disdain that I couldn't help but stiffen.

I was no psychic, but I was positive there was a double meaning to Casimir's accusation. Nigel, however, did not seem affected. He chortled, clearly accustomed to the prince's prejudices and elitism.

"So, Lana, can she read your mind? Your familiar?" Casimir asked as if he hadn't just said something offensive.

"I'm not sure," I replied through clenched teeth.

I wanted to stand up for Ryker, but the threat that Prince Casimir would relay that information back to my father was too great. If Finn's revelation had taught me something, it was that coming face to face with our prejudices was uncomfortable.

What if my father took offense? A part of me knew I shouldn't care, but there was also the abandoned little girl inside me, who I'd tried to quiet for years. That little girl wanted to know him and please him, and dammit, she deserved to have *some* say when she'd waited so long.

So, instead of telling Casimir that Ryker was a great guy, I simply answered his question. "Naela's ability to do what I want has increased since coming here. I feel like I can sense her displeasure more, too. You know, because I'm spending so much time training and not flying with her."

My eyes followed Naela. She'd abandoned me

when I didn't provide her an arm to perch on. Now she was all the way across the courtyard, soaring through the sky with Kane.

Casimir nodded knowingly. "Xerxes can sense our father's will at short distances. He was of great help to our father in the last battle we fought. Talons can do substantial damage, as I'm sure you're aware."

"I once shot a hawk double the size of yours," Nigel said, his tone boastful. "It was my first hunting trophy. I had her stuffed and mounted in my room."

My jaw tightened. Was this what impressed his aristocratic friends back home? How could this conversation get any worse? I had to get out of here.

Casimir's lips pursed in displeasure. "I wouldn't mention your love of hunting the winged beasts in this court, brother. Our father appreciates creatures of the air, and those who have an affinity for them."

Nigel seemed to ascribe to the belief that all attention was good attention and grinned despite the prince's chiding. "Of course he does. He's sleeping with one, isn't he? Can't say I blame him. She's as fit as they come. Where are you hiding the rest of the fae ladies like her? Or are you keeping them all for yourself?"

Nigel raised his eyebrows, and Casimir chuckled lightly. The two continued on in this vein, revealing that there wasn't any difference between these brothers and some disgusting men I'd met at Trinners. What a letdown.

I was about to excuse myself before Prince Casimir could make another icky marriage reference, when a dull pressure against my temple caught my attention. It was a pressure I recognized; a pressure Gran had inflicted upon me so I'd know when a malicious psychic was around.

Someone was trying to read my mind. My breath hitched. One of my siblings had developed mind magic. My eyes snapped back to Nigel and Casimir, still lost in their conversation.

I discounted the Crown Prince right away. Casimir had no reason to hide his powers. It gave him no edge in the Successional since he was not competing. Nigel had a motive to be sneaky, but I highly doubted anyone gaining a brand-new ability could do so without total concentration. Both were out.

Gio and Dak were still asleep. My gaze traveled to Crystal next. She hadn't moved from Ryker's side and was giving their conversation her all. Even more amazing was that Ryker was grinning from ear to ear. Was it possible he was *interested* in Crystal? I never would have guessed that. Their personalities were so different.

Finn was still flying our hawks. He wasn't a prime candidate anyhow. I doubted very much Finn would want to infiltrate my mind right now when he was doing his best to ignore me.

Finally, my eyes swung to where Wikolia, Arlo,

and Victoria were resting on the grass. I bit back a gasp.

Victoria stared back at me, her dark blue eyes narrow. The instant our gazes met, she smirked. I sucked in a breath and whirled around to face the men. Plastering a smile on my face, I pretended to be listening to their conversation.

The sense of pressure against my skull had not diminished. Someone was still trying to break in. Obviously, the worker of the mind magic—who I hypothesized was Victoria based on her wicked smile—was oblivious to the fact that I had years of practice keeping a psychic out of my mind.

Victoria didn't understand she was wasting her time trying to read my mind. She'd given her new power away by targeting me. A smile crept over my face. Most importantly, she had just given me an advantage over the other Successional contenders.

CHAPTER TWENTY-SIX

"Tomorrow is your ritual day of rest to prepare your body and mind for what is coming," Meegra's commanding voice rang out through the training hall as she paced before us.

Not for the first time, I wondered what she did when she wasn't terrorizing us. I hoped it was something that took her far away after the Successional was over.

"As it's the final day, today's training is special. It will be the culmination of your experience thus far. You will work to defeat or evade all the Feathered Fae."

My gaze shot up from the ground. We'd seen Meegra and Oren, the wardmaker, every day, but the rest of the Feathered Fae had been largely absent. This would be the first time we'd get to witness the powers that made the group so special.

Meegra snapped her fingers, and the doors behind us flew open. A line of ten figures marched in, their black velvet capes fluttering behind them. They were dressed for battle with armor covering their torsos. Two etched metal feathers ran the length of their armored collarbones with the frayed ends stopping at their shoulders. Another feather was etched on their breastplates, over their sternums. Black leather covered their arms, allowing for increased mobility, while retaining some protection. Meegra's uniform was more elaborate, but the Feathered Faes' armor spoke volumes. Their decorated armor was a status symbol, putting them above the common fae and other guards of the castle who wore simple black.

"We shall be outside today. Moving into the elements will better mimic the Successional arena. Of course, do not imagine everything will be *exactly* the same." She popped an unimpressed eyebrow.

"Only the king can be sure of what will be in the arena. I trust you locked up your familiars for the day, as requested. This is an exercise and we do not wish to run into a vengeful hawk who does not respect the rank of a Feathered Fae."

That explained why Garret had requested I lock Naela up that morning. I'd done so, but only once he insisted Sai would return to her post to guard my door. After one break-in and murder attempt, I wasn't taking any chances with my familiar.

Since I didn't speak up, Meegra's eyes locked on me. I nodded to indicate I had caged Naela. Down the queue, Finn did the same.

"Good. Follow me."

We filed out of the castle. Meegra led us into the barren woods surrounding Castle Phoenix. Dead trees littered a landscape almost devoid of green. The only life-form that seemed capable of thriving here was a fungus grown out of proportion, its black tops the size of ottomans.

What struck me as most curious was that some of the plants clinging to life resembled those outside Mam's house. Then again, should it really be curious? Faerie, no matter how odd, was still derived from the Old Land. The land I stood on was once located in the same dimension as the human world. Performing incredible magic, powerful fae, the Sinkers, sank the islands to a new plane and smashed them together. In finding their kind a new home, they gave their lives.

"There is an identical clearing five kilometers east." Meegra said as we stepped into a clearing. She pointed to the flag of Lyonesse, which hung behind my father at every meal. Someone had stuck the flag in the clearing's center. Its white background with a black and gold phoenix rising from red flames provided a welcome pop of color in the unadulterated bleakness.

"Your mission is to make it to that clearing, using

whatever magic necessary," Meegra continued. "The Feathered Fae will hunt you."

Himari let out a little gasp. I knew just how she felt. My heart rate seemed to have doubled.

"If we incapacitate you, or you surrender, you're out. If by some miracle you actually incapacitate a Feathered Fae,"—Meegra allowed a lengthy pause—"then you're in elite company. We shall give you a two-minute head start. When you hear the screech of an eagle, the hunt is on. Expect no mercy. Questions?"

"Which way is east?" Gio asked, his dark brows furrowed.

Meegra smirked. "It appears *that* will be your first challenge. Feathered Fae, transform. The rest of you, your time starts now."

All around us fae were transforming. Ellette became the sparrowhawk I'd seen the night she'd brought me the scroll and changed my life forever. Oren, the wardmaker, transformed into a brown owl. Another Feathered Fae named Ash, who had a reputation among the guards for being less than pleasant, morphed into a red-tailed hawk. The other members of the Feathered Fae transfigured into winged forms ranging from a common crow to a bird I could not name but whose bright plumage suggested it belonged in a rainforest.

Meegra was the most impressive. She became a

massive harpy eagle with talons as long as my fingers and unyielding green eyes. The birds beat their wings, rising about three meters above the ground to wait for Meegra's signal.

"So, does anyone know which way is east?" Gio repeated, his eyes widening as he took in Meegra's vicious talons.

Everyone except Nigel, who disappeared behind an illusion, turned on the spot attempting to get their bearings. Had I been in any other scenario, I might have taken pleasure in informing Nigel his illusion would do no good. Many species of hawks could see heat trails left by their prey. Presently, my heart and mind were racing too fast to care about Nigel.

This was not only a training exercise, but a power play—a reminder. Though after the Successional three of us would rank above her, Meegra wanted there to be no question who was the most powerful. From the corner of my eye, I saw one of the Feathered Fae soared higher than the rest and an idea hit me.

"Arlo, fly high. You should be able to see the clearing."

Arlo's face lit up, and within a second the ginger-haired young man had transformed into a golden eagle and soared above us. He hovered on the wind for a heartbeat before taking off in the direction I assumed was east.

"This way!" I sprinted out of the clearing first. I didn't make it far before a bone-chilling screech broke the stillness of the dead forest.

Our head start was up.

CHAPTER TWENTY-SEVEN

My feet pounded the dirt at a ferocious pace, trying to put distance between myself and the Feathered Fae—particularly Meegra. The Master Feathered Fae had something to prove and that was a dangerous thing.

A rush of wings sounded, and I glanced up just in time to see two falcons speeding ahead to catch Arlo first. Good, that bought me some time. With two Feathered Fae busy that left nine; nine against thirteen. I was faster than Himari, Victoria, and Kate, so any Feathered Fae who worked from the back forward would get them first. I had a chance—albeit a slim one.

A yip echoed through the woods and my eyes darted around wildly, searching for the source of the sound. I found it quickly. Meegra had dive-bombed a wolfy Wikolia and tore into her flesh with sharp talons. They were ahead of me, in the precise direction I needed to go.

I dismissed my earlier judgment of Nigel and produced an illusion to hide behind. It may not hide me from Meegra, but it *would* keep me hidden from Wikolia. I watched as the harpy eagle dove upon the wolf time and time again, lethal and fearless. More than once Wikolia nearly caught Meegra in her snapping jaws, but the harpy eagle always darted away at the last second.

My progress forward was frustratingly slow. The last thing I wanted to do was clue Meegra or Wikolia in to my presence. While hawks had poor hearing akin to that of humans, Wikolia did not, especially in her shifter form. If I made enough noise to alert her, she may be able to sniff me out. To have Wikolia discover I didn't come to her aid wouldn't help our relationship, which was already strained thanks to the Successional and Wikolia's friendship with Crystal.

My jaw clenched as the harpy eagle soared away, pulled back through the trees in a wide loop, then returned like a boomerang, talons extended. This was not going to be good.

Wikolia froze, clearly unable to work out how she'd catch the massive flying bullet without ripping her jaw off. Instead of fighting, she turned tail and ran back toward the clearing where we'd started.

But it was too late; Meegra was already upon the wolf. With a victorious screech, the harpy eagle sank her talons into Wikolia's fur and ripped out a massive chunk of skin. A wolf's howl morphed into a scream as Wikolia transformed into human aspect.

Before Wikolia could surrender, I sprinted away. Invisible or not, there was no way in hell I wanted to be anywhere near Meegra when Wikolia waved the white flag. I ran all out for a full minute without becoming harpy eagle prey before I chanced a glance behind me. No one was there. Thank goodness. A relieved smile was just blooming on my face when my toe caught on something and I tripped.

My hands kissed hard ground, catching me, and my concentration broke, releasing my illusion. I turned to see what had stolen my momentum and froze.

Gio lay on the ground. Someone had knocked his chiseled jaw to the side, his nose was bleeding and most likely broken, and a slash on his arm oozed blood.

Crawling toward him, I examined the cut. It was clean, not resembling punctures made by talons. Meegra hadn't mentioned the Feathered Fae would have weapons, but then again, she didn't want to spoil her fun. I shuddered. If I didn't already believe they meant business, there was no denying it now.

Feeling far too visible and vulnerable, I wrapped

another illusion around me. The instant the illusion was complete, a twig snapped nearby. I squinted past the blackened trees. No one was there—or at least no one *visible*. I wasn't the only illuminator in the woods.

Quickly, I propped Gio up against a tree so that no one else would trip over him, and moved on. I made it only a short distance when a flash of red light among the trees caught my eye. I gasped.

Finn was battling Ash, a Feathered Fae with a notoriously bad attitude. Though he'd practiced little magic while trying to keep his demon born status under wraps, Finn had improved remarkably in just a few days. I had a hunch that a guard had been giving him tips. No one could become *that* skilled with their magic so fast—or at least no witch I'd ever met. Then again, before Finn, I'd never met a demon born.

Unfortunately for Finn, Ash had had years of practice and wielded all four elements as naturally as he breathed. He whirled and struck, a hurricane of raven black hair and armor, clobbering Finn in an elemental carousel of pain. Rocks slammed into Finn's shins, thighs, and gut. Air blew him off his feet. Water blinded him and opposing fire danced around him.

Part of me wanted to keep running; let Finn handle it himself. I doubted he wanted to be indebted to me when he could barely look at me. A larger part, however, couldn't stop watching.

So I was still there when Ash launched a rock the

size of a softball at Finn's temple, and Finn collapsed to the ground with a heavy thud. A smile bloomed on the Feathered Fae's face. I recoiled and prepared myself to slink away. But then Ash moved closer to Finn, and I tensed. The Feathered Fae called a grouping of small boulders to him and floated them to hover directly over my brother.

Over my dead body, I thought, dropping my illusion and sprinting for Ash. I called infrared light as I ran, praying that if I was ever to have success creating a weapon out of light, it would happen now. Any other tricks I had up my sleeve may work against my siblings, but they'd be pitiful against Ash, a powerful Feathered Fae.

I'd halved the distance between us when the light heeded my call in one sweltering ambush of energy. I gasped, overwhelmed for a moment, before snapping back to the present. The light was with me, and now I only had to make it usable—make it solid. A practiced request and visible light was there, too, bright and blinding before me. I wove the two together, never breaking step as I thundered through the trees.

I felt the second the two wavelengths meshed into perfect harmony, white light stabilizing infrared and making it visible to the human eye as a red flash. The light was insistent: I would either use it, or the energy would dissipate as it had in my lessons with Casimir. The sensation was almost enough to pull me off my game.

Almost.

I forced another surge of power into the light around me and something clicked. The wavelengths, already woven together, straightened, forming a laser. Not breaking step, I reached out and grabbed the weapon hovering before me.

Holy shite. I was holding an infrared sword.

But I didn't have time to dwell on my victory as Ash turned around at that exact second. His cruel smile grew larger and he rushed forward to meet me, his feet skimming the ground, the mess of boulders he'd threatened to drop on Finn trailing behind him. Obviously, he was looking forward to tangling with an illuminator.

It was a sure sign I should *not* be engaging him. Nobody intelligent entered a fight they couldn't win. And Ash had just bested a demon born, the strongest type of witch. Still, I had to do *something*. Shakily, I lifted my sword and drew it through the air in a vicious swipe, hoping to scare the fae off.

My hopes crashed and burned when Ash *laughed*. His teeth were as sharp as a shark's—gleaming white and menacing against the nut-brown of his skin. My mind screamed for me to run, while my body pushed me forward like a noble idiot. If I could just injure him enough so that he'd leave Finn alone, then maybe—

I let out a yelp as a boulder flew from out of nowhere to clock the Feathered Fae in the head.

Ash fell like a bag of bricks and I whirled about, searching for my savior.

Maria stepped out from behind a tree.

An exhale gusted out of me as I lowered my sword. "Thanks. He looked like he was ready to have some real fun with me."

"Ash is an ass. I saw him gouge Victoria in the face earlier. Didn't want the same to happen to you."

I cringed. There wasn't a worse thing one could do to the vain vila-elf. I hoped the healers excelled at cosmetic fixes. If not, Victoria would be a terror to live with.

"He did a number on Finn, too, which reminds me . . ." I released my sword into the atmosphere, strode over to Finn, and propped him up against a blackened tree.

He didn't even flutter an eyelid. Well, shite. He wasn't waking up soon.

Unwilling to just leave him there with Ash lying so close by, I wove an illusion. Finn disappeared beneath a blanket of light masquerading as the tree I'd propped him against. It wasn't a perfect solution. If someone stepped on him it would hurt, and without me around to manipulate it the illusion would break as soon as he stood from this spot. Still, it was better than nothing. I wished I could hide Finn in such a way that hawks circling above couldn't see him, but that was beyond my capabilities.

All I knew was Finn had never actually surrendered. Protected by the illusion, if he came to before the training exercise was over, he could move on.

Maria's eyebrows lifted as my gaze met hers. "That was nice, considering what a jerk he's been to you—and recent revelations."

There was no need to tell her Finn had been playing the jerk to protect his own heart. And as much as my witchy intuition agreed about having a demon born in our midst, I didn't want to propagate a prejudice that I was trying to overcome.

"I saw Meegra tear into Wikolia's flesh earlier," I said. "If I can spare him that, I will. Even if he is a demon born, he was my best friend for years. And he's not evil now, just . . . conflicted."

Maria gave me a curious look.

I squirmed. Time to change the subject. "Do you know which way is east?"

She tilted her head, her brown eyes full of questions.

I waited, expecting Maria to probe.

Instead, she knelt to touch the ground. A second later she pointed to the right. It was the exact opposite way I would have gone. "That way."

"You can feel the earth's electromagnetic pull?" I asked, amazed.

"I've never been able to until I came here. Never able to manipulate metal either, but that ability popped up yesterday in my room." A sheepish look flashed across her face as she admitted to doing magic outside the training hall.

"Don't tell anyone." Maria's eyes darted to Finn at the mention of forbidden practice. "I don't think I'm the only one who practices after hours. I wanted it to be my secret weapon."

"You just saved my butt. It's our secret," I replied, suppressing a sigh. First Victoria had a secret skill, now Maria. Bloody hell, did I ever wish I had a secret weapon. "But we should probably start moving—get this thing over with. Hopefully, unmarred."

"We can try," Maria agreed, and we picked up our pace.

With each step, I was sure a Feathered Fae would appear at any moment. Minutes passed and nothing happened. After what had to be ten minutes, I was beginning to think it was miraculous that we hadn't run into anyone hunting us. Or perhaps it was an omen—probably a bad one. I glanced around like a sheep who knew the wolves were coming.

"Can you chill out? Your twitching is making me nervous," Maria snapped.

Her breath was short because of our clipped pace. Before coming to Faerie I wasn't much of an athlete, but even I was in better shape than Maria. She often reminisced about her night spent drinking margaritas with the elite of Mexico City's art scene. She continued her partying habit here and could often be found staying up late, playing cards, and indulging in elven wine with our guards in their room in Half-Elf Tower.

"Sorry." I darted another glance around. "Don't you think it's weird we haven't seen anyone, though?"

"Of course it's weird. Why haven't they flown over us? But even so, you're radiating stress. It's making my jaw hurt."

The part of the forest we found ourselves in was more attractive than the land closer to the castle. Sparse grass budded from the base of almost every tree, and I'd even spotted a sapling making its way out of the ground. I was wondering how it had seeded and survived when everything else was so dead, when I saw it: a flash of copper through the bleak black.

I squinted. Less than two hundred meters ahead, Crystal was standing around talking to Nigel and Arlo.

"Maria, look!" I pointed at the trio. "They must be in the clearing. There's no way Crystal would just be standing around chatting if she was still in the game."

"Thank God," Maria muttered and crossed herself in the Catholic manner, before breaking into a run alongside me. We didn't make it far when I felt the shift. The movement of air, the sound of beating wings all around.

I glanced up and gasped. A flock of five birds soared above us, one of them a horrifying mash-up of a woman's head and harpy eagle's body. There was a reason no one had sought us out in the woods. They'd been waiting for us here.

"So close, yet so, so far," Meegra said, shooting a blast of fire at us as she descended, half-transformed.

Maria and I split, leaping to the side, away from the inferno. Meegra's high, cold laughter flew through the air. I groaned, realizing our reactions were exactly what she'd wanted. Our best chance of reaching the clearing had been to fight our way forward together. Could I make it back to Maria's side?

Before I could even look to see where she was, pain shot through my arm. I let out a shriek and a peregrine falcon swooped skyward, my blood trailing from her talons. As if I'd done it a million times before and not just once, I conjured infrared light, wove it with visible light, and clicked the energies into place. The infrared sword bloomed in my hand yet again, but not before another hawk dive-bombed me. I flailed away from the bird, not even bothering to swing the sword, focused only on avoiding its sharp talons.

"What's the point of having light—pure energy— in your arsenal when you can't even use it properly?"

I whirled about. Meegra was in fae aspect a mere two meters away. Her lips curved up in a cold smile and a wall of fire, blazing hot, shot up from the black-ened earth between us.

Shite! I jumped back and screamed as another falcon's talons dug into my sword arm. I was surrounded. A shriek came from behind me. I glanced, searching for Maria. Blood dripped from her shoulder as the falcon she fought darted skillfully through the rocks she hurled.

"Shame so few of you made it," Meegra said, and my attention snapped back to her as she walked through the fire she'd conjured, impervious to its flames. "Not that it was unexpected. Being from where you are—growing up *weak*. I suggested to King Oberon he should have made the clues harder, narrowed the herd further. It's a pity he didn't listen."

Without warning, a ball of flame flew from her hands, catching my shirt on fire. I pounded the flames out, wincing with each blow.

Meegra laughed. "You think that hurt? Just wait until the Successional." Meegra moved closer and leaned in, her face centimeters from the flames, taunting me.

I swung my sword, aiming for Meegra's arm, which had only a layer of leather covering it. My blade hit, slicing open the leather and filling the air with the scent of burnt skin. But instead of retreating backward, Meegra grunted and lunged *forward* through the flames, blood dripping from her arm, a hard grin on her face.

"It will take more than a burn to bring me down, witch. It will take a *force of nature*. Remember that." She grabbed me by the throat.

I gasped, and my sword dissipated with my

concentration as she squeezed tighter. Her touch was hot from the flame she'd wielded, painfully so. I struggled to get away, but with every wiggle and shift Meegra's grip constricted, burning the thin skin of my neck, stealing my breath, until everything dimmed to black.

CHAPTER TWENTY-EIGHT

The day before the Successional was our second free day, and I slept the hours away. After training with the Feathered Fae, I needed the extra rest to heal the wounds Meegra had inflicted. They were wounds I would never forget, no matter how skilled the pixie healer had been at erasing the burn marks from my neck.

Because I'd rested all day, I ended up tossing and turning the night before the Successional. When dawn came I was already awake to witness the sun spraying its light over Lyonesse.

They served breakfast and lunch earlier than normal to allow us time to digest and prepare before the late-afternoon tournament. The meals, though meant to be celebratory, were blurs and everyone—servants, guards, nobles, Prince Casimir, and my father—was more excited than I'd ever seen. Only my siblings and I were quiet. After eating, we were confined to our rooms, where I filled the hours practicing with a dagger—my weapon of choice to bring into the arena. I doubted I'd use it now that I could create an infrared sword, but its heavy presence on my hip was still welcome.

Naela watched me wield the blade with fascination and worry I found easy to read. The last two weeks had changed things between us. Before arriving in Faerie I'd considered my bond with Naela close, but nothing more. Now I knew better. Naela was my familiar. She was as in tune and affected by my feelings as I was with hers.

"I've come a long way, haven't I?" I said, taking a break to sit in the chair next to the hearth.

Naela's head bobbed up and down.

"Who knows what we'll do after this? It'd be grand to do some exploring—maybe even hiking in other realms. I've read that not all the kingdoms look as dead as this. You may fancy flying in other realms more."

Naela tilted her head, her gold eyes full of caution and wisdom.

"You're right, I'm getting ahead of myself. Let's take it one day at a time."

I laid my head over the back of the chair and closed my eyes, allowing the heat of the fire to wash over me. I'd almost succumbed to the cocoon of warmth and lack of sleep when Garret, recognizable by his signature knock, tapped on the door.

"Come in," I called, not moving a muscle. I needed to save every iota of energy I could for the tournament.

There was a soft creak, followed by Garret's deep voice. "It's time."

I took a deep breath before opening my eyes and lifting myself from the chair. Walking to the bed, my fingers grazed the official tournament uniform I'd been given that morning. Unlike my dark sparring attire, this was true armor—crafted of white metal and supple white leather. The thin, flexible metal meant to shield my torso resembled fish scales and reflected light brilliantly. Although the white leather that covered my arms was a little restrictive, I was glad for it. Only a thick leather would save me from getting ripped open by talons, claws, and blades. Slipping both protective layers on, I clipped the sides of the metal together to tighten the uniform around me reassuringly.

I was ready as I'd ever be. It was time to show my father, all of Faerie, what I could do.

<hr>

MEEGRA HAD CALLED THE SUCCESSIONAL A gladiator-style competition, and from what I could see, the arena reflected that aesthetic. My mouth hung open as I stared into a ring that resembled the Colosseum of Rome—had it been made by magic.

The arena was an oval and at least a kilometer long. It smelled of dried dirt, which was the only feature inside the arena. Much like the expansive training room, it was easy to imagine my siblings and me battling it out in the open space.

The gate we'd entered through had been blocked off by a retractable wooden fence, presumably to keep out the crowds of people chattering outside the stadium. I tried to ignore their laughter and excitement. Thinking of onlookers only made my stomach flip uncomfortably.

Stands made of what looked to be glass encompassed the arena. Situated ten meters above the ground level where we'd be battling, the rows of seats climbed upward toward the twilight sun of Faerie. However, instead of angling away from the ring as stands would in a football stadium, these seats slanted sharply inward. The better to observe us from, I assumed.

Even more fascinating were the large islands of gold and glass floating above the ring. Unsupported by anything, the islands reminded me of the top box from the faeball match, but larger and with no seats. Placed just below the stands and glass-bottomed, nothing could block their occupants' views. The largest island, no doubt my father's, floated in the precise center of the ring. I wondered if they moved at the king's whim, enabling him to view whichever fight he desired.

My siblings and I stood beneath individual recessed arches lining the perimeter of the ring. Two larger arches were uninhabited and blockaded by heavy stone doors. One was directly across from mine at the opposite pole of the oval. The other was at a right angle from me. I was about to ask for what was probably the hundredth time when we'd be starting, when the guards manning the wood gate pushed it to the side.

Fae filed in, their poverty as plain as it had been the day of the parade. It clung to them, like the dozens of children at the heels of each mother and father. Most were clad in loose-fitting clothes that hung off their bodies. Their cheeks were sunken and their coloring was dull and lifeless.

Their eyes, however, were bright.

"They're so excited," I breathed.

"Many will not have attended a Successional before," Sai replied from her position behind me. "It's likely the best entertainment they'll ever see."

Entertainment. I still couldn't wrap my mind around the fact that this, a fight that would likely result in injuries—was entertainment. But I supposed it had been that way for the Romans, too. From what little I'd seen of Faerie so far, the fae lived in line with the old ways more than modern times.

The angled stands were filled, and a handful of fae dressed in finer clothes were entering the arena. I recognized some of them from the faeball match and meals at the castle. The nobles moved to stand at the center of the ring, beneath the floating islands of metal and gold.

Not a minute later a trumpet sounded, and everyone froze. A rumbling of rock reverberated through the stadium, and the large, arched doorway across from me opened much like a modern garage door. King Oberon and Prince Casimir stood behind it, their clothing pure white and their long blond hair whipping around in the breeze coming off nearby Choral Bay. The king and prince emerged to a roaring crowd. Meegra and the rest of the Feathered Fae followed in their wake like living shadows.

In the sunlight, King Oberon was blinding—like a gem shining too brightly. Prince Casimir looked nearly as impressive but lacked the charisma our father exuded in spades. The king waved and smiled and the crowds loved him for it, blowing kisses and clapping. When the royals reached the center of the ring, my father held up his hands, fingers splayed, and the crowd fell into an expectant hush.

A tingle ran up my spine in anticipation as the king lifted his arms to the sky. I furrowed my brows, but before I could even guess what he was up to, he yanked his arms back down. The floating islands plummeted and slammed into the ground centimeters from where my father stood. A hundred gasps muffled the sound of the fall.

It was one of the few times I'd seen my father use magic. He was strong.

King Oberon and Prince Casimir filed into an island first, followed by the Feathered Fae.

"Join me," my father said, his voice magically amplified throughout the stadium.

The nobles rushed the remaining islands, each wanting the ones closest to the king and dispersing only once those were full. When every noble had found a place, the king lifted his hands with a flourish and the islands lifted into the sky, as steady as hot air balloons, to still just below the stands.

The crowd murmured, and I saw wide grins on the children's faces. They were magical beings, but with Lyonesse being as depleted as it was, I doubted they saw grand displays of power often.

"Welcome, fae folk of Lyonesse, to the first Successional in over three hundred years," King Oberon's charismatic voice rang out. The crowd's screams and claps rose again, cutting the king off until finally, he raised his hands.

Silence fell once more and fae leaned forward in their precariously angled stands. There was an energy in the stadium unlike any I'd ever felt. The air was practically vibrating with it.

Just when I thought everyone in the stadium may burst from excitement, my father swept his arms wide, beckoning the Feathered Fae to join him at the railing. "Shall we get the arena in working order?" The king thrust his arms forward and each of the Feathered Fae followed his lead.

The ground shook beneath my feet, and trees erupted from the dirt. My mouth fell open as the desolate arena transformed into a lush jungle. Things had just become a lot more interesting. Much more dangerous, too.

I shot a glance to my right. In the alcove closest to mine, Wikolia cracked a smile. There was no doubt she'd enjoy this twist. A jungle wasn't exactly the same as the wooded winter forests Wikolia prowled in Alaska, but her wolf aspect would manage.

My brows furrowed. But if our father could do this, why couldn't he transform his own barren lands? A flash of white from high above the canopy caught my eye, and I had my answer. The king, who minutes before was standing tall and proud, had faltered. He clutched at the sides of the metal island, his chest heaving. Apparently, the effort it took to create the jungle had been immense. Still, he'd done it to entertain his people—to give them a show and an heir to protect them. All eyes pinned on him, King Oberon, well aware that everyone in the stadium was still watching, struggled to bring himself upright.

"As always, the Successional is a tournament of royal blood." King Oberon patted his rumpled white shirt and jacket into submission. "There are no rules. An heir can only truly be safe after they are lifted from the arena or can no longer fight. However, it would be a folly to think *this* Successional the same as all others in the history of fae."

He sounded a tad tired, but there was no embarrassment present as there would have been in my voice if I'd collapsed in front of all these people. No, his words were laden with pride. That told me something, too. Even to *struggle* with magic was considered elite when so few could work it at all.

Anger rose as memories of the hundreds of wan fae I'd met during the parade—some of whom were surely in the crowds above—came flooding back. Remembering them reinforced my desire to win and actually change Lyonesse. Determined to appear the dutiful daughter and potential princess general, I straightened my spine and devoted my attention to my father's speech.

"Unlike in the past, no royal heir taking part in this Successional today is full fae." Unlike Meegra, who scorned our half-blood status, he sounded proud of that fact.

"Nor are they steeped in the ways of Faerie." As

he spoke, the island pivoted slowly so that he could look upon all sides of the crowd. "You may wonder, will they fight for a crown they have little attachment to? Will the spectacle be great for you—my cherished subjects—who *deserve* to see their future princes and princesses in all their glory? The uncertainties crossed my mind as well. Hence, I've added another little twist for my heirs. A taste of what Faerie offers, if you will."

My father whipped about to face the second massive stone arch. It was the only door that had remained closed since we arrived in the arena. "Unleash the prisoners!"

Prisoners? My shoulders tensed as the doors groaned open. The lush vegetation made it impossible to tell what was happening, but the crowds above went wild.

I rubbed the nape of my neck, trying to ease my growing tension. Whatever was making them so excited couldn't be good. I was about to question Sai and Garret when I caught sight of something that shot ice through my veins.

A giant head—a literal *giant's* head—appeared above the treetops. Straggly hair swayed as the giant entered the arena, her (or at least I thought it was a her) teeth bared. As if responding to the rowdy crowds, the giant let out a roar so booming it shook the pebbles at my feet.

My hand flew to my mouth. Moving on autopilot,

I took a few steps backward, right into Sai. This was a bloody nightmare.

From what I'd read, which at that moment I suspected was far less than I should have, giants didn't have magic. At least they didn't have magic in the way witches or fae did. Nor were they gifted with the elevated senses of shifters or chimera.

What little magic the giants possessed was embedded in their skin. It was a protectant of the strongest sort, making them difficult to injure or kill. They were creatures of brute force, able to withstand almost any assault. Their strength had been the species' ticket into Faerie, where humans wouldn't hunt and kill them. The fae allowed them into this realm as long as they built the castles, plowed the fields, and cleared the roads the other races desired.

But I can evade brute-force, I thought, working to get over my shock quickly and enter the Successional on an even keel. I could always cloak myself in an illusion and hide from the giant.

I took a deep breath and had nearly brought my heart rate back to normal when a creature with a ten-foot wingspan, deer-like legs ending in cloven hooves, and a human torso burst out of the trees, spiking my pulse yet again. As if aware the Successional was a performance as much as a challenge, the creature flew in corkscrews above the highest stands, an arrow notched and pointed at the crowds, who screamed in shock and delight.

"Shite," I whispered, mesmerized by the chimera's wings, black and shiny as obsidian. We weren't just up against each other, but a giant and a chimera archer.

"I heard mention of a few other creatures when the guards brought them up from the dungeons," Sai's voice was quiet, hesitant, so unlike her usual outgoing nature. "Rumor has it they are to put on a convincing show—drawing the line only at your surrender. They fight to earn their freedom."

I whipped around to face her. However, Sai's violet eyes were not seeking mine, but Garret's, the question in them plain.

Will you rat me out if I tell her?

I bit my lip. The more I knew, the longer I would last in the tournament. I was already middle of the pack. I needed more information to outlast my siblings.

Please, Garret, for once in your life don't be such a stickler for the rules, I pleaded mentally.

Unnamable emotions rolled over his face as he took in what Sai was asking. His silence stretched on for what felt like forever. Unable to take much more, I laid my hand on Garret's shoulder.

He softened, his eyes meeting mine. "I won't say anything."

Sai exhaled. "Besides the giantess and chimera, there are two spriggans, a pooka, and a naga loose in the arena. The naga, unlike Kumar, is *not* opposed to fighting. She relishes it. However, the spriggans are the most dangerous. They were swords for hire who snuck into Lyonesse and were imprisoned after being declared guilty of two murders. They're more skilled with blades than half the guards in the castle. As the chimera has a bow and arrows, I assume the spriggans, too, are armed."

The reasoning behind my father's insistence that we use the library and research Faerie clarified. He'd figured most of us would surrender to avoid drawing blood or injuring others. But my father couldn't have a showing like that.

He needed to see our powers in action, to assess them, because he was looking for a second heir. And, of course, that wasn't all. The Successional was a beloved ritual and competition that boosted the morale of a kingdom. It was a genius stroke, really. In one event, my father could secure that his royal bloodline remained in power, give his subjects hope for the future, *and* provide them with an afternoon of entertainment like they'd never seen. It sucked for us, but I understood his motive . . . and, in hindsight, all the warnings he'd given.

I'd never met any spriggans in the castle, but thought I recalled that their kind preferred to live in the eastern Faerie, in largely mafia-run districts of the Free Realm.

Spriggans . . . Finally, an image from a book Kumar had shown me arose in my mind: A withered old

man's body with a childlike head grinning malevo-
lently up from the page.

Ugly as hell, spriggans had nasty dispositions, and
apparently the two running about the arena were
master bladesmen. Nothing about their magic was
coming up. I'd just have to deal with whatever they
threw at me, whether it be metal or magic. I
moved on.

"A fecking pooka?" Bloody hell, why didn't I have
a memory like Finn's?

Sai opened her mouth, but Garret answered first.

"A shapeshifter who can become many beastly
and human forms. They're historically from your
home island in the Old Land. From what I've heard,
this one prefers to shift into anything with large claws
and teeth."

Wonderful. Just bloody wonderful. As if I didn't
have enough to worry about facing off with a lion,
wolf, eagle, and two nagas—albeit one of them reluctant to fight. Now there was the threat of a creature
who could transform into *any* beast.

My worries were cut short when a crimson firework
exploded high in the sky. It was our signal for the beginning of the tournament, as well as any endings we may
face. I whirled about. The giantess released a soul-shattering roar, an eagle soared through the air, and a flash of
white fur to the side of me disappeared into the foliage.

The Successional had officially begun.

I turned back to Sai and Garret. "Thank you—both of you."

"Good luck. We'll see you after the tournament. Do us proud." Sai clapped me on the shoulder.

"Sinkers be with you," Garret echoed Sai's wish of luck in the fae manner, though unlike Sai he couldn't mask the note of fear in his voice.

CHAPTER TWENTY-NINE

The jungle was silent, ominous. Spooky. Even the giantess, who had been roaring as though her life depended on it just minutes before, wasn't making a sound.

Everyone had slipped into stealth mode.

I bit into the side of my cheek as I took my first steps into the dense vegetation. Was it best to hone an illusion right away? Or to save my energy until I needed it? For all I knew, the Successional could last minutes or hours. In this sort of environment, my illusion would have to be ever changing and hence more energy zapping. Why hadn't I thought up a game plan before? I decided I may as well use an illusion right away. If I didn't and was eliminated from the competition early because of it, I would be furious with myself.

I'd just finished bending white light and cloaking

myself beneath it when a scream ripped through the air. I jumped and searched the surrounding mess of green, trying to discern the direction of the sound. Not far ahead, a glint of metal slashed through the foliage. A hideous fae with wrinkled arms and legs and the face of a toddler leapt into view. He ran straight for Maria, his sword raised.

One of the spriggans. Shite. I was torn. Remain hidden? Or help Maria? She'd saved me in our training exercise. Like Ash, this spriggan looked like he wanted to cause serious damage.

But this was the *Successional*—the main event. My dream of getting to know my father hinged on my choices. As did my desire to help his subjects. What if Maria turned on me after I helped her, eliminating me?

My eyes followed Maria as she hurled stones and shook the ground. Although the spriggan's spine curved into a hunchback, he was spry. He wove in and out of the rocks and took Maria's blows with a menacing grin.

I still hadn't made my decision when suddenly Maria released a bloodcurdling scream. The spriggan had darted close enough to slash her arm open. Blood sprayed everywhere as Maria's knees buckled and she hit the ground. My reservations flew from me. I sprinted to her aid, horror growing as the spriggan's blade rose high over Maria's head. He was threatening to bring it down with a death blow.

"Surrender or die!" the spriggan demanded, his voice high and cold and full of glee. His sword wavered as if caught in a strong gust of wind.

Was Maria testing her new skill of manipulating metal? If she was, her new power didn't seem strong enough to divert the sword. Maria must have realized that too, because she switched tack and flung another hailstorm of rocks at the spriggan's face. He dropped his weapon and batted the rocks away frantically.

"Insolent royal bastards," the spriggan growled as he fought through the rocks to kick my sister in the gut.

Maria collapsed, and the last rock in her arsenal thunked on the ground alongside her. She groaned and blood stained the earth. She was fading fast.

"No one can say I didn't give you a choice." The spriggan's blade rose once more—faster, surer this time.

I called light and launched myself at him. My infrared blade flew through the air. With a hiss of melted metal, my sword sliced the spriggan's blade in half at the hilt.

My mouth fell open. The most the sword had ever done was burn someone. How had I cut through metal? The question had barely formed when the spriggan whirled in my direction, his eyes searching for me. I snapped back to reality and took another swipe at him, burning a deep gash across his chest.

The spriggan howled. "Show yourself! You

coward! Show yourself! I demand—" A rock collided with his skull, knocking him to the ground and cutting his demand short.

"That's becoming your signature move." I dropped my illusion and jogged to Maria, whose arm was still bleeding profusely.

"Princess of the rocks." She winced as I helped her up. "Thanks for that. I think that asshole, whatever the hell he is, would have killed me."

"A spriggan. There's another like him in here. A shapeshifter, chimera, giantess, and a cruel naga, too."

Maria raised a single eyebrow. "You know we're fighting against each other, right? You'd have been better off if you didn't tell me that."

"I figured you may need a heads-up." I gestured to her arm. Plus, she told me about her new power before the Successional. This made me feel as though we were even. "Are you gonna continue?"

My sister's black curls, bound in a high ponytail so they would stay out of her face, bounced up and down as she nodded. "At least until the first—"

A single crimson firework erupted in the sky. Aided by magic, it was shockingly visible, though the sun had only just started its slow descent. The beacon bloomed from a spray of light into a dragon that released a roar and soared over the stands.

The crowd went wild.

It was a sign that one of our siblings had surrendered.

Or died.

Though I'd only known most of them two weeks, I didn't believe any of my siblings capable of murder. Masterful mental games, threats, and fighting to get what they wanted, absolutely. But killing? I couldn't see it. However, I held no such faith in the other creatures in the arena.

"Thank God. I would have been mortified if I was the first to go," Maria whispered and gripped her arm. "I may wait a couple minutes more."

My gaze ran over her arm, red all the way to her fingertips with blood. Her face had become pale and was covered in a sheen of perspiration. It seemed likely the spriggan had sliced open a large artery.

The armor I wore was too strong to rip and make a tourniquet, and I didn't know enough about the nearby plants to be sure that they'd stop the bleeding. If only Kate was here, she'd know, I thought, rubbing the back of my neck.

"Don't worry," Maria sighed. "I'll surrender soon. I'm just . . . competitive. Who knows what luxuries one rank higher could afford me? You should keep moving."

"Are you sure?"

"Absolutely. If I feel even close to fainting, I'll just surrender. Until then, I'll wait on this rock."

"All right, then. I'll see you later." I waved and started to leave.

"Hey, Lana!"

I turned back toward my sister. "Yeah?"

"Watch out for Nigel. I can't be sure, but—" She tapped at her temple.

My mouth gaped. Not only had Maria's earth powers grown since arriving in Faerie, now she was admitting that—like Victoria—she was gaining a psychic ability. She'd heard *something* in Nigel's mind.

"I think he has something up his sleeve," Maria added. "Something he's kept hidden during training, which means it's powerful."

She was right. Nigel trained as though each sparring practice was his last, wanting to win every session. If he hadn't revealed his skills in practice, it would have been a strategic move. I wondered how many other siblings downplayed their powers to have the upper hand during the Successional.

"Thanks." I threw her a concerned look as she gripped her arm tighter to slow the blood.

"Go on. Stay in the game," she urged. "I'll be fine."

I nodded in thanks and left her to fight her own fight. As I moved through the jungle, I marveled at how it was indistinguishable from a real jungle—at least as far as I could tell. It even felt more humid in the arena than before the tournament, as evidenced by the beads of sweat on my forehead despite my slow pace. Only the lack of animal noises hinted I wasn't in a lush, thriving Amazonian rainforest. I suspected my father had somehow deadened the sounds in the arena—ensuring we had to be close to hear a friend or foe approach. Minutes passed with only the thumping of my heart for company. It struck me as odd that I hadn't run across more of my siblings; the enclosure wasn't *so* huge. Then again, the vegetation was rather thick.

Boom!

The ground shook beneath me, and I lowered into a crouch. Was Maria starting an earthquake? A last-ditch effort to force someone to surrender before her?

Boom. Boom. Boom. Boom.

Victoria shot past me, her usually perfect hair disheveled and face glistening from tears.

Boom! Boom! Boom! Boom! Boom!

The noise picked up the pace, rolling into a precise canter. I tensed and twisted to gaze in the direction Victoria had come from. Trees downed as an enormous figure emerged, running after my sister.

Shite! I leapt backward just in time to avoid being crushed by a foot as large as a sofa. That had been far too close.

I trembled and pulled my illusion closer. I should have already run the opposite way, but the creature demanded my attention. The giantess' hands were the size of a four-person kitchen table, her teeth like chipped bricks. There were gashes and scars on her face, two of them fresh and oozing.

Someone had beaten her. I gulped. Father had called the creatures in the arena with us prisoners. No doubt it had been his soldiers who beat the giantess.

Fighting my rising tide of sympathy, Sai's warning echoed through me, reminding me. The fae, naga, chimera, and giantess were fighting for their freedom. Their liberty depended on the quality of the show they put on. Which meant they were exceedingly dangerous. I should not pity them. Or at the very least, I needed to restrain my pity and prioritize survival.

A scream tore through the jungle, pulling me back to the moment.

Bloody hell. Victoria! I glanced up to find my sister hadn't made it far. In fact, she'd gotten herself stuck on a massive rock in the middle of a sizable river our father had magicked into the arena. She perched there, glancing at the water surrounding her and then at the giantess in fear. The lesser evil was obvious to me, but I guessed my sister didn't know how to swim.

Victoria and I hadn't clicked, but that didn't mean I wanted her killed or mangled by a giantess who got carried away. For a creature of that size, hurting Victoria would be far too easy. My fists clenched and unclenched as I decided what to do.

The giantess' ear-splitting roar was deterrent

enough to stay away. Her nails, like jagged swords cutting down thick vegetation with a swipe of her hand, definitely didn't entice me to get closer. Even so, Victoria *was* my sister. I'd barely teetered to the side of helping when she threw up her hands.

"I surrender! Get this ugly ass thing away from me!" Victoria screamed at the top of her lungs. Her armor glowed blindingly white, marking her as out.

The giantess slammed her fist into a tree. The resounding crack startled me into dropping my illusion.

A firework exploded in the sky a second later, transmuting its vivid red sparks into the shape of a unicorn. Another followed before the unicorn vanished, a gryphon. Maria's firework, I hoped.

Before the gryphon faded, I was on the move again. I didn't want to be the giantess' next target. An indeterminable distance later I slowed to a pace dictated by my breath. Finally, recognizing that like the prey Naela hunted, I hadn't taken in my surroundings since sprinting away, I paused. In an arena such as this, my actions bordered on idiotic. It took only a moment of stillness for me to sense it.

Someone was watching me.

My eyes flitted across the vegetation, from top to bottom, but found nothing. Then, remembering Arlo and the winged chimera, I glanced up and gasped.

I'd stopped below one of the lower stands. Since I had yet to recreate my illusion after the giant scared me into dropping it, I was visible. *Super visible.* Dozens of fae stared down at me. My eyes roved over the variety of creatures, latching onto a little boy with huge pointed ears I hoped he'd grow into and bluish skin. A massive grin split his face as he waved at me. Garret was right, Oberon's subjects were enjoying the show. I waved back, and the boy blew me a kiss which I caught and slapped to my cheek. His mouth opened in delight, revealing a black, forked tongue.

I smiled. He was odd looking, but cute—shite! I hit the ground as a soul-shattering roar rolled through the jungle like a wave. A new one started before the first even ended. Judging by how the leaves next to me shook, the source wasn't far away. I wanted to avoid it at all costs.

Inexplicably, I glanced up at the little boy again. He pointed to my right, his eyes wide. My chest warmed. He was helping me.

I mouthed a "thank you" and went left, choosing instead to face the dangers unknown.

CHAPTER THIRTY

I ran as fast as my feet would carry me in what I thought was the opposite direction of the monstrous sound. So, when I rushed into a clearing and came face to face with a white lion, it was a miracle that I didn't scream. Dak's eyes widened, and he let out an ear-shattering roar as he slammed his paw into my chest.

I flew backward through the trees, landed with a thump on the ground, and froze in fear. I was fighting Dak, but he hadn't been the only creature in the clearing. I cursed myself for misunderstanding the fae boy.

My heart pounded wildly as the seconds passed. Neither the albino lion nor the monster, the beast I suspected Dak had just pushed me away from, appeared. Only the sounds of growls and the scent of something musty assaulted me. I was about to crawl away when a deep, feline yowl cut through a rumbling of predatory fighting.

Dak . . . I stared at the leaves blocking my view. Did I really want to see what was behind them again—fully this time? There was a hiss, another feline yowl, and I couldn't help myself. I nudged a massive leaf to the side, peeked into the clearing, and winced.

It was worse than I could have imagined.

Dak was battling the pooka—the shapeshifter. The creature was transformed into a hydra, a hideous, scaled monster with three heads. And from the vicious gashes staining Dak's white fur, it was obvious he was losing.

I trembled, releasing the leaf as my mind raced ahead, picturing Dak at the monster's mercy—or lack thereof. Through my fear for him, my rational brain was screaming for me to cut and run before the monster caught wind of a witch in the bushes.

Could I live with myself if Dak got injured or died? The spriggan would have killed Maria, and there was no way I could be sure that this monster wouldn't do the same to Dak. Plus, he'd *just saved me*.

I chewed the inside of my cheek, drawing blood. Blood. Dak was blood. I closed my eyes briefly.

Slowly, I let out a breath and teased the enormous leaf blocking my view back once more. I'd barely created a window large enough to see through when the branch the leaf sprouted off of snapped—exposing me. I froze as the hydra tensed and one of the creature's three heads turned my way.

A squeak of fear escaped me and the other two heads whipped around, too, all eyes searching for the creature thick enough to sneak up on it.

Dak went for the kill, launching himself, claws outstretched and teeth bared. Reacting to the threat, the hydra's heads snapped back to face the lion. Then the hydra shifted. The scent of smoke filled my nostrils, and I recoiled in fear as Dak soared closer to the beast.

A dragon, smaller than the one kept in the castle courtyard but still terrifying, stood before me. Its leathery hide glinted like armor and its teeth gnashed menacingly.

I cringed as the lion collided with the dragon's chest. The

dipped its neck and tore into Dak's back. Blood shot high and Dak's roar of pain rumbled through my ears. I shoved my fist in my mouth to keep from crying out as his body, now half crimson, thudded to the ground. The dragon lumbered forward. Smoke seeping from its mouth caught the wind and fluttered by me, filling my nostrils with its putrid scent. The dragon was preparing to light Dak on fire. At that distance, it wouldn't miss.

My body vibrated with tension. I have to save him, I thought, shoving aside my instincts of self-preservation and calling my infrared sword. Inhaling,

I steeled myself to take on the dragon. I'd just lifted a trembling foot when Dak transformed into human aspect with remarkable speed and threw up his hands.

"I surrender!" His blood-stained armor lit up, a glaring white that beamed through the canopy of trees.

A firework flew high above the arena and burst into life in the shape of an ouroboros—a serpent eating its own tail. Meegra's voice followed, echoing above the stadium. "Nine contestants remaining, battling for the rank of general and second-in-line to the throne of Lyonesse!"

The crowd tossed around magically conjured leaves and sprays of water like confetti. I shot back behind the foliage and strained to tune them out as I waited for the subtle sounds that would tell me the dragon's next move.

Would it recall hearing me and investigate? I shook as nervous energy rippled through me. After minutes that felt like *years*, I couldn't take not knowing anymore.

I pulled back another massive leaf and nearly cried from relief. The dragon was plodding away, disappearing through the trees.

Dak shot me a warning look and gestured for me to leave. Like hell I'd leave before I was sure he was fine. I waited until there were no longer sounds of the dragon crashing through the jungle before approaching my brother.

"You all right?" I asked, taking in Dak's many lacerations and the copious blood staining the clearing.

Dak nodded and tried to give me a reassuring smile that materialized more like a grimace. "It didn't hit anything vital. It—what the hell?!"

Suddenly, Dak floated a meter off the ground. I glanced up to find one of the metal islands—the one holding my father and his Feathered Fae—above us. Two fae were working magic and levitating Dak out of the arena—away from danger.

All his muscles loosened. "Good luck. See you when it's over."

A part of me wished I was going with him, while another part was grateful still to be in the game. This bloody Successional was messed up. I couldn't wait for it to be over. As I continued through the jungle, I hoped the payoff was worth it.

It appeared I had a gift for trouble as less than two minutes passed before I stumbled upon my next obstacle. Or rather, my next opponent dropped out of the sky to stop me.

"Hello there, little witch," the chimera said. A smirk bloomed on his face as his cloven hooves graced the ground. He had long black hair and an ultra-masculine face, which might be handsome if he didn't look like a straight up killer.

Still high on adrenaline from my near miss with a dragon, I recovered from the surprise quickly. An infrared sword appeared in my hand as if I'd been wielding it all my life. Before I knew it, I'd already lunged at him.

He rose in the air, evading my attack with grace. "Now, now. That was not the welcome I would expect from a royal. What do you say I show you what we do to rude fae where I come from?"

Lightning fast, the chimera pulled an arrow from his quiver and notched it in his bow. "Surrender. Or die. Your choice."

My options flashed through my mind, one after the other. If he loosed his arrow, would I be fast and dexterous enough to destroy the arrow with my sword? It was unlikely. Should I disappear? Despite how helpful illusions had been in the past, I didn't think I could bear hiding behind one now. After seeing so many of my siblings fight, an illusion felt cowardly. Not something a princess, and certainly not a general, should rely on when facing a foe. I widened my stance, preparing to take him on.

"Finally, someone with grit," the chimera said.

My senses heightened as the chimera's string eased back. A twig cracked somewhere in the jungle. I could taste the dirt from the arena on my tongue. A breeze fluttered across my face and I savored it, hoping it wouldn't be my last. That I'd somehow be able to stave off the chimera's arrows and fight him on the ground, face-to-face, where my chances would be better.

The first arrow flew at me. I extended my sword and sliced my blade through the air. A shaky grin bloomed on my face as it struck and the arrow's halves fell to the ground, filling my nostrils with the aroma of burnt wood.

The chimera scowled. "No one ever said freedom came easy."

With that he fired a hailstorm of arrows, one after the other. My heartbeat raced as I darted, leapt, and swung my infrared sword at the arrows in rapid succession. I barely made it out of the way too many times to count. Still in motion and trying to determine how much longer the chimera would have an upper hand, I took my eyes off the bow and peeked into his quiver. Only two arrows remained. A sliver of hope bloomed from the depths of my fear.

Then, an arrow sliced open my left shoulder.

I screamed and a cry from the crowds echoed. I refrained from flipping them the bird. Ignore them, I thought, gritting my teeth. This is what you signed up for. This is your fight.

Blocking out the pain, I raised my sword, determined to make it through the last two arrows. To force the chimera onto even ground and into a fair fight.

But fate had another plan in store, for the next second Arlo in his golden eagle aspect swooped down from nowhere and knocked the chimera's bow from his hands.

And he wasn't alone.

Naela was at his side, her fury plain as she screeched and clawed at the chimera's long hair and face.

I jumped as high as I could, swinging my sword in the air. I missed the chimera but hit his bowstring, slicing it in half, leaving him weaponless. As much as I'd have liked for him to recognize I'd bested him by muttering a curse or loosing a growl, the chimera was no longer focused on me. His sights had shifted to Arlo, soaring away to safety. Thankfully, my familiar had flown into the trees. She was hidden from the chimera, though not from me. I could feel her watchful presence. I hoped Naela stayed back.

"Damn shifters." He launched into the sky after my winged brother.

"Naela!" I held out my good arm for my hawk, who perched but did not relax. Her feathers were puffed higher than I'd ever seen them. Her eyes latched onto the sky, searching for the chimera. "How do you always get out of your cage?" I shook my head, incredulous that of all the things I focused on, it was *that*. This bird had been a bloody Houdini for years, and I had more important things to worry about. "Actually, it doesn't matter. Thanks for your help."

Naela did a little head bob before her eyes shot to the sky once more.

I followed her gaze. Arlo was just noticeable through the canopy as a glimmer of gold dodging and weaving away from the chimera.

"Boss, can you help the eagle? He's my brother and I don't want that chimera to get him. My other siblings are fair game to fight the eagle, but not that vile creature."

Naela didn't need to be asked twice. She launched off my arm, intent on wreaking havoc on the creature who'd tried to kill me. I watched her disappear and hoped that I hadn't made a horrible mistake by involving my familiar in the Successional.

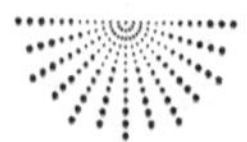

CHAPTER THIRTY-ONE

No one crossed my path for a long time. I was thankful. I needed the respite to nurse the gash in my shoulder. The bleeding was slowing, and I'd started to wish Naela was back with me when I caught a hint of smoke in the air.

In any other scenario I'd worry about avoiding a forest fire, but in this unnatural arena I leapt onto a large rock and whirled around, searching for the source. I found it almost immediately, though not because of the fire.

Instead, a tornado caught my eye.

It was *massive*, climbing above the treetops, its whistle growing ever louder as it flung burning branches about inside its funnel with increasing speed. The crowd had noticed it, too. Hundreds of fae leaned forward in their seats to get a better glimpse of the conjurer of the tornado.

A tornado indicated one of two people. Either Himari or Crystal was fighting the only one of us able to produce fire—Finn. Judging by the size of the tornado, my money was on the weaver witch. Despite Crystal's rapid ability to learn her fae magic, Himari had been an air witch her entire life. The weaver possessed more raw power and better control.

Should I join the battle? This—unlike my encounters with the chimera, giant, spriggan, and pooka— was a fair fight. It was *exactly* what we'd been training for. I took another glance at the tornado. It had already diminished in size. I could barely see the top of it over the trees now. Whoever the wind worker was, they were weakening. Perhaps Finn was losing steam, too.

And that was an advantage I would take.

Generals should be masters of strategy, right? And what was more strategic than saving your energy until your opponent was completely knackered? I hopped off the boulder, wrapped myself in an illusion so I could jump in when it best suited me, and made my way toward the tornado.

To my surprise, I came across the sounds of fighting sooner than I'd expected. I glanced up and saw the fae in the stands were still leaning at a precarious angle, their attention directed far from where I stood.

Apparently, I'd been close to another quarrel and not even realized it. I suspected that the noise of the tornado had muffled the sounds. I picked my way through the vegetation, hoping I'd be able to use the element of surprise to my advantage twice in rapid succession.

Soon enough I came across Nigel and Kumar. They were fighting tooth and nail, their eyes glinting, sweat dripping off their skin. I crouched in the bushes and watched as Kumar slithered and darted about, fangs extended while Nigel hurled beam after beam of red light. After one near graze of infrared light against the naga's scales, Kumar lunged at Nigel, fangs dripping with venom. Silently, I cheered for my kinder, gentler brother. To my dismay, Nigel whirled out of the way just in time and threw up a protective wall of vivid green light—ultraviolet radiation.

"Couldn't beat me as a man, you snake?" A sneer flashed across Nigel's pale face. "Had to transform into a beast? How pathetic."

"Pathetic that I wouldn't let you control my mind as you did to Wikolia?" Kumar's words ended with an eerie hiss, though it was what he said, more than how he said it, that got my attention. "I saw how you manipulated her! What else have you been hiding from us? A penchant for sneaking around in the dark, perhaps?"

Nigel was developing psychic powers? An image of Maria tapping her temples flashed in my mind, and I nearly let out a gasp and gave myself away. I was such an idiot! Maria hadn't meant *she* was becoming physic. She'd been warning me about Nigel!

"Sneaking?" Nigel barked out a laugh and hurled another beam of light at Kumar. "You mean our sister's bloody bird? That's a bit dramatic, don't you think? Although, top marks to you for being the only one bright enough to piece it together. Never thought a serpent could be clever."

Bird? Did he mean Naela? I clapped a hand over my mouth as all the pieces clicked into place.

Sai had sworn that she'd been at her post that entire night. I'd believed her, and now that belief was reinforced. Nigel would only have had to use his budding mind magic to convince Sai he'd never been near my room. He may have used an illusion to cover his tracks more thoroughly.

Then there was the odd sensation that someone was trying to break into my mind the day I flew Naela. That hadn't been Victoria, but Nigel. He took advantage of my assumption that he wouldn't be able to talk and use a new power simultaneously.

Heat rose in my face and anger coiled deep within me. More than anything, I wanted to fling myself out from behind the trees, but *something*—a familiar, dangerous sensation in the air—stopped me. I backed away as Kumar lunged at Nigel again, fangs bared, ready to grab the witch by the throat and end it. Instead of retreating, however, Nigel just stood there, his arms spread in a gesture of surrender that I didn't trust for a second. Nigel confirmed my suspicion a moment later, when a sword of bubbling, poisonous green light materialized from thin air, stopping the naga in his tracks.

An ultraviolet sword.

My eyes popped open in shock. Both Casimir and I could create an infrared sword, but I'd never seen anything like *this*. Every time an illuminator worked with higher energy wavelengths, it took more power and drained the witch faster, but it was also deadlier to their opponent. My infrared sword could cut through metal, as I'd discovered against the spriggan. Following that logic, ultraviolet light could be even more destructive. The details were not something I wanted to entertain as the tip of Nigel's sword hovered centimeters from Kumar's neck.

"It's over," Nigel sneered, so sure of his victory. "Surrender, snake. Time to let the better man win."

Kumar jerked back. In retaliation, Nigel dropped the sword to Kumar's chest. The sharp tip kissed Kumar's skin.

Kumar screamed as blood gushed everywhere. Smooth skin that would probably never be the same, bubbled viciously and the scent of burnt flesh filled my nostrils. I wanted to vomit. Nigel repositioned his sword centimeters from Kumar's jugular.

"I *said*, surrender, snake."

Salty blood filled my mouth as I tore at my bottom lip, waiting, silently pleading for Kumar to listen.

After what seemed like years, Kumar dropped his arms to his side. "I surrender," he said, his words coming out in a long, defeated hiss.

"Now, that's what I like to hear." Nigel held his brother's gaze for a moment before slashing open Kumar's throat.

A firework exploded above.

My breath stalled, shuddering in and out of my mouth in gasps as tears blurred my vision. Vomit threatened to climb up my throat, but I swallowed it back down. Stopping to puke meant that Nigel had a better chance at finding me.

Nigel, who could cloak himself in light and hide better than me. Nigel, who had slit Kumar's throat despite a clear surrender. Fratricide. Brother killing brother. Cruel, senseless murder. Nigel, *my brother,* the murderer.

What had been the point of killing Kumar? How had I not seen that Nigel was dangerous or considered him as a suspect when I'd thought someone had killed Naela? What had he done to Wikolia? A strangled sound left my throat as tears spilled over my eyelids.

I had to find everyone else. I had to warn them about Nigel and convince them we *needed* to band together. At least until we found Nigel, knocked him unconscious, and turned him over to the guards. Then we could continue this ridiculous Faerie ritual.

But did I even want to continue after what I'd seen? I'd been prepared to fight, to injure, but never imagined one of my siblings would aim to kill. Now that I'd seen it with my own eyes, the Successional was taking on a darker tone.

I stopped running. I wasn't sure which way I'd gone after I'd bolted. Before I did anything else, I needed to reorient myself. I stood beneath one end of the stands laden with the poorer fae of Lyonesse. I was performing a scan to discern where most of the crowd's attention was when two fireworks burst into the sky above the stands. One took the shape of a pegasus. The other assembled itself in a form identical to the chimera flying about the arena.

"Two more suckers down! Only five to go until I win!" A voice, confident and haughty, shrieked from somewhere nearby.

Crystal.

Of course, the first person I'd come across and have to warn about Nigel *would* be Crystal. I rolled my eyes; how ironic. She was still laughing like a lunatic in between bouts of taunting whoever her opponent was, so I simply followed the sound of her voice. I'd just caught a flash of red through the trees when I realized it was probably best to have an illusion up. That way no one attacked me before I got too close.

Cloaked in invisibility, I crept closer to find Gio pummeling Crystal with waves of water. My lips twitched. Every time she got doused, Crystal's scowl grew wider. But our brother didn't let up. Not for a second. His water bent through the air in every shape imaginable: a galloping horse, a diving bird, a hammer, and the most terrifying of all—water bullets that tore toward Crystal.

Still, Crystal had not been an Olympic gymnast for nothing. For every hit Gio landed, Crystal dodged five others, often by using gravity-defying flips that must have been bolstered by air magic. They were each a force of nature and both were playing to win.

Well, their duel would just have to wait. At least until we booted a cold-blooded murderer out of the arena. I stepped out from behind a tree, exposing my body to their elements while remaining invisible. Visible light pooled in my hands, ready and waiting for the moment Crystal slowed, so I could incapacitate their vision simultaneously. My redhead sister launched herself in the air once more, and I spotted my opportunity. I dropped my illusion.

Crystal stuck her landing and her gaze darted to the side, latching onto me. Gio was slower, turning only once he realized Crystal had faltered in her assault. Once I saw the whites of their eyes, I let the light fly. Both opponents wrenched their eyes shut.

"I call a temporary peace!" I yelled as loud as I dared. "I have to tell you something potentially life-saving. I'll stop blinding you, but you have to promise not to attack me—to listen. If you don't, well, I can do this for a long time. Raise your hand if you agree."

Gio's hand shot into the air first, then Crystal's.

I ceased blasting light into their eyes.

Crystal recovered first, opening her eyes, blinking away the spots. She looked at me, then at Gio, who was still rubbing his eyes.

I should have seen it coming. Should have made them agree not to attack *each other.* But with Nigel's murder fresh in my mind, I was a bit frazzled. Instead, I watched helplessly as Crystal shot at Gio with the speed of a racehorse, plowed her muscular body into his, and landed a fist right upside his jaw.

He didn't stand a chance against her perfectly placed punch. His armor lit up like a pinball machine, and a firework exploded above. Gio fell to the ground, unconscious. The crowds went wild, leaping and pointing at the glowing, red sea creature lighting up the sky.

"What a show!" Meegra exclaimed, sounding more amused than I'd ever heard. "Five contestants remain to battle for the rank of general and second in line to the throne of Lyonesse! If you haven't placed your bet, do it now!"

Crystal turned on me. "It's about to be four. Thanks for the help against the diviner. He was proving to be more work than I'd planned for. I'm sure I won't say the same for you." She hurtled toward me, wrenching her dagger from her scabbard. A crazed smile spread across her face.

"No! Wait! I seriously have something important to tell you!"

But Crystal was long gone, replaced by a wildly competitive young woman with the laser-like vision that had honed her into being the best in everything she did. She was nearly upon me, blade poised to plunge, when my nervous system kicked into "flight mode."

Hastily, I pulled my illusion around me and darted left, then right. I'd seen enough action movies to know serpentine movements helped people evade bullets. I hoped they would help me evade a competition-crazed, violent sister, too. I shot a spray of bright white light behind me as I ran away, not bothering to aim, certain something would hit.

A stream of colorful curses validated my method, but they faded quickly as I pushed my muscles to breaking and sprinted through the trees.

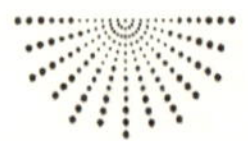

CHAPTER THIRTY-TWO

What if Nigel found Crystal next? Could I live with the guilt of knowing he killed someone else? Even a person who'd come after me with a blade glinting in their hand? Why hadn't I just blurted out Nigel was a psycho murderer as I ran away from Crystal? Then guilt wouldn't be weighing me down with each step.

I kicked a rock and plopped onto a boulder. The sky above was darkening, which was an unwelcome sign. In Faerie, the sunlight was different from the light in the human plane. Just as in many of the old fairy tales, it was the land of perpetual twilight. Sunrises took longer and sunsets were faster than on the human plane. Hours of prolonged darkness would follow. In this arena, darkness was just another danger working against me.

"Nigel, Crystal, two mystery siblings, and me." I

counted the remaining Successional contestants on my fingers. Between Nigel and Crystal, the prospect of winning was daunting, and that wasn't even counting the two others still in contention. My cheeks puffed out, and I released a long sigh.

"Don't forget to count us *poor* prisoners. We're still here, too," a voice hissed.

I shot off the rock and whirled about to find the naga hovering behind me. Unlike Kumar, who had always kept his humanity when he shifted, this creature looked and smelled feral.

Over her human torso, she wore a leather band to cover her large breasts, but the rest of her was bare and caked in dirt. The serpent half of her body was a bright, poisonous blue, tapering into a rattle. Blood covered her scales—though no cuts marred her body. She'd met someone else in this jungle and injured them.

"I've been looking for *you* everywhere, little light witch." She played with her words, elongating the ends.

"Why? There are loads of others in here."

"True." She smiled, showing off fangs, four inches long and slick with venom. "But I've always *loved* the taste of lightworkers best. I haven't had one in years and couldn't pass up this opportunity for dwarf or elf. Once I'm freed, I can get those any time. But you, the way light spills from you when the life leaves your body . . . *ahhh,* that is something special. Let me show you."

She lunged at me.

I brandished my infrared sword. I knew from sparring and talking with Kumar that an illusion would be useless against this naga. Like a hawk, a transformed naga could sense body heat. However, that meant a hot sword might be confused with my limbs, depending on how fast I moved, which I hoped was fast enough to avoid her fangs.

The naga didn't seem fazed by this additional hurdle. In fact, her lips actually *broadened* into a crazed smile as she took in the bright red sword. "Wonderful. You can do more than work with just visible light. Lightworkers with a wider range always have more depth of flavor." Her rattle shook.

I clenched the white-light hilt of my sword tight as I poured power into it and urged it into the blade. It had to be blazing hot to dent her magically imbued scales.

When she came at me again, I was ready. My sword flew straight for her face as I pivoted like a wild ballerina, twisting and arching my torso away from her deadly teeth. As I'd hoped, the naga dodged the blazing light, protecting her face and slithering away from it. Watching Kumar, whose primary method of defense was to slither away, had taught me that if one half of their snake body slid one way, the other half moved in the opposite direction. And this naga's tail was long. Long enough for me to plunge the infrared blade into it, burning her flesh open in a rift of seared scales.

An otherworldly wail pierced the forest. Blood spurted everywhere as the naga thrashed about, coating everything with hot, sticky liquid.

Despite the blood flinging its way into my mouth and making me gag, I kept my sword aloft, my eyes on my opponent. Even with the hilt of pure white light making it safe for me to touch, I felt how fiercely my weapon burned. I dared the naga to come at me again, to steal my light.

Instead, the naga turned to face me, and I watched her own light dim in her eyes—the life leaving them. Disbelievingly, I glanced down and gasped. I had cut all the way through her bone and out the other side. A meter of blue tail lay on the ground, blood pooling around it. With that much blood, I had to have severed a main artery. Was she bleeding out?

As if in confirmation, the naga dropped to the ground, a dull hiss dying on her lips.

My head spun and my arms shook. I'd just killed a creature. *Killed her.* The Successional was turning out to be one massive nightmare. But before I could even try to come to terms with my new status as a murderer, a shriek rang through the jungle.

"Help! Help!"

Immediately, I placed the voice. I knew it because I'd cherished it so much these past two weeks.

Kate.

I sprinted toward the sound, knowing it might be a death sentence but unable to flee. What felt like a marathon later, I spotted a flash of red light. Without thinking, I careened through the vegetation right at Nigel and tackled him from the side. Our bodies toppled as one. As soon as we hit the ground, I rolled away, pulled my dagger from the scabbard, and rose just as a pair of strong hands pressed me back down into the ground.

There was a scrambling sound, and I caught Kate darting backward to retrieve her dagger. Vines littered the clearing, giving me hope. Kate hadn't surrendered. She'd been trying to fight back, which meant she wouldn't disappear from the arena. That was a boon, because now I needed her to fight for me, too.

"Idiot woman," Nigel breathed, his face an inch from mine.

"You're a murderer!" I screamed, wanting Kate to know, so she could proceed with caution.

"Don't you fools get it?" Spittle flew from his mouth. "We're battling for a chance at a bloody crown! Ultimate military power! No one will take that from me."

The air shifted. A faint green hue filled the air, congregating around us. Nigel was calling his magic to him—magic I recognized straight away.

Ultraviolet radiation.

"Kate!" I screamed, flailing about and kicking my legs to free myself.

"Yes, Kate. Why don't you help me?" Nigel whispered, his tone oily—persuasive.

I stilled. Help him? I tore my gaze from Nigel to land on Kate. All my breath flew from me.

Kate's blue eyes were glazed over, just as Gran had warned me mine would look if a psychic ever got control of my mind. I'd forgotten about Nigel's burgeoning psychic magic. A deadly mistake.

"I'll hold her, Kate." Nigel's eyes sparkled with a lust for power. "You stab."

Kate's arm shot up like a puppet's, her dagger held aloft. I became a whirlwind of limbs and terror. With every breath, I pleaded with Kate to stop, hoped that my voice would cut through Nigel's influence and reach her.

But Kate only stepped closer, her movement almost robotic. There was a thunk of knees against rocks as she knelt at my side, her gaze still hazy, unresponsive. I couldn't take it anymore, couldn't watch my sister stab me. I wrenched my eyes shut. Still, the scent of her chamomile lotion filled my nostrils, and her hot breath washed over me as she leaned closer.

Suddenly, the weight of Nigel's hands on my shoulders *lifted*.

I gasped. My eyes flew open. A glint of metal

raced toward me. I rolled to the side, stood, and thrust my hands out, ready to defend myself against Kate.

Instead, I found my sister still on her knees, her dagger plunged into the ground, where I'd just lain. Her eyes were horrified and filling with tears. "Oh, my G—G—God, Lana! I didn't m—mean to!"

"I know, Kate! Just . . . pull yourself together." I didn't have the time to comfort her, not with the sounds of heavy breathing and grunting nearby.

"Get up," I urged her. "He's a murderer. We have to fight him."

Though there was technically the option of surrendering to Nigel, I couldn't bring myself to do it. He'd killed Kumar and just tried to kill us too. Someone like that couldn't win such power. He wouldn't use it properly. Wouldn't help the people.

Kate nodded, her eyes now totally clear. Sure that she was herself again, I whirled about to see who'd come to my rescue. My heart nearly stopped.

Finn was pummeling Nigel with his fists. He seemed to have forgotten he was capable of magic, but it didn't matter. For the moment, he was besting Nigel.

I swung into action, dashing forward, conjuring my infrared sword, and trapping Nigel between Finn and me.

"Surrender!" I yelled at Nigel, not bothering to wait for Finn to stop throwing punches. Nigel deserved every one of them.

"Never!" Nigel screamed, shoving Finn back and leaping just out of his reach. "I'd rather die than lose to any of *you*."

I already had one death on my conscience; I didn't want any more. Knocking Nigel out was the only option I could stomach. My eyes sought Finn's, and he met them for the first time in days. An unspoken connection formed between us, and Finn nodded. We may have been broken, but for a moment we were a team once again.

"Cover us!" I shot at Kate as Nigel charged me, an infrared sword materializing in his hand.

Our blades met, sizzling and colliding with one another rather than cutting through. It appeared illuminator magic could cut through anything—except other illuminator magic. Within seconds I found myself in a precarious squatting position while Nigel loomed over me. His sword angled above mine. His biceps strained to press down as I reciprocated upward.

One hard thrust and I'm dead, I thought, my teeth grinding together as I pushed against his opposing force. Nigel was physically stronger, so the threat was all too real.

Then, unexpectedly, Nigel shot to the right, out of reach of my sword. His hands flailed, trying to put out the flames on his back as he spewed a foul string of curses.

I engaged again. Finn joined, and together, we

trapped Nigel between us. Kate followed a heartbeat later. We bombarded Nigel, with fire, rocks moving fast as bullets, and searing flashes of red light, demanding he surrender with each blow.

Nigel did no such thing. Instead, he ran back and forth between us, fighting our trio off with all his might. I hated that he could take us both on, but he'd spent a lifetime of training—*really* training with magic. His practice showed with every well-aimed beam of light we dodged.

After a few minutes, Finn and Kate were visibly tiring. They needed to recover, so I'd stepped forward to take Nigel on solo. That's when the foliage behind me rustled. I sucked in a sharp breath. Someone was there, watching.

It only took a second to peek—a second for Nigel to do something unexpected. The instant my head was turned Nigel leapt away from me, extended his blade of light, and slammed the sword straight through Kate's gut.

Kate moaned.

My sword fell from my hand, still solid as it hit the ground and rolled away. Vaguely, I heard Finn exclaim, and a collective intake of breath from above: Onlookers watching us, appalled and fascinated as my sister fell to her knees.

Nigel, knowing he had us right where he wanted us, shot a searing beam of light at Finn to incapacitate him, pivoted, and charged toward me.

I scrambled for my weapon, but he was too fast. Before I could breathe, before I could even *think*, Nigel's sword was above me, not a meter from slicing my neck in half. I crouched and squeezed my eyes shut, pulling all my remaining power and tossing up a plea to whatever higher power would listen.

My power flared with an alien intensity—a last gasp, my final chance before I was completely spent. It was like nothing I'd ever experienced. The light was hot and defensive, flocking to me, bolstering me to live. It had barely touched my skin when I redirected it and flung it upward at Nigel in a spray. Even through my closed eyelids, the intensity of the beams left an imprint on my retinas, burnt through them like a solar flare. I'd just manipulated more light than I'd ever harnessed in my life.

I had only a second to take in the revelation when heat covered me. I cringed and pressed myself closer to the ground, thinking Nigel was retaliating. That he was manipulating infrared light and pouring it over me like liquid in a final, evil act. But then I heard the hitch of a breath, a gurgling, and finally weight, *solid dead weight*, fell on top of me.

A firework exploded and my eyes flew open. Nigel lay on top of me, warm and wet with blood, an aura of the deadly green light he'd nearly cast upon me dissipating into the air. There was a gash through his stomach from my spray of magic, and his back was covered in flames—Finn's flames.

He was dead. We'd killed him. *I'd* killed him.

Muffling a scream, I pushed Nigel's body off me. His blue eyes stared back at me, cold and lifeless. I shivered.

Someone moaned—a low, wretched sound.

Kate.

I scrambled to my feet, desperate to get to my sister, to see if she was still alive and was knocked back to the ground by a solid fist.

"God, that went on for *forever!*" Crystal chirped. With her brown eyes wide and half her hair burned off, she looked mad. "I almost took on all of you, but thought it better that you wore yourselves out first." She pulled me up, put me in a headlock and squeezed, shielding her body from Finn's retaliation and cutting off my air supply in one fell swoop. Defending myself was as impossible as getting a full, nourishing breath of air. Kate's low moans continued to run through me, the only sounds I could hear over the thrumming of blood in my ears.

Or was it?

I strained to pick up on something rushing toward us, a movement of air, a flapping.

A gasp escaped me as Naela and Kane swooped into view and attacked Crystal. My escape artist hawk must have freed her friend to help save Finn and me.

Red hair rained from above as the hawks ripped, soared up, and dive-bombed Crystal's head again and again. My captor released a terrified scream. Her grip loosened ever so slightly as the onslaught of talons persisted.

But slightly was all I needed. The second her hold slackened, I wrenched myself free, whipped around, and slammed my fist into Crystal's gut, her side, and finally, square on the jaw. She fell with a moan after the third punch. Her white armor lit up, indicating she was unconscious—she was out. Naela landed on the center of Crystal's chest, her feathers puffed to the heavens. Kane, seeing his job was done, flew to circle over Finn.

A firework exploded in the sky, but I didn't see it. My attention snapped to Finn, the final contender. All I wanted was to get to Kate's side, but would Finn turn on me unexpectedly like he'd done when he'd defended Crystal in training? Finn was used to being the best at everything, and as a demon born he probably had tricks up his sleeve I couldn't even fathom. Maybe a new lust for power, too? We'd never been here before, and if I knew one thing, it was that Faerie had changed us both.

And when I locked eyes with Finn, I saw I was right.

He dropped to his knees and raised his hands to the sky in a gesture of defeat I'd never seen from him. "I surrender!"

His suit of armor lit up, marking him as out just as another firework burst in the night sky. Again, I didn't see what sort of creature it was, didn't care one iota.

Single-mindedly, I rushed to Kate's side. I fell to my knees and placed my hand on her shoulder. "Kate?"

"Lana?" Her voice was little more than a whisper.

"All you have to do is say you surrender. Someone will come to help. I saw they did it with Dak."

"Far, huh?" Kate choked out, and I noticed blood bubbling from her mouth.

"Yeah, we made it farther than we expected. Hurry! Surrender and someone will come. They'll save you." I started to stand so I could force the matter and call down help.

"Sis . . ." Kate grabbed my hand, and I stopped, waiting for her to finish. Instead, her blue eyes fluttered closed.

A firework—a blazing red phoenix—burst in the sky.

CHAPTER THIRTY-THREE

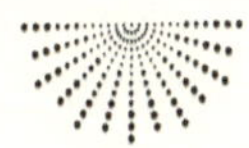

The Burnings took place the next day, but none of us were permitted to watch. Fae law forbad it.

When a fae died only their parents, mate, and sovereign were present at their Burning ceremonies, which were analogous to funerals. Under fae law, Kate, Kumar, and Nigel burned with only our father to mourn them.

I found the death ritual a relief. There was no way I would have been able to sit through the Burnings—certainly not for Nigel, whom I would never forgive. In lieu of attending the death rite, my siblings and I got the option to collect a bone from each deceased. It was a literal piece to remember them by.

"Won't they crumble into dust and ash from the fire?" I'd asked the burner, a fae specialized in Burnings, who informed me of my choice.

He'd explained that fae did not use regular fire for Burnings but enchanted fire. It was a fire only certain fae could produce, usually those with a long family lineage of being burners. It allowed the bones to remain white. It even polished and shaped the smaller ones in the hands and feet into perfect spheres. Those were the bones most often claimed by grieving family members, for portability's sake. Though, apparently, the sternum was popular, too. Some families hung it on their walls, a token of remembrance to cherish.

The burner said the bones of the deceased held great power, much like the bonekeys that brought us to Faerie. In fact, bonekeys were formed by the same ritual the burner was performing on my siblings' bones. The bonekeys were simply spelled further at the request of the kings or queens who reigned after the Sinkers sank Faerie.

Burners did not perform the same enchantments for normal fae bones. The power within most deceased fae bones was restricted to the powers that had flowed through the fae when they were alive. So they were still considered magical objects, just less powerful than bonekeys.

I committed to care for the bones of Kumar and Kate and requested the most circular ones from their hands. A circle to trick my mind into seeing it as a rock eroded by the sea, rather than the bones of my dead brother and sister. From the hand because it felt right. I requested the burner take a bone of Nigel's and bury it for me.

The burner was flabbergasted by my request. He insisted that as we were both illuminators, Nigel's bone would provide me with the most power. He tried to press the memorial token upon me.

What he didn't understand was I didn't want Nigel's bone. I wanted nothing to do with someone capable of murdering their own kin out of spite and a desire for power. Someone who had made *me* a kin killer, too.

I never asked where the burner buried the bone.

AFTER THE SUCCESSIONAL, KING OBERON'S TEN living demi-fae children chose to stay in Faerie. Only Victoria's firm "yes" surprised me.

After having her face marred by Ash and being chased by a giantess during the Successional, I'd expected her to demand a one-way journey back to Toronto. Apparently, Victoria was stronger than I gave her credit for. That, or she *really* wanted to find a prince.

Our father thought it wise that we send a second letter to our mothers. In it, he would explain what had happened since he contacted them upon our arrival and tell of our new rank within the kingdom. The letter would also assure them that in time we could travel to and from the Old Land as we desired.

Kate's, Kumar's, and Nigel's families would receive a very different letter. The correspondence would be delivered by one of the Feathered Fae, and in true Faerie fashion, a bone of their lost child.

My heart broke to think of their parents holding the bones of their child, knowing they'd never see them again. Probably they'd wonder why their son or daughter had made such a thick decision. For looking back, I realized what a *stupid choice* the Successional had been for most of us, untrained and unknowledgeable as we were. They'd warned us of the dangers and told us to study the fae in preparation. I'd even received hints from Garret as to just how different fae culture was from my own. And yet, I dove right in— sure it was the right thing to do.

The ceremony when our rank would be announced to all of Lyonesse, the Pinning, was the day after the Burnings. It was not a private affair—a fact I couldn't help but be nervous over as I walked down the hallway to the throne room.

The throne room was stark white, luminous with firelight, and brimming with Lord and Lady fae. There was the odd fae of lesser wealth present, too, obvious by their rough-spun attire sticking out among the silks and gems of nobility. However, whatever their status, every pair of eyes followed as my siblings filed in, all clad in crimson save for

Crystal, Finn, and I, who were dressed in bronze, silver, and gold, respectively. They announced me last.

The attention of thousands of eyes was like nothing I'd ever experienced. My cheeks heated, and I stared at the hem of the golden gown Sai had delivered that morning. Gold that was the same shade of my eyes—Fullfeather eyes.

After what felt like forever, I made it to the center of the throne room and took my ceremonial place next to Finn. It still felt odd being next to him, all our secrets bare, but his quick surrender in the Successional had cemented one thing in my mind. Finn may be a demon born, but he wasn't a monster. I needed to get over my prejudice. It was the first step to recovering a relationship with him.

The announcer, an old dwarf with a booming voice, called Wikolia up to the dais to receive her title.

Princess and General Lana . . . bugger, that's a lot, I thought, watching Wikolia stride up the steps to our father's throne. Eyes followed her and Wikolia's black, wavy hair rose slightly, a warning bristle reminiscent of her wolf aspect. She may desire the status that came along with being a royal, but she clearly did not appreciate the staring.

The vows were simple, three short sentences, and in the end the king deemed Wikolia a princess and knight befitting her royal and militaristic duties.

Finn shook his head and grumbled something under his breath.

I smirked. Though I couldn't hear what he'd said, I had an idea what it may have been. However royal titles and military ranks correlated in Faerie, it was most likely different from where we came from. Faerie had offended Finn's sense of military history.

Victoria, Maria, Dak, and Arlo were also named princesses, princes, and knights. Himari was the first to claim the rank of captain, the same rank as Garret. Gio received the same ranking with a massive grin on his face.

Crystal was next, her back straight and proud as she climbed the steps to Oberon's throne. Her title was major second order.

The fae girls swooned when Finn disappeared from my side to approach the throne. He looked every bit the royal standing before our father, clad in dark silver military attire. He received the title major first order.

It was my turn.

"And now, for the winner of the Successional." The dwarf announcer bowed, and his tone turned grandiose, sweeping. "Lana Fullfeather, please rise and join your king!"

My knees shook as I climbed the marble white steps. The torch light reflected off my dress and gold spots danced on the white marble walls. This was the moment I'd been waiting for. The moment my father would really, finally, *see me*. I was still shaking when I reached the top of the dais.

"Thank you for coming here and taking part in a foreign ritual." My father rested his hand softly on my shoulder. I relaxed a touch, recognizing the pride in his gaze. "I recognize that, for you, it was a choice, rather than a duty—as it had been for me. I appreciate your effort. And I must say, your performance was extraordinary."

"Thank you," I said, barely more than a whisper. I could hardly believe this was happening.

"I'm pleased you are the winner." Father smiled. "Your abilities, bravery, and willingness to put yourself on the line for others will do great things for this kingdom. Most of all, I'm pleased our relationship can bloom."

Victory sang in my chest. Without hesitation I swore my oaths—to my father, my king, to Prince Casimir, and to the kingdom of Lyonesse.

My father's moon white fingers pinned a small golden crown with a phoenix rising from the center on the thick strap of my dress. He lifted my hand, still clasped within his, and together, we turned to face the crowds below.

"As your king, it is my great pleasure to present to you Princess Lana, General of the Lyonesse army and second in line to the throne." My father inclined his head toward the crowd.

Applause erupted from below.

CHAPTER THIRTY-FOUR

"Lana!"

My eyebrows shot up as Finn's voice rang down the hallway.

I'd shaken more hands and given more hugs in the last half an hour than I ever had in my life. Now that I'd snuck away from the aftermath of the Pinning, I wanted nothing more than space to breathe and prepare for my first meeting with my father.

I certainly didn't want yet another conversation that left me feeling graceless. As this would be our first real conversation after all the awkwardness happened between us, I didn't see how it could go any other way. Still, Finn had helped me defeat Nigel. We had each others' backs in the arena. I should, at the very least, thank him.

"Hi," I said once he caught up. The greeting

came out strangled, much like the gamut of emotions rushing through me.

"Hi," Finn replied, his cheeks flushing pink at the single word. He was as awkward as me, which I was *positive* had never happened before.

"So . . . . General Lana? Princess? I heard Garret call you princess general? What do I call you now? It's weird not to be accompanied anymore, huh?" Finn's mouth snapped shut, halting his babbling.

In actuality, it was *wonderful* to walk the halls of the castle alone. Now that the Successional was over, diminishing the threat of sabotage, our term of being guarded all day and night would end.

As for what I wanted to be called, that was a great question. I imagined Finn calling me Princess General Lana and recoiled. No. That just wouldn't do.

"Just Lana. I guess if we're on a mission you can use general, but only if others are around. Princess is too weird."

Finn nodded and his shoulders relaxed. "We didn't get to talk yesterday."

Actually, I'd told Garret and Sai I didn't *want* to talk to anyone yesterday. All I'd wanted to do was think about Kate and Kumar and honor their Burning. My guards had respected my wishes, denying everyone access to my door.

"I want you to know," Finn said, "these last two weeks have been hard on me. Especially after finding out I was a demon born . . . and recalling what you'd told me about them when we were kids."

"Finn . . ."

"Wait." He held up a hand. "I have to get this out."

He took a huge breath. "After seeing Nigel nearly end you, I realized I couldn't hold you to your poor opinion of demon borns. Or let anything go unsaid between us any longer. You didn't even really know one. Let alone that I am a demon born . . . and I miss you, Lan. I'm sure it will be awkward for a bit, but still, I'd like to be friends. We can work at it, if you want. If you don't want to, then I understand that too. It might be too uncomfortable for you."

My heart fluttered. *Friends.* God, I wanted that more than anything. I'd missed him, too. Terribly so.

"But in case it's not," Finn continued. He sounded more like me than ever, his speech stuttering and stopping. "Too uncomfortable, that is . . . I was wondering if you wanted to hang out tomorrow? Fly Naela and Kane together like old times? The woods aren't much, but some normalcy would be nice."

Normal. The term was laughable, seeing as we'd never be normal ever again. Still, looking into Finn's familiar, genuine, blue eyes, I knew we had to try to find *our* new normal: a friendship, a familial bond. No matter how uncomfortable it might be, we needed to start working through our issues.

"I'd like that. Naela would, too." I paused, and my cheeks heated as I steeled myself to say what I must.

"Also, I really want to apologize for bad-mouthing the demon born witches," I said. "I grew up hearing how terrible they were, but I had no personal experience with them—except you, of course. It was wrong of me to judge and I'm working on it. Forgive me?"

Instantly, Finn nodded. "Everyone fears what they don't know or understand. It's natural. If history has taught me one thing, it's that. I wish I could have gotten over my personal wound sooner."

I released a breath. "You're too good to me, Finn." The tension coiled within me loosened. "Can I ask you something?"

Finn nodded again.

"Once it was just the two of us, why did you surrender? You could have bested me. I was spent, and you're a demon born. You have vast, raw power even if you don't have a lot of control yet. And I *know* you, Finn. You *hate* being second best."

His eyes dropped to his shoes and the red of his cheeks deepened before he met my gaze again. "It's true. I bloody despise being second best. But I'd dislike it even more if my best friend didn't get what she'd dreamed of her entire life. Plus, let's be honest. Where magic is concerned, I'm not the best—*yet.*"

I mock scoffed at his cockiness, and his lips quirked up in a wry grin. They flattened out quickly though, becoming serious once more.

"After the Successional, Maria told me you helped her. And Gio said you were about to warn them about something when Crystal knocked him out. In the end, *you* bested Nigel and Crystal. *You* fought harder."

He shrugged. "In the arena, I was focused on saving my own skin. I had a fair bit of luck, too. Just like I've had all my life. As much as I want to be the best at everything, it didn't feel right to take your dream from you because I have a habit of being in the right place at the right time."

Warmth filled me at his admission that for once, I'd been better. Though Finn was a kind and, generally positive person, he'd never blown smoke up my rear. Finn said what he meant.

"Thank you," I whispered and wiped a tear threatening to fall from my eye. Then, desperately needing to pull myself together before meeting my father, I added. "I think I need some alone time before my meeting."

"Well, I guess I'll leave you to it, then." He gave a little wave and took off down his hallway.

I'd nearly rounded the corner when I heard his voice again.

"Lana?"

"Yeah?"

"I wanted you to know, I really am proud of you. You earned it."

My chest loosened and fresh tears pricked in my eyes. Those words meant so much to me.

"Thanks," I whispered, suddenly sure that no matter how much time it took, or how many clumsy conversations we had, Finn and I would be normal again.

———

It was ethereal, being led to my father's private chambers. Chambers I hadn't even known about until today. Chambers that Garret informed me the king allowed only a select few to enter. Among them, his Feathered Fae, Prince Casimir, and now—*me*.

White surrounded me and hints of gold peeked out from the crown moldings. Sparse figurines made of white marble and gold lined the alcoves. It appeared like everywhere else in Castle Phoenix and yet completely different. Because this moment was what I'd been waiting for my entire life.

Garret's heavy footsteps were an anthem, pounding in regular intervals, a sound I would never forget. He stopped, and I realized we'd reached the end of the hallway.

"We're here, Princess." Garret stepped to the side, his eyes down though his lips twitched at the title.

I rolled my eyes but refrained from whacking him on the shoulder. "We're friends. It's Lana."

"Only until we are on a mission—Lana."

I could live with that. Garret was a soldier, after

all. It would be disrespectful to ask him to disregard the military ranks.

"Thank you. You'll be here when I come out?"

"I won't leave, unless you ask me to."

Heat crept up my neck as I sensed something deeper in Garret's words. A feeling I wasn't ready to acknowledge despite the pull I felt toward him. "Good."

Before me was a door unlike any other in the castle. Made of a shining white metal, there was a massive gold feather cast into the door. Its downy image spanned the threshold from ceiling to floor. At the bottom of the feather onyx flames rose to engulf the plume, almost like it was a full phoenix. This was it—the moment I'd been waiting for.

I exhaled a slow breath to calm my nerves and then I knocked.

<u>Spellcasters Spy Academy Series (Magic of Arcana Universe)</u>

A Legacy Witch: Year One

A Rebel Witch: Year Two

A Crucible Witch: Year Three

An Academy Witch: Prequel

The Complete Spellcasters Spy Academy Boxset

<u>The Wonderland Court Series (Magic of Arcana Universe)</u>

Alice the Dagger

Alice the Torch

<u>Standalone Novel</u>

Stealing Maid Marian's Heart (Magic of Arcana Universe)

<u>Fanged Fae Series - A Bonegates sister series</u>

Blood Moon Magic

Faerie Blood

<u>The Bonegates Series - A Fanged Fae sister series</u>

Hawk Witch

Assassin Witch

Traitor Witch

Illuminator Witch

<u>**The Royal Quest Series**</u>

Dragon Prince

Dragon Magic

Dragon Mate

Dragon Betrayal

Dragon Crown

Dragon War

<u>**The Starseed Universe - An Irish Witch Urban**
Fantasy</u>

Prophecy of Three

Souls of Three

Rising of Three

The Starseed Universe (five-book boxset)

ABOUT THE AUTHOR

Ashley lives in Portland with her husband, Kurt, their dog, Flicka, and the house ghost that sometimes makes appearances in her charming, old home.

When she's not writing, she enjoys traveling the world, reading, kicking butt at board games (she recommends Splendor and Dominion), and frequenting taquerias.

For all the latest releases and updates, subscribe to Ashley's newsletter, The Coven, today!

As a Coven member you will receive a weekly update from Ashley and exclusive teasers, information about giveaways, and sneak peeks into her author life. You can also find her Facebook group, Ashley's Reader Coven and join in on the fun there!

ACKNOWLEDGMENTS

Thank you to Kurt for always believing in me, championing me, helping me out, and being patient with me. You keep me thankful for your love, unyielding compassion, and support everyday. I love you, babe.

I would not be where I am today without my critique partners and fellow authors Kelly N. Jane and Jaci Miller. Thank you for your help in making this book better. You ladies rock and I LOVE talking books with you!

Jennifer Roop, my editor. You've brought my work to a new level and gave me valuable and kind input when I needed it. You're the best.

To Kim Cunningham of Atlantis Book Design, thank you for beautiful cover art and being a delight to work with.

Thank you to my beta readers Olivia Petris and Alkisti Kal. You two gave such great advice when it came to refining *Hawk Witch*. Thank you for your keen eyes and minds.

Finally, I want to thank all my family and friends who have supported me, stood by me, and cheered for me. Not every creative can say the majority of people in their life support them, but I sure can. There are honestly too many people to name here, but if you are reading this book, just know, I mean you.

All the magic,

Ashley McLeo